THE CURSE OF *The Winwoods*

The Curse of *The Winwoods*

Puja Miri Yajnik

LiFi Publications Pvt. Ltd.
New Delhi

Published by:
LiFi Publications Pvt. Ltd.
211, 2nd Floor, Gagandeep
12, Rajendra Place, New Delhi–110 008, India
Phone : (011) 2574 1000
E-mail : info@lifipublications.com
Web : www.lifipublications.com

ISBN 13: 978-93-82536-68-0 ISBN 10: 93-82536-68-X

First published in 2014

Cataloging in Publication Data—DK
[Courtesy: D.K. Agencies (P) Ltd. <docinfo@dkagencies.com>]

Yajnik, Puja Miri.
The curse of the Winwoods / Puja Miri Yajnik.
p. cm.
Novel.
ISBN 9789382536680

1. Adventure stories. 2. Indic fiction (English). I. Title.

DDC 823.92 23

Printed in India by D.K. Fine Art Press (P) Ltd., Delhi–52

Acknowledgements

My sincere thanks to my father Professor Mrinal Miri for the guidance, to Sam and Garima for all the help. This book is for Bundle Divvij, Nik, and Aks and for everyone else who enjoys a good, old-fashioned adventure story. I hope you all enjoy it!

1

It all started one Friday afternoon when we, a small group of friends, sat together on one of our school balconies wondering how to entertain ourselves. Winwood Manor School was established in 1870 by Lord Charles Devon Winwood on the premises of his own stately home. It was a large rambling building, most of it in Tudor style, but, as is the case with most old houses almost every generation had added to it, so what one saw now was a mixture of various styles which our teachers loved to remind us of. It had survived extremely hard times, including the recent war, that many of us had memories of.

We had magnificent state rooms which still housed the Winwood family portraits by famous artists like Van Dyke. This was forbidden territory to us, students. Only special guests and delegations were allowed a glimpse of the sacred rooms. The headmistress was very proud of the old building and prodigious care was taken in its maintenance. Mrs Weston was a tall, well built woman with grey hair that was always confined to a small bun at the back of her head. She had a clear bright complexion, regular features, which, in spite of having no claim to beauty, were handsome enough to give her a distinguished look. Small glasses sat on her prominent nose, and yes, more often than not, she wore grey. She was extremely efficient and ran the school like a well oiled machine. She managed the school through the tough years of the war; and in spite of the shortages, we were all relatively comfortable, even though, at times, we had a lot of new children arriving from the big cities to tide over the difficult periods. The staff looked up to her; indeed, there seemed to be no problem that was considered unsolvable by Mrs Weston. When all else failed, the problems, whatever they happened to be, were taken to her and everyone relaxed in the knowledge that all would be well.

My attention was claimed by Edward, a rather large boy of fourteen. Edward always gave the impression of being unable to know how to carry his huge frame, as if he was taken by surprise, by his own largeness. He had big brown eyes and dark hair, broad shoulders and long legs, yet he was not fat, just large.

"Where are you Emma? What are you thinking of?" he asked.

"Oh, nothing really, just generally about school," I answered.

"We thought of exploring the forbidden dungeons again, what do you say?" he asked.

Now this was a favourite pastime of most of the children in our school and therefore we all were very familiar with the dark and rather clean dungeons! I suspected them to be nothing more than hidden cellars, but everyone loved to imagine terrible events associated with them.

"Not again, Edward, we have done that far too many times. Let's enjoy the sunshine," I said.

"Lazy bones," said Julia, a fat short girl, whose trademark was that she was always eating something and lazing around somewhere or other.

"Let's play a game or something, should I bring 'clue' down from my locker?" asked Floppy, a short thin boy with large spectacles, his hair flopped about his face, therefore earning him his nickname. Floppy was different from all of us. He was a foreign Prince! He came from an Indian Princely province called Rajdevnagri. Aside from the fact that his father, the Raja, would, once in while, arrive in a large Bentley, with four ADCs, always dressed immaculately, and walk majestically down the corridor to Mrs Westen's study and talk in a loud, booming voice, you would never guess his royal connection. Floppy, himself, was a boy of mild manners and preferred not to make much of his royal background. His full name was Veer Prathap Bhavani Jawahar Singh! He was the most brilliant boy in the school. Even the teachers brought complicated mathematical puzzles to him. We were rather proud to have him as our 'particular' friend. I got up from the bench on which I was sitting, stretched my arms a bit and yawned.

"Emma, that's rude, say sorry," said David, my little brother who, though seven years old, had this horrid habit of reading me constant lectures on how to conduct myself in society!

David was an extremely 'handsome' little boy, with beautiful large eyes and light brown hair, clear well defined features and an angelic expression on his face which made him a favourite with all my friends.

"So cute!," the girls chorused, when he said something to them, even the boys tolerated, no matter what trick he played or tried to play on them!

"Its getting a bit cooler," I said ignoring David, "Shall we go into the common room and play a game as Floppy suggested?"

"Lets go for a walk into the forest," David pleaded, "Please!" looking beseechingly round at us.

"Isn't allowed," I said.

"Miss Lewis might come to look for us, she did say an hour only," said Julia from the corner of the balcony where she was half sitting, half lying down on an uncomfortable bench made of wrought iron.

"Oh, she won't bother us till tea time," said Edward "will be enjoying a bit of quiet herself with all the crowd away."

I should perhaps explain that it was school break time and only a few children, whose parents could not take them for some reason or other, were at school. Basically the whole school was out on vacation save for a few mistresses and about twenty children, of whom our group of friends comprised five.

Edward went up to Julia and roughly pulled her. "Stop it," she mumbled, "we're so comfortable, lets just stay here."

"I thought you called Emma lazy bones a while ago, or was it my imagination?" Edward said with a sly look. Julia made a face at him, her large plump face breaking into a smile.

David jumped up and down clapping his hands. "Lets go to the forest and have an adventure, forward march!" he squealed excitedly treading on Edward's feet who did not even notice!

Floppy got up from the stone ledge where he had been sitting, bending down to pick up one or two books from the steps which led up to the balcony.

"I will just put these away and meet you all at the gate," he said making his way towards the huge wooden door that lead directly from the balcony into one of the school corridors.

"Here David, take your jumper along," I said. "It may get chilly in a while."

"Don't need it," said David, and ran down the steps towards the green, and well kept lawn. We all began to follow him.

"Feet off my grass," said a gruff voice. We turned and saw Mr Peters, our old, rather surly, head gardener.

"So sorry," I said, trying to smile appeasingly at Mr Peters, but to no effect. He continued looking angrily at us as if we were some insects on his favourite flowers or something. We moved off the grass immediately but David looked back at Mr Peters, waved at him and proceeded to execute a dance on his precious grass. Mr Peters frowned thunderously and shook his fist at him. David laughed louder.

"Ho, Mr Peters, lovely day, isn't it? Would like to lie down on the lawn. Very comfortable. It will be like a soft bed," he said giggling all the while and acting as if he was about to lie down on the lawn.

Mr Peters's tall thin frame shook with repulsion at the thought of any one lying down on his much loved grass, he made as if to run after David, waving his spade in the air.

David laughed louder, but turned and ran all the same. We all followed suit and soon reached the small wooden gate that separated the school property from the forest around it. David was the first to reach it and quickly scrambled up and was on the other side. Edward reached the gate but waited to assist Julia who came, huffing and puffing up to the gate and had to be helped to jump over. I executed a smooth jump which every one applauded, after which Edward just put one of his legs over it; no jumping needed for him to cross such a small little hurdle.

Mr Peters was still far behind as he was rather old, and thought running was bad for his health. He was scowling, pulling at his own beard and saying something, but seemed to have given up the chase. Floppy was the last to come up to the gate as he had not caught up with us as yet. We looked at each other as he coolly lifted the latch of the gate and walked through, carefully pushing it back before joining us.

"Come on gang, lets go," he said.

✦ ✦ ✦

2

Winwood Manor School had beautiful extensive grounds. We were told that the famous Francis White created the landscape in the 1700's, giving it sweeping lawns, borders and majestic specimen trees. We even had an 18th century orangery, which was one of my favourite haunts. The land outside the school boundaries, in contrast, was acres and acres of unkempt forest. As a result we were not allowed to step outside.

As we stood looking around us, for a moment I felt a twinge of apprehension. The sunshine coming down, through the thickset trees caste strange shadows around, it was very quiet, we could only hear the chirping of birds. Floppy was the first one to move forward, and his footsteps, as he walked over the leaves and twigs that lay on the ground, sounded very loud and somewhat menacing.

"I am not sure this is a good idea," I whispered.

"Shall we go back?" whispered Julia.

"Why are you whispering?" asked Edward, "Are you both scared?"

"We are not allowed to come here, I think we should go back, we may get into trouble," I said a little louder.

"Adventure, it's an adventure!" squealed David jumping excitedly on the ground.

"Come on girls, just a little walk in the forest will do no harm, let's explore a bit," said Floppy coaxingly, looking at, Julia and me.

Since neither of us wanted to admit to being frightened, we quietly began to follow Floppy into the forest. There was no clear path and we had to find our way by pushing against branches of trees and bushes. I was behind Floppy, followed by David, then Julia, Edward was the last one.

"Careful now," said Edward, from behind us. We all stopped and turned back.

"Those bushes look like thistle," he said, pointing to somewhere near Floppy. "Stop Floppy, you are too close."

Floppy stopped, but bent down to look at the bushes near him "you are right old man, they are. How could you tell from such a distance?"

"Saw some like them near home, can be a pain if you go nearer," said Edward and they both laughed.

I took David's hand as we walked past the thistle bushes, surprisingly he let me guide him, I was half expecting him to want to touch them just to see what could happen. We went a little further into the forest, it was really quite beautiful. There were tall trees with thick branches, little bushes in different shades of green, some had wild patches of white flowers on them. We walked about forty minutes, enjoying the beauty of our surroundings.

"Look, berries!" said David pointing at some bushes "can we pluck them, can we?"

"No, better not," said Floppy bending to look at them, "may be poisonous, can't be sure."

"I want some, I want some!" said David, beginning to get excited.

"No David, you may get sick, now be a good boy," I said in my grown up voice.

"I don't care, I want some," said my brother, his voice getting louder and more urgent.

"No means no, you must listen to us, it is not safe to eat anything here," I scolded.

David pulled his hand out of mine and sat down on the ground. "I will have some, I don't care, I am not scared," he said.

I tried to pull him up and he began to cry, we all looked helplessly at each other. Just at that moment we heard a strange noise coming from ahead, we froze, even David immediately stopped crying.

It was an eerie sound something between a sneeze and a laugh. "Is somebody there?" said Floppy, trying to peer ahead yet not walking further. All was quiet, not even a branch rustled. He called again "Is anybody there?"

Edward moved past Julia, David and I. He whispered something to Floppy and they both looked ahead and turned to us.

"We think it's time to go back, may not be such a good idea to continue," said Floppy, "what do you say?"

Julia and I assented, at heart, rather relieved to turn back. We returned in the same order we had come, with Floppy leading and Edward bringing up the rear, except that our steps were a bit hurried this time.

The silence was broken by David, "may be it was a dog..." he said in a brave voice.

"Or any animal," said Julia hopefully, "after all we are in a forest, may have been a squirrel."

"Didn't sound like one," said Edward, "sounded suspiciously human."

I looked around, although there was nothing save the forest sights, we had become familiar with in the past hour or so, I had a strong feeling that there was someone watching us.

"Do lets hurry," said Julia, looking over her shoulder, "are you sure you know where you are going Floppy?"

"Don't for heaven's sake take a wrong turn," I said anxiously.

"Relax, I am just retracing our steps, we made this path ourselves by walking through and pushing at the bushes...."

His voice suddenly trailed off, and he stopped.

"What's wrong?" I shouted.

"Turn back," he said, "I think this isn't our path."

"What?" said Julia, in a horrified voice.

David's little hand crept into my hand, I held it tightly, and looking reassuringly at him, then looked at Edward who was looking back over his shoulder.

"Are you sure old man?" he asked.

"Yes, yes," said Floppy pushing his glasses up his nose, as was his habit when he concentrated on anything. He walked back towards Edward, and passed him by, and went on ahead.

"Shall I go and look around a bit, you can all wait here," he said over his shoulder.

"No," I said firmly, "we had better stick together."

We all moved towards the direction we had first come from. As the trees and shrubs all looked similar to each other, in half an hour we got thoroughly confused.

"I'm sorry," said Floppy, "I should have left some sign somewhere. I thought we would be able to walk back by simply turning back on the path we had made for ourselves."

"In other words," said Julia in a low voice, "we are officially lost!"

"Be calm everyone," I said, looking around at them all, "first thing is not to panic. Let us not wonder to far from here, we will, sooner or later, find our way, as we did not walk for that long after all."

"The question is, since we didn't see any path as we started, how come we are on this one now," murmured Floppy half to himself.

"I think..." began Julia.

Edward signaled to us to keep quiet, but Floppy paid no heed to us and began to retrace our path. He was looking at the branches that had been broken as if to clear a way ahead.

"Just as I thought, these have been broken recently; perhaps if we follow this path we will meet someone who will be helpful."

"I don't think I want to meet anyone, because you know there is always a chance they may be quite the opposite," I added my bit.

"May be a villain," emphasized my brother, "or even a wolf like in Red Riding Hood."

"I shouldn't like to meet a wolf, they are alright in story books, but not in real life," said Julia looking back over her shoulder.

"Oh yes there will definitely be wolves here," said Edwards absentmindedly. Julia and I exchanged a look of sheer panic.

We were all walking along the same path where we had discovered that we were lost. Floppy was not taking notice of anything we said, he seemed to be intent on finding our way back. We lapsed into silence. Only the sound of our footsteps on the ground crushing the dry leaves and twigs that lay there, could be heard.

"I am tired," declared David suddenly. His loud and decisive voice shattered the silence, and brought us to a sudden halt.

"Do let's rest for a while," Julia urged. "I am not accustomed to so much walking."

Nobody called her 'lazy bones' as we normally would have, so worried were we at our plight.

"No, no we can't afford to do that," said Floppy, "must find our way back as quickly as possible," he said, looking up at the sky.

Edward moved forward and lifted David in his arms. "Like a ride on my shoulders old boy?" he asked, grinning sympathetically at the tired child. He lifted him effortlessly on to his shoulders. David put his arms around Edwards's neck and we once more began our search for the way back to school. We had been walking only for about ten minutes when the silence was broken by a loud sneeze.

"God bless," said Floppy mechanically without turning back.

"Who was that?" I asked looking back at Julia, Edward and David.

"Not me," sighed Julia, too tired to even to look up as she walked.

"Not us," said David. We all came to a sudden halt and look around wildly.

"Is anybody there?" said Floppy trying to sound as if he was not scared. There was silence, no one spoke, we stood still looking at each other, now seriously scared. Then it happened – a sound, not loud, but of a branch being snapped. It was enough for us, we turned in the direction opposite to the sound we had just heard and ran, as fast as we could. Julia was ahead, followed by Floppy, I kept as close to Edward as I could, who ran forward holding both David hands as he bounced up and down on his shoulders. All of sudden Julia came to a halt, we all collided with each other, as we too, stopped.

"What the...!" said Floppy.

Then we saw what had brought her to a halt. We were gazing at an unexpected but wondrous sight. There, set in the middle of the dark and lonely forest, was the most beautiful house I had ever seen.

✦ ✦ ✦

3

The large, majestic, iron gates opened up to a winding drive way. There was a green lawn, in circular shape, in the centre of which was a fountain. The statue was of a child holding up a torch, but the fountain lay barren. Around this circular lawn was a narrow gravel walk, and opposite to us, that is, behind the now-dry fountain, there was what seemed to be, the foyer of the house.

The house itself seemed to be perfectly proportioned, it was large but not too imposing, had solid, high walls, a few chimneys, and from what we could see, long French windows. It had very pretty and colourful flowers creeping up its walls but in a wild unkempt sort of way, as if no one preened them.

For a few minutes we stood still, taking in this unexpected sight. Then, I remembered the reason for our fright and looked over my shoulder but could see nothing. All was still, not a sound could be heard. Floppy was the first to move towards the house, we all silently followed.

As if by instinct we got of the gravel and unto the grass, so as not to make any noise. As we silently crept up to the house, we looked around apprehensively.

"Do you think there is anybody here?" asked Julia to no one in particular.

"It's awfully quiet," whispered Edward.

"There is no bell," I said, "look."

We all looked at the large wooden door, there was a massive door handle made of iron, but of any bell, there was no sign.

"This is it," said Floppy, stretching out his hand above. We looked up and saw an old style door knocker, we had something similar up at school.

"Shhh," whispered Edward suddenly, glancing at the rest of us, "come on," he turned and began to walk away, as stealthily as he could on the gravel, we looked puzzled at each other but obediently followed him and David as they went.

Edward crept along the wall of the house till he reached the corner of the house, he then peeped at the back of the building and with his hand beckoned us to follow him.

We crossed the lawn and went towards some thickets in the garden, once hidden from view, Edward lifted David from his shoulders and put him on the ground.

"What?" whispered Floppy, "what's the matter?"

"Do tell, why did we not pull the bell?" asked Julia excitedly.

"Ask David," said Edward.

"David?" I cried, "What's the matter?"

"Shhh," said Edward, "not so loud."

I bent down next to David and held his arms, "Speak up, did you see something?"

"Let me go, Emma," said David pushing my hands away. "I was high up on Edward's shoulders, right?" he said.

"Yes," I said, trying to be patient.

"Well, when you were all looking for the bell I was trying to see if I could peep into the house..."

"And...?" whispered Julia excitedly.

"There was a gap in the curtain high up, just a small one..." he continued.

"And...?" squealed Julia.

David gave her a look, she grinned sheepishly and put her finger in her mouth.

"And," said David, "by stretching my neck I could see a little into the room."

"What did you see?" I said impatiently, "Come on David speak up, it might be important!" I said firmly.

"A very odd sight," said the little boy looking as he was feeling, very important! I moved towards him, he retreated towards Edward.

"Come on old boy, no more suspense," said Edward coaxingly, crouching down next to David.

"There were three people in the room, two women and one man. It was quite dark as the curtains were all drawn, a candle was lit on one table."

"Strange," I said.

"You haven't heard the strange part yet," whispered David, his voice now highly excited. "One woman was standing behind the other who was sitting on a chair, her hand covering the other woman's mouth!"

"My god!" I said.

"What can it mean?" Said Floppy.

"Let's get out of here," said Julia.

Edward moved towards the bushes and peered towards the house. Although the sun had set, there was still light and we could see pretty well.

"David, are you sure you are not mistaken?" I asked suspiciously.

"I'm sure; I looked very carefully, then whispered to Edward as much as I could."

"I didn't understand, but thought it best to move away and talk it over," said Edward.

"What was the man doing?" asked Floppy.

"Just standing looking down, as if listening for something, they were not talking," said David frowning and trying to remember the scene he had seen.

"Wonder if they saw us approaching the house?" said Floppy.

"We'd better leave," said Julia looking frightened.

"Most peculiar," said Floppy reflectively "have we walked into a real-life adventure?"

"I don't want a real-life adventure, let's go, come on," urged Julia, moving away from the thicket.

Just then there was an interruption, a voice said, "excuse me!"

We all jumped out of our skins. Julia stood paralyzed with fear, I turned towards the voice, Floppy pushed his glasses up on his nose, looking quite scared. David was hiding behind Edward, who was gazing in a shocked way at 'the voice'.

We found ourselves looking, quite simply, at the most 'beautiful girl on earth'. There was no other way to describe the vision before our eyes. A young girl, maybe eighteen or twenty years of age, with glorious golden hair, a heart shaped face, dark eyebrows, greyish blue eyes that were framed by thick lashes. She was dressed in a white skirt and long sleeved top, her wavy hair was wild and unkempt, and she wore thick black boots.

No one spoke, we just stared at her, and went on staring for what seemed an age.

"Who are you?" finally said the beautiful girl.

"No one!... I mean we are nobody, just leaving, sorry for trespassing!" said Julia incoherently.

The 'girl' looked around at us puzzled.

"Is this your house?" asked Floppy.

"No, are you lost?" she asked, looking at him a little curiously.

"He is a Prince," said David, in an explanatory manner.

"Is that so," She mumbled, politely.

"Yes, yes, we're just leaving!" said Julia.

"Are you a ghost?" then said David, putting into words with the innocence of childhood, what had been in all our minds from the minute we had seen this vision in white. The girl's beautiful face broke into a smile, which made her look even prettier, if that was possible!

"Did I startle you? I'm sorry," she said in a soft musical voice, looking around at us, "I'm no ghost, just as human as you all are, I hope...see?" she smiled stretching her hand towards David. We continued to stare at her as she looked at David and said coaxingly. "Come touch my hand, I won't disappear, unless," she pulled back her hand, "you all are ghosts, are you?" she looked skeptically at David. "We're not," he said, "we're human," he answered seriously.

"I'm relieved to hear that," she said in mock seriousness, "being, as I am, I must admit, of a little timid nature. Come, shake my hand and let us introduce ourselves," she smiled invitingly.

David looked at me, as if to make sure it was safe, I nodded and he went up to her and shook the hand she was holding out.

"My name is Marianne," she said.

"I am David," he said. He then pointed to me, "she, is my sister Emma."

"This is Julia and that is Floppy," I said.

"And I am Edward," said our tall burly friend, a trifle eagerly, staring fascinated at the 'vision'!

For a moment we took stock of each other. No one said anything. I was wondering to myself, that if this was not her house, then what was she doing here, then again who were those people David had seen and what was their relationship to Marianne. The whole setup seemed very strange to me.

"Are you all lost?" said Marianne in a soft voice after what seemed an age.

"Yes," said Floppy, "we had just come for a walk and couldn't find our way back, can you help us with directions?"

"I wish I could," said the lovely girl, "you see this is the first time I have come here, in fact I have no idea where I am."

We all looked at her, puzzled. 'How very odd,' I thought to myself.

As if reading my mind she said, "I suppose you think it odd, that such a grown up girl has no idea where she is."

"Frankly yes," I said, "perhaps your parents brought you."

"I have no parents. 'Till last week, I lived with my grandmother, but she died," said Marianne in a sad low voice.

We all were looking curiously at her. Her eyes filled up with tears, she looked away trying to wipe them.

"We are sorry to hear that," said Floppy politely.

She turned to us, attempting a smile, "well, that's life I suppose, so here I am, in the middle of nowhere and quite unable to assist you all."

"But who are...?" began Edward, and suddenly stopped.

I noticed that he was looking at Floppy who was frowning at him. Floppy doesn't want us to tell her what David saw, perhaps he doesn't trust her, I thought to myself.

Marianne seemed to be lost in her own world and didn't seem to have noticed what Edward said. I looked in the sky, it was showing signs of getting darker, "we're in a soup," I thought.

"Is there no one in the house," asked Floppy gesturing with his hand, towards the house and trying to sound as casual as possible.

"Oh yes, how stupid of me, perhaps they can help," she replied sounding very doubtful. We exchanged alarmed glances with each other.

Marianne looked at us, then looked over her shoulder in the direction of the house. Suddenly her voice changed, "can I trust you?" she said in a low urgent whisper, drawing close to us.

My heart was beating loud in my chest, as I involuntarily stepped backwards treading on Julia's feet who said "ouch!"

"Who is there?" said a loud, unfriendly voice, from somewhere quite close.

We all looked at each other in dismay, the beautiful girl looked crestfallen, she put her fingers to her lips, then whispered to me as I was closest to her. "I will try to get away again, wait here, PLEASE."

So saying she moved out of the thicket and stepped back into the lawn.

"Its only me Mr Goddard."

We heard a rough voice saying "I thought I heard something, what are you doing out here, you should be indoors."

"Just wanted a bit of fresh air," said Marianne in her soft way, "anything wrong?"

The man's voice seemed to change a bit as he said, "Nip in the air is not very good for you, better for you to be indoors. Come I will escort you as its getting dark." His voice trailed off. Our group, standing quite still with bated breath, in the now familiar thicket, looked at each other.

"Gosh!" said Julia.

"What shall we do?" I said looking at Floppy.

"We'd better get moving," he replied glancing at his wrist watch. "It is getting late."

"But she's clearly in trouble, shouldn't we try and help?" said Edward, a worried look on his kind face.

"She did ask us to wait," I said a little doubtfully.

"Right now we are in trouble, don't you realize, we have to get back to school," said Floppy.

"If only she had been able to tell us her story..." murmured Edward half to himself.

"I want to help her too," said David suddenly.

"Shhh, not so loud," I whispered to him, looking fearfully around.

"Let us at least wait for a while," suggested Edward, "give her a chance to come back."

"What if 'that man' comes instead and discovers us, doesn't sound like a pleasant character," said Floppy sarcastically. "Come on," he looked round at us all, "good sense says we get on with finding our way back to school. Don't be a fool, Edward."

We all realized the sense in Floppy's words, even David didn't make a fuss as we slowly began to move out of the thicket back in the direction of the forest, away from the strange house, and it's even stranger in-mates. We had reached the end of the grounds and were about to get back to the forest, when Edward gave a start!

"Gang, look!" he said, staring at the house.

"What?!" said Floppy annoyed by the disruption.

I looked at the direction of Edward's finger as he pointed. For a moment nothing registered, then I saw, in a flash, what he had seen. I froze. It was an upstairs window; someone had stuck, or was holding, a large white paper against the window pane. On it, with bold capital letters, was written only one word–'HELP'! Edward and I exchanged shocked glances, the others were still looking around, trying to figure out what we were looking at.

Then Floppy said, "gosh" and pushed his spectacles up on his nose. Edward made a move as if to go back towards the house, I caught his arm and shook my head.

"No, no, let us discuss it, we should get out of sight of the house quickly," I whispered urgently.

That seemed to rouse Floppy, who seemed to be genuinely shocked into immobility by this new development.

Meanwhile David and Julia had not seen what we had, so were looking wildly in all directions over their shoulder as we hustled them into the forest. Once out of sight of the house we stopped and looked at each other.

"Hope no one saw us," I said breathlessly.

"What is it?" whispered David tugging at my hand.

"Didn't you see?" said Floppy excitedly.

"If it was something scary, please don't tell me," said Julia, "I've had enough excitement for a day!" she looked at the trees around us fearfully.

"A paper, at one of the upstairs window, it said 'HELP'," whispered Floppy. "That's what made Edward stop."

"I just glanced over my shoulder to see of Marianne was looking for us, and my eye caught sight of the white paper," explained Edward.

"We'd better get out of here," said Floppy, half to himself, as he looked around.

"What, and not do anything? Marianne is obviously in trouble," said gallant Edward.

"We cannot help her, being so hopelessly lost ourselves, be reasonable this is out of our league. Besides the teachers will have discovered us missing, will be looking for us, we must try and reach school as soon as possible, we owe it to them!" said Floppy.

"Yes, yes," urged Julia.

"I think it is the sensible thing to do," I added my bit. "Floppy is right, we cannot delay any longer, it is getting dark as we speak."

There was nothing else to do. It was a subdued group that made its way slowly past the trees, into the forest. I went up to Edward and squeezed his arm, "I know you don't like to leave, but look at it this way, if we reach school we can get help and come back," I whispered.

He visibly brightened up, "Yes, let's leave some marks along the way," he said.

David, who was once more perched on Edwards shoulders, pulled his hair to attract attention.

"What's the matter?" said Edward, wincing and looking up.

"I've got some marbles in my pocket," said David.

"That's great, give them to me," said Edward, "and listen old man, try not to pull my hair, that hurts," he grinned as he put David on the ground, we waited as David took out some marbles from his pocket and handed them to Edward.

"One, two, three, four" counted Edward. There were only six.

"Julia," I said, "give us your hair ribbon."

"We can tie this on some tree, and mine too," I said undoing my ribbon.

Floppy held out his hand for a ribbon, and then tied it to the branch of a tree.

"Space the clues," he said, as he moved on, that'll make it easier to come back.

It was not very pleasant to be in the forest again, as it was not as bright as it had been earlier. In the fading light, the forest, with its tall trees, wild flowers and bushes, seemed even more sinister. I must say that all of us tried to be brave, we stayed calm and kept walking behind Floppy who would try one direction, and then another, hoping to come across something that looked familiar.

We must have gone on for a whole hour at least before anyone spoke. It was now even darker and by now even Edward was dragging his steps. We had disposed of all our 'clues' a long time back. Tired and hungry we had almost given up and had no idea what to do, when we heard some rustling sound coming from quite close to us.

"Stop!" said Floppy.

Each of us collided with the person in front of us as we abruptly stopped.

"Is anyone there?" shouted Floppy.

There was no reply; we all looked at each other in panic, remembering our earlier experience. Then all of a sudden there burst out, through the bushes, what looked at first glance like only a 'lantern'.

"Oh!" I screamed.

"Oh God!" screamed Julia, louder than me, clinging to Edwards arm.

"It's okay, kids, don't be frightened its only me, Mr Greenwood," said a deep friendly voice.

We all breathed a sigh of relief as we recognized our school's security officer, Mr Greenwood, who habitually wore a dark uniform; hence we couldn't see him at first.

"You've found us, you've found us!" said Julia.

"Been looking two–three hours at least," said a grumbling voice next to Mr Greenwood. It was the school Janitor, Mr Smith. We took no notice of him as he was always grumbling anyway.

"Got lost, did you? You obviously know how naughty you have been," scolded Mr Greenwood looking round at all of us sternly. Something in our exhausted faces must have affected him as his expression softened, and all he said was, "Come on then, let's get you lot back to school. Here Edward, give me your load." He took David from Edward's arms, and began to walk. We all followed, in a line with Mr Smith bringing up the rear.

"What a day," I thought to myself as I walked, "little did we think it would be this 'adventurous' when we set out in the afternoon. We are in for a lot of trouble when we reach school."

We entered by the same gate, we had left from, this time it was open and one of the school gatekeepers was standing there, a most forbidding expression on his face.

"Found them, did you? They're waiting," he said jerking his thumb towards the school building.

We looked at each other, now, no longer brave. I felt dreadful, suppose our parents are called in, suppose they send us down from school, oh God, no, please don't let that happen, I prayed silently.

We followed Mr Greenwood up to the main school entrance, as all other doors were shut every evening. There, standing on the top of the stairs leading up to the great door was, Miss Lewis, and next to her was Mrs Weston, herself. I was too nervous to even look at the head mistress's face, we just went up the stairs and stood in front of her in a line, our heads bent down.

"Oh children," she said a tremor in her usually calm voice, "thank God you are safe, you have been very naughty but no doubt you have an explanation for me..." she looked round at us. Floppy made a sound as if to say something. Mrs Weston held up her hand, "No Veer Pratap, not now, I would have thought that at least you would have known better! Now what am I to tell His Highness? You know full well that you have to be careful." She put a hand up again, as we began to say something, "the explanation can wait. You are all safe and unhurt. I want you all to get indoors, go to your respective rooms have a bath and some food. We will talk tomorrow, go now."

We fled and made our way to our rooms. No one said anything, we were just relieved to be back and dying to have some supper as we were all starving. Matron was not of the same mind as Mrs Weston and did not spare us. Her plump round face was red; she was furious and let us know it. On and on she went about how wicked we had been, how thoughtless and reckless. Julia and I hung our heads down and just listened, we felt awful, it was now that we realized how terrible it would have been had they not found us!

✦ ✦ ✦

4

The next morning was bright and sunny, the birds chirped, the bees buzzed, even the flowers seemed to be smiling. Yet when I looked out of my window at the lush green lawn outside, I felt a sense of sadness, a gloom, which was hard to explain, even to myself. Breakfast time saw all of us lined up in the dining hall as usual with young Madame Gustave presiding. Madame Gustave was our new French teacher who had been with us about six odd months, she was, quite simply, the prettiest teacher in school. Most of the older boys had a soft corner for her and were always volunteering to do chores for her. She took their devotion in good spirit and was basically considered a 'chum' by most of us.

The dining room was large, with wooden floors, a row of faded white gold pillars stood at each end, and in the centre were long wooden, solid looking tables with chairs all around. There were tables standing at the far end on which was placed the food in huge bowls with long serving spoons resting on little plates placed next to them. We would pick up our plates from our places which were allocated according to our forms, and serve ourselves. It was rather a noisy business, accompanied with constant chattering. The teachers were not overly strict about noise, especially during holidays.

Julia and I filled our plates and went and sat down. From the corner of my eye I looked at Madame Gustave, she had not said anything about our escapade when we had wished her. "Bonjour," she said, merely smiling in her usual way. She was busy moving between the tables and greeting late comers.

Julia was busy eating, whereas I found myself unable to swallow much. I couldn't see Floppy anywhere, but Edward was at his table drinking his hot chocolate and looking pre-occupied with his thoughts. I looked around for David and couldn't find him; "perhaps he has finished," I thought to myself. Just then I felt a hand on my shoulders. It was Madame Gustave who was laughing at something and looking over her shoulder. She turned to me and smiled, then sat down next to me, "Not hungry, *mon amie*?" she said in her heavily accented voice, an understanding look in her eyes.

"Not very," I mumbled.

"Julia is okay," she laughed.

"Julia is always okay, food wise," I replied.

"True," said Julia. "I love eating, can't help it," she added good naturedly.

"Madame Gustave," I said "have you seen David this morning? He isn't here."

"Oui, David is having breakfast in his dormitory, special instructions from the head. She said yesterday was too much exertion for a little boy," she answered.

I looked up at her in alarm, but she was still smiling. She reached out and squeezed my hand reassuringly. It was then that she dropped the bombshell, "You are to go to Mrs Weston's study after breakfast, all of you."

We must have looked dismayed for she added, "Don't look like that, she won't eat you, you know!"

"No, of course not," I murmured unconvincingly.

"You must tell her everything about yesterday, after all you were all very naughty," said Madame Gustave getting up from the chair, "you owe her an explanation."

Julia's spoon had fallen down with a clatter; I gripped the edge of the table. Madame Gustave looked at us silently for a minute, gave a half smile, and said, *"ne vous inquiétez pas,"* (don't worry) she said and walked away.

"What will we say?" whispered Julia in panic.

"Gosh," I said "wish we could meet the others and decide," I looked around for Edward, but he had left, "come on. I dragged Julia on to her feet, as she seemed to be frozen with panic. We rushed out of dining room, down the green corridor (so called because of its green walls) and up the side stairs. On the second landing was the door of the boys common room, where the boys were usually to be found after breakfast in the holidays. Without ceremony we literally burst through the door. There were only two senior boys lounging on twin armchairs, they looked up instinctively at us but didn't bother to say anything.

"Excuse me," I said politely, "have you seen Edward or Floppy?"

"Nope, never heard of them," answered one of boys and looked glumly ahead.

"They're usually here," I persisted.

They stared at us blankly, Julia pulled my arm. I looked at the two in exasperation.

"Really," I thought "boys!"

"Come on, let's look somewhere else," said Julia still pulling at my arm.

"I wish you would give up this habit of pulling people's arms," I said, "most irritating."

"Where now?" she said a little breathlessly as we had been running.

"Library," I said. We ran down the same stairs we had come up from, towards the centre of the school. As we passed various doors I tried to peep into as many as I could. The billiard room, the music room, the painting room, the sculpture room, all with no luck.

I felt a tug on my arm; I looked back irritably at Julia, "Now what?" I said, a little rudely.

"I...can't...run...any...more," she whispered breathlessly, her plump arms leaning on the nearest wall for support.

I looked at my watch, then at Julia, "yes, better head to Mrs Weston's study, else we'll be hauled up for being late!"

Mrs Weston's study was at one end of the school tucked away in a corner, so to speak. Her office was a large impressive room extremely formal looking in the centre of the school, which you could reach fastest by the main school entrance. This room was small and comfortable in total contrast to her office, which was quite daunting, to say the least.

There was no one outside the door, my last hope of meeting the boys there, was thus dashed. I looked at Julia's scared face, took a deep breath and knocked on the door.

Let me take a moment to describe the room into which we entered. It was quite small, long French windows opened out onto the rose garden, the curtains were dark green, there was a large desk in one corner with a lamp on it. In one corner of the room were a couple of huge plants, (Mrs Weston was an avid gardener), there were two comfortable armchairs in front of the fireplace and two stiff backed chairs in front of the desk. Mrs Weston was sitting behind the desk and opposite her stood Floppy and Edward.

She looked at us as we hesitatingly entered and joined the boys. I didn't dare look at the boys, although I was dying to.

"Well Emma, Julia?" said Mrs Weston. Her voice sounded neutral, neither angry nor friendly. Nobody said anything. "Who is going to tell me the story?" she asked looking round at us all.

At this point I tried to sneak a look at Floppy for I wanted desperately to gauge how much he must have told. Mrs Weston caught my glance and immediately summoned me to her side. I walked round the desk and stood next to her chair.

"Well! Come on, I haven't got all day," she said a little impatiently.

I looked at the others, who looked utterly blank, no help from there! "Oh, well, here goes," I thought to myself and began a confused explanation. "It was nothing really Mrs Weston, we are very sorry, of course we ought not to have, but it was just that we were so bored and had absolutely nothing to do..." I went on relating the events as they had taken place. She listened attentively, without interrupting me. "And so we got scared of the strange sound and ran until we reached..." I continued.

"A clearing...," suddenly interrupted Edward. Mrs Weston turned sharply to look at him. So did I. He was red in the face as he took over the story from me. He described the rest of the walk without a single mention of 'the house' or Marianne.

Floppy and I exchanged glances and then held our peace. Why on earth was Edward hiding this part of the story I wondered.

"And that's all?" enquired the Head Mistress in a disbelieving tone, "are you sure there is nothing else you need to inform me?" she looked round sternly at us.

Again Floppy and I exchanged glances, we were later to regret the silent decision we took then, at that very moment there was an interruption.

There walked in, very unceremoniously, through the open French windows, a story book 'Prince'. There was no other way to describe the young man, very tall and muscular with big blue eyes and blonde hair. He wore a long black buttoned coat, over brown trousers that were tucked in black boots. With his arrival Mrs Weston's whole body language underwent a miraculous change. She blushed and moved awkwardly past me, straight into the arms of the 'Prince'!

"Where have you been?" she said, giving him a brief hug "I've been waiting all morning, I was feeling worried...." He kissed her on both cheeks, and laughingly embraced her.

"Aunt Agatha, you look well," he said looking round at us as we stood blatantly staring at them.

My eyes met his for a moment he winked at me and grinned, it was a most disarming smile. I smiled back involuntarily. Mrs Weston suddenly realized our presence, and flushed scarlet, she turned round at us and tried to get back to her formal self. "Well children, here is my nephew come to pay me a little visit. I shall have to leave you all now. Although...," she looked sternly at us, "let me tell you I am not too happy with the account you have given me, this is certainly not the end of the discussion." So saying she nodded dismissal at us, we all trooped out thankful to come out of it so easily thanks to the interruption!

"So Mrs Weston has feelings..." whispered Floppy excitedly.

"Horrid boy, of course she has!" I whispered back. No one knew much about Mrs Weston's personal life, we didn't even know who Mr Weston was, or had been. So, there was a strong curiosity about her background in the entire school. From time to time, rumors circulated about her family or past, but there had never been any credible verification of any story, the arrival of a nephew was, therefore, a huge event.

We made our way back to our part of the school. A little noise attracted my attention and looking out, I saw a motorcar parked on the driveway outside, Mr Smith and Mr Peters were taking some luggage out of the boot and talking to each other. Automatically we made our way to our favorite balcony (where we had been setting yesterday at the start of our adventure)

"What's the matter with you?" Floppy said suddenly.

I looked at him in surprise; he was looking at Julia as he spoke. I too turned to her. "Julia! Whatever's the matter?" I echoed Floppy.

Julia was looking quite strange, her round plump face had reddened, as if she were blushing, and her eyes looked glazed, a far away look in them. She didn't seem to have heard either of us. I went up to her and put my hands on her arms and shook her.

"What...?" she said.

"Julia, come back to us!" I said.

"Stop it Emma," she said.

"I will not unless you become yourself again," I said.

"Of course I'm myself, what's wrong with you?" came the answer.

Floppy looked slyly at her, then smiled and said "Julia's fallen in love."

"What rubbish!" said Julia angrily "nothing of the sort." Poor Julia, her face became redder still as she threw her jumper at Floppy (there was nothing else to throw)

"Come on gang, stop wasting time we need to discuss what is to be done," interrupted Edward. I realized then, that he had been standing quietly all the while.

"Discuss what?" I asked.

"We've got off pretty easily," added Floppy, still teasing Julia by looking knowingly at her.

"What?" said Edward in an outraged voice, "have you all forgotten about Marianne?"

Floppy turned at this, "Julia's not the only one in love," he said mischievously.

Edward turned to him and made as if to grab his collar, Floppy ran down the stairs and made a peace sign to him, from a safe distance, then slowly made his way back to us, keeping a wary eye on Edward.

But Edward had lost interest in doing him any mischief; he was totally preoccupied with the problem of Marianne.

I looked in surprise at Edward, then at Julia who was again looking lost, Floppy was looking at me, looking at them, a most irritating look on his face!

✦ ✦ ✦

5

That evening brought in a thunderstorm. The rain beat at the windows panes and the thunder, well, thundered! As I sat in a cozy common room listening to my favourite music, I couldn't help thanking God for our safe return the previous evening.

"Imagine if we had been out in this weather," shuddered Julia who was sitting nearby, darning, or at least trying to darn, a sock.

"Hideous," I agreed.

"Still, I must say I wish we could have helped Marianne, poor girl, I wonder how she is," said Julia.

"Why do you think Edward did not want us to tell her story to the Head? I mean she may make a push to help the girl," I murmured.

"Hmm, I too have been thinking about that," said Julia, "and do you know what I think?" she said excitedly putting her stitching down on a nearby table and moving forward on her chair.

I looked at her, not that I expected anything brilliant from my sweet friend, but I didn't want to disappoint her by being uninterested.

"Well," I said, "go on," as Julia was just looking at me, a strange look on her face.

"Yes, yes, well listen; I think he has got a plan of his own," she said in a dramatic voice.

"Oh no, don't say that," I said genuinely worried. "I hope not, I am sure you are wrong. What can he possibly do on his own?"

I was working at my maths book the next morning in the same common room, when there was a knock on the door. I looked up in surprise as most people just walked in, no one knocked.

"Am I interrupting something stupendously important?" said a deep voice from behind the door.

"Who...?" I said.

"Only me, the mysterious stranger," laughed aunt Agatha's nephew as he came into the room. To my embarrassment I actually blushed as I tried to say something polite.

"Hmm, they do keep the school beautiful, excellent taste," he said looking approvingly at the floral curtains and Mahogany furniture arranged tastefully in this much-used room.

"Lovely, isn't it?" I said trying to sound normal, as if it was an everyday event to have a handsome young man walk into our common room, while I was working on some maths problem!

He was standing in front of my desk now, looking down at me thoughtfully. I tried to meet his eyes, but looked away immediately; there was something disconcerting in his look. "He suspects something," I thought to myself.

"Well," he said.

"Well?" I said.

"Well," he laughed, "shouldn't we introduce ourselves."

"Oh yes, of course," I replied, "I'm Emma."

"My name is William," he said "come here on a visit to my aunt, your Head, as you know already. May I sit down Emma?"

"Of course," I said embarrassed at my own awkwardness. "Oh God I am behaving like a stereotypical, blushing schoolgirl!" silently I scolded myself.

He pulled up a chair close to the desk at which I was working and sat down. There was a moment's silence as I fiddled with my pen.

"Is something worrying you?" he said suddenly. I looked up in alarm. His look softened as he smiled in a friendly way at me, "listen, sorry to be nosy but it looks to me as if you and your friends are worried about something." There was a moment of indecision as I debated whether or not to tell this stranger our story.

"No, whatever gave you that idea?" I replied in a nonchalant voice.

He looked intently at me for a moment as if he was about to say something, then abruptly got up as if to go. At that moment the door was rudely flung open and a human hurricane, in other words my brother, burst in.

"Hey, hey, hey," he sing-songed and ran around the room in circles, three times, God knows for what purpose. I noticed that William was looking at him in surprise. In his own time David came to a stop near me.

"Hello Emma, what's up, shall we play a game, I'm bored," he explained loudly.

"You don't look bored to me at all," I said sarcastically, "where are your manners, say hello," I said gesturing towards William. David seemed to notice him for the first time. He looked him up and down, then appeared to like what he saw, as he put his hand out.

"I'm David," he said.

"I'm William," said the other, bending down to shake hands. "Would you like to play with me?" smiled William.

David stared at him thoughtfully.

"I'm not at all boring," coaxed William.

"Oh, all right," said my brother putting his little hand in William's large one. I stared behind them as they both walked out.

It was that very night; I had just about managed to get to sleep when I felt someone prodding me. As it often happens, when one is in a deep slumber, it took a while to wake up. I felt I was on a ship which for some reason kept swaying wildly!

"What, what?" I said.

"Wake up Emma, its important," said a strange, whispering voice.

I opened my eyes and looked up, I sat up with a jerk, for it was Floppy, in his night gown staring angrily down at me. The bedside lamp had been switched on, Julia who shared the room with me was standing next to Floppy, chewing her nails and looking dazed.

"Whatever's the matter Floppy? Have you taken leave of your senses? What are you doing here?" I said, or rather whispered angrily.

"You take an awful long time to wake up, sleeping beauty," retorted Floppy quite rudely.

"Well, I wasn't expecting visitors!" I flashed back.

"Okay, okay, just listen," he said.

"No, go back to your room, matron will be MAD if she comes for a surprise round or something..." I mumbled, panic gripping me.

"Do stop talking for once, Emma," said a timid little voice. I looked in surprise at Julia, who had spoken for the first time.

"What's happened, you two?" I asked suddenly, getting really worried now.

"Its Edward," said Floppy pushing his spectacles up his nose.

I grasped my blanket tightly, "What's the matter with him?" my voice sounded strange even to my ears. There was a moment's silence, only the ticking of the clock could be heard as the three of us looked at each other.

"He's gone," said Floppy in horribly final voice. We looked at each other, nobody said a word. A dog barked somewhere, the clock kept ticking, we three just couldn't think of anything to say.

"I knew it, I knew it," my mind kept saying.

Julia had sat down on the foot of my bed, Floppy started walking up and down in the little room. I noticed he kept walking into furniture, sometimes the bed, sometimes a chair. He would bend down and rub his knees or his leg automatically and continue moving around.

"Are you sure?" I blurted out suddenly breaking the silence.

Floppy gave me a contemptuous look, "Emma, really, would I come here without making sure?" he said looking round at the girl's room.

"I know, I know," I said placatingly, "but maybe, he's playing a trick on you..." my voice trailed off. It sounded half hearted even to my own ears. I realized I had known all along that he would not sit idle and do nothing about the beautiful Marianne!

Here, let me mention that our room was on a sort of raised ground level. There was a large balcony, (with a beautiful old fashioned stone railing) outside it. There were tall trees outside and their branches sometimes knocked on the windows if it got too windy.

"Floppy," I said suddenly, pushing my blanket away, and getting out of bed, "tell me how you found out." I put my dressing gown on and tied the sash tightly round my waist as if getting ready to tackle this disaster!

Floppy smiled in spite of himself, "That's the spirit, Emma," he paused, "it's quite simple really. We got to our rooms at about eight o'clock, got ready for bed, read for a bit and put the lights out at about 8.30. I got up an hour later for a drink of water and put my lamp on, I looked casually at Edward's bed, he seemed to be sleeping."

Julia was staring at Floppy with her mouth open, "close your mouth, Julia," I said trying to defuse the tension a bit. She scowled at me.

Floppy continued, "Felt something is wrong and for some reason got up, yes I think it was the fact that I couldn't hear his breathing (he's usually a noisy breather in his sleep) Sure enough when I lifted his blanket, there was no Edward, only the pillows arranged to give that impression! An old trick," Floppy concluded.

"But maybe he's gone for a walk or a midnight feast with some others..." I said hopefully.

"Without telling me? Impossible," said Floppy.

"Why wouldn't he tell you if he planned to go there?" I asked.

"I wouldn't let him," he said simply, "you see..."

At that moment there was a huge crash from somewhere outside our window.

"My God!" squealed Julia.

Floppy and I both ran to the door that led to the balcony. "Wait," said Floppy, holding my hand back as I tried to push the curtains in order to peer out.

"Quick Julia," he said looking back at her, "put the lamp out! Come on, move."

As soon as the light went out we both peered out from the two corners of the curtains, into the darkness outside, and what we saw shocked us.

I fully expected to see nothing, thinking that a dog must have knocked against something. I certainly didn't expect to see what I did. For what Floppy and I both saw was the figure of a man in a long dark coat running from our balcony across the lawn outside! Floppy tried to open the door.

"It's locked," I said.

"Open it," he said, "hurry." Someone banged on our door. There was a tense moment; three of us, standing almost in three corners of the room, exchanged stunned glances. By now there was quite a bit of noise in the corridor outside, looked as if people were getting out of their rooms to investigate the loud crash!

"Emma, Julia," said Matron's loud voice, "open up girls."

"Quick Floppy, get under the bed," I moved towards the bed and lifted the blankets and bed valance, I turned and beckoned to him.

"No, no, I will explain..." he whispered, but He looked pale as he said the words.

"You may be sent down from school," suddenly said Julia.

"And what would your father say to that?" I warned.

"Well done, most likely. You know what a grave disappointment I am to him.... 'At last', he will say I am 'carrying on the family tradition.' " Floppy tried to make light of the situation. I could not help smiling, as he had told us many stories of his father and his uncle's narrow scrapes at their respective schools.

Matron had been knocking on other doors outside, she now came back to ours this time there was a magnificent rap. I went up to Floppy and pushed him towards his hiding place. Dumbly, he did as I bid him.

"Open the door Julia," I said in a calm voice as I adjusted the bed valance once Floppy had hidden himself.

"For god's sake Emma, is it okay?" said Julia looking fearfully over her shoulder, one hand on the door latch.

"Of course it's not!" I gave her a look. At the same time there was a humongous bang on the door as Julia moved to unlock the latch.

"My God, you do sleep lightly, don't you?" Matron's voice boomed, as she came into the room. I hugged my dressing gown tightly and stood rooted to my bed in front of Floppy's hiding place.

"What's the matter Matron?" I said quickly, trying to sound normal.

"Didn't you hear the noise?" said our classmate, Sally, from the door. Another girl popped her face in, "it was awfully loud, C-R-A-S-H!" she added melodramatically obviously enjoying herself hugely.

Matron was straightening the curtains, I was looking at her all the while, suddenly she lifted one end and looked out, "the plant stand, is broken outside. Drat, must have been the dog again. That's the third in the last two days," she said. She turned the door handle. "Good it's locked, keep it locked girls, just to be on the safe side," she moved towards me, I held my breath, but she walked past the bed and went to the door.

'Phew,' I thought to myself, Matron was standing in our doorway, frowning, "You didn't hear that noise?" she asked in a suspicious voice, I shook my head, looking back sweetly at her. She gave a searching look to Julia who (to my annoyance) went red, like an apple!

For a moment no one spoke, when the door closed behind her. We stood still waiting for the noises outside to abate. The girls were all very excited so it took a while to get back to their rooms. When it had been quite some five minutes, I silently opened our door and looked out into the corridor, there was no one there, it was now quiet and rather dark with only one night light on. I shut the door and ran back towards the bed, quickly bending down on to the floor, I whispered urgently and a little rudely to Floppy.

"Now go Floppy, if you are caught here, you've had it."

He slid out quite easily (as he was rather slim) "She wasn't convinced you know," he said rather nastily.

Julia came up to me and pulled at my sleeve, ignoring Floppy's remark, "But, what about Edward?"

"I don't know Julia, I really can't think of what to do," I answered.

"Unless" said Floppy "we go and make a clean breast of it."

"To the head, you mean?" I whispered.

We looked at each other.

"God! Why couldn't he let it be?" I sighed.

"Let's go now, before Edward gets into some serious trouble," whispered Julia really scared for Edward, "that man was very nasty, I can't get him out of my mind," she shuddered.

"Floppy, I'll make sure the coast is clear and then you run out of the girls' dormitory thus getting rid of one problem."

Floppy had the grace to blush. "Then," I continued "Julia and I will meet you in the green common room in ten minutes, okay? It's too dangerous to talk here, as you said Matron wasn't convinced, she may come back anytime."

I looked cautiously out into the corridor; it looked all right. I beckoned to Floppy who peered out and then just sprinted out of our sight.

My mind wasn't working as I pulled on my warmest grey trousers and dark blue jumper. Automatically I pulled up my socks and tied my shoe laces. Julia hurriedly did likewise. It was awfully dark and quiet outside.

"Lets take a torchlight along," I said suddenly.

Julia jumped at the sound of my voice and then gave me an angry look. "Really Emma!" she sighed. I grinned at her and moved towards the door.

"Coats," said Julia.

"Do we need them?" I turned towards her, "after all we are indoors."

"Okay," she shrugged and followed me out.

The green common room was just two or three passages away from our sleeping quarters along the green corridor, and consequently did not take us long to reach. It was quite strange to be entering the room in the dark, I clicked on my torch and shone it round the room; there was nobody there, the light created strange shadows, which made the atmosphere very eerie. We waited for what seemed to be an age and still no sign of Floppy.

"Let's go back, I don't like to stay here in the dark," whispered Julia, pulling at my sleeve as usual.

"Five more minutes," I whispered back.

Still no Floppy. We looked at each other in silent agreement, and crept out of the room, shutting the door carefully behind us.

There was no one about as we walked down the corridor. One or two bulbs lit the passage now and then, the rest was in darkness. We turned to our left, towards our bed rooms; I paused. I could hear a faint scratching noise. Julia, too, seemed to have heard it, as she too, paused. We both strained our ears trying to concentrate and listen. Yes, there was a distinct sound, not loud, but it could be heard. I turned towards the direction of the sound. Julia pulled vigorously at my sleeve, all the while shaking her head at me. I smiled reassuringly at her, but continued, this time towards the noise and away from our sleeping quarters. Poor Julia, what could she do, to continue alone was as frightening as following me. Sure enough, after a second's pause, she came up behind me.

I walked hesitatingly, pausing to listen every two or three minutes. At first the sound grew stronger. We were now walking down a long passage with windows on one side and a wall lined with photographs on the other. Julia looked fearfully around but did not say a word. Suddenly the noise stopped. One minute I could hear it clearly and the next minute it was all quiet. By now we were next to the dining hall, the door of which stood ajar. I sneaked up to it and peeped in, rather nervously, I must admit. At first I saw nothing, it was all as usual, the large tables and chairs arranged all over the room, could be seen vaguely because of the moonlight that peeped through the half drawn curtains. I looked around the room first quickly, then again with more concentration. My instinct told me that the noise came from somewhere here.

"Nothing," whispered Julia turning away.

"No, wait," I said. "See, Julia," I said again this time more urgently.

"Where?" said Julia.

I pointed to the row of golden pillars that stood at the far end of the room. Somewhere to the right hand side between two pillars, there was a disturbance. In plain words, between the two pillars, instead of seeing the wall with its usual white coloured elaborate carvings, what we now saw was a gaping dark hole!

I felt a thrill of excitement. This was a real adventure. Without a moment's hesitation I moved into the room. I kept my eyes on the wall and moved cautiously towards it; close behind me I could feel Julia's frightened presence.

All of sudden, when we were quite close to the 'hole' in the wall, we heard sound of footsteps. Without a word, we both ducked under the nearest table, and literally held our breaths. From where I sat, crouched on the floor under the table, I looked in the direction of the sound we had just heard; we now could hear distinct voices. Two male voices could be heard, they were not bothering to speak softly, so we could hear every word.

"What exactly did the chief want?" said one voice, it sounded coarse and uneducated.

"Must be after something big, or wouldn't bother down here," said the other in a slightly more cultured tone.

Then I saw to my shock two pairs of legs step coolly out of the 'hole' in the wall. There was a pause and one person seemed to move sideways, the other stood still for a moment. There was a buzzing sort of noise and I actually saw the wall moving to close the gap. It stopped with a click. Once this happened, the men simply walked off, out of the dining room, they didn't pause for a moment, as if there was no fear of being discovered at all!

Julia and I just sat where we were, hardly daring to breathe for fear that they may decide to come back. At last I turned towards her and gave her a nudge. We crawled out from under the huge wooden table and slowly straightened. I looked awestruck at the wall; it looked as it always did. Who could guess that it could open up? Silently we walked towards the door. We peeped out into the corridor, our hearts pounding loudly in our chests. "Suppose they came back, suppose..." was the only thought in our minds at that point.

Thankfully we reached our room without meeting anyone. As soon as the door shut behind us, I heaved a sigh of relief. I turned to look at Julia, to my surprise she was looking very excited.

"What?" I said.

"Oh Emma!" she said.

Her face was red and her eyes gleamed with a strange light.

"What is it Julia?" I asked alarmed.

"Did you not realize it? Couldn't you make out?" she mumbled, still whispering.

"For God sake, 'make out' what?" I said urgently.

"You didn't recognize the man?" she asked.

"What man?" I said fearfully "please tell me!"

"One of the men who came out of the wall was Marianne's horrid Mr Goddard!" she declared.

I stared at her aghast. "Are you sure? I mean we couldn't see the men!" I said.

"We didn't see him that day," she reminded me, "but I could recognize that horrid voice anywhere."

"No doubt?" I asked.

"None," she said flatly.

Now Julia had a talent for voices; not only could she do different voices, she could recognize people by their voices, it's a game we often played. If she said it was Mr Goddard, it simply was. We looked at each other, for a moment unable to say anything. Then I said looking around helplessly, "Gosh! What in the world is happening?"

"Where is Edward?" said Julia.

"Where is Floppy?" said I.

✦ ✦ ✦

6

Floppy meanwhile had been having his own adventure, which he told us about later. I will take a moment here to recount his experiences.

After he left us, he went back to his room. It had occurred to him that he should check if there was any sign of, or from, Edward. Finding none, he decided to change his clothes thinking that he should be properly attired if he was to meet the Head! Having completed this formality, he set off in the direction of the green common room.

As he rounded a corner in one dark passage he heard some voices. He wondered who it could be, walking around the school in the middle of the night. Instinctively he hid himself behind a large plant stand. Two men, and one lady walked by, the lady was silent (dressed in a dark skirt and jacket), but the two men talked together constantly.

One man who seemed rather large and thickset said to the other, "I'm sure it's a wild goose chase, Guvnor."

The other, a considerably smaller man, replied, "you do as you are told, leave the thinking to us."

"Come on, Guvnor, loosen up," said the large man.

"You talk too much, get you in trouble one of these days," threatened the smaller man.

Floppy couldn't catch any more of their conversation as they went out of his sight. For a moment he stood still, quietly listening in the dark. He was very puzzled. "Who were these people? Why are they here? What were the school security up to?" Suddenly he remembered us and quickly made his way to the common room. He entered the room and switched his torchlight on, there was no one there. He sat down on a sofa and waited. He says he was about to doze off when he felt, rather than heard, a little noise. Pointing his torch towards the door, he saw the door knob moving. Here it may have been instinct again, or the fact that he had just seen strangers walking around in school, but he put the torchlight off and ducked behind the sofa he had been sitting on.

Someone entered the room. All he could make out was a tallish form. Immediately he realized that it was not Julia and myself. This someone seemed to know his way about the room as he or she didn't use any light but made his way towards the far end of the room, where a long heavy wooden case containing books and manuscripts was kept. Floppy was looking intently at the dark form of the intruder, when the door was suddenly thrown open and some people burst into the room. The astonished Floppy looked back towards the book case, the first intruder had miraculously disappeared! Now he could see two people making their way towards the same book case. One person bumped into a table and loudly mouthed an oath, the other, more cautious, felt his or her way about and reached the book case without incident. Once there, one person switched on a torchlight, now Floppy could see that they were two men in darkish coats and hats. They appeared to be rummaging for something in the book case. Again one of the men began abusing in a rough coarse voice.

"Keep your mouth shut," ordered the other rudely.

"I'm not the man for this kind of job, I'm used to bigger stuff," said the coarse voice.

"No doubt," said the other sarcastically.

"Woman's job, this is, get her to do it," replied the coarse voice, one thumb gesturing towards the door.

"You keep your mouth shut or we'll do it for you," said the other in a soft silky and yet, ugly voice. Somehow that voice sent a chill down Floppy's spine. For the first time, he was scared. He held his breath as he watched the two men leave the room. They didn't bother to shut the door behind them.

Floppy looked around the room trying to see where the 'first' intruder was, but it was too dark without the flashlight and he was too frightened to switch it on. He decided to creep out of the room. He was just about to crawl forward on his hands and knees, when suddenly someone drooped down on top of him.

"Oh hell," said a male voice as a huge form fell, half on top of poor Floppy and half on the hard floor.

"What the hell?" repeated the intruder in considerable irritation. Floppy tried to get up, he wanted to run but couldn't move, as half of him seemed to be buried under the other.

The intruder somehow managed to grab his collar and they both struggled to vertical positions. Poor Floppy tried to struggle out of the intruder's clutches but couldn't move, as the other man was too strong.

"What have we here?" said the man to himself. "Let's see." He put on his torchlight and aimed it towards Floppy.

"A school boy, hmm, what are you doing up at this hour, I wonder?" he said.

At this point Floppy felt a vague sense of familiarity; he managed to croak out, as he felt half strangled. "Who are you?"

As an answer the intruder walked to the door, carefully shut it and then put the electric light on. Floppy found that he was looking at Mrs Weston's handsome nephew, William. For a moment neither of them spoke.

"Well?" said William looking intently at Floppy. "Where have I seen you before? You look familiar."

"Just came up for a book," mumbled Floppy, rubbing his neck and struggling to get to his feet.

"Is that so?" said the other incredulously.

"For that matter what are you doing here?" said Floppy trying to turn the tables, a little bolder now.

"The same, came up for a book," grinned the other. They both laughed. The tension in the room eased a bit. There was a pause.

"Saw the men?' hesitatingly asked Floppy, "who the hell were they?" blurted the other.

"Lord knows, saw them in the corridor on my way up, seemed to be going all over the school," said Floppy reflectively.

"Do people come and go just like that?" asked William, "what are your gatekeepers up to?"

"Never heard of such a thing," said Floppy.

"Did you really come up for a book?" asked William.

"No, did you?" replied Floppy.

"No," said the other ruefully. "Well then, I'll go first," said Floppy, "my friends are in a spot of trouble and were to meet here to discuss what to do. Actually we thought we would go to the Head and make a clean breast of it, something like that, what about you?"

"That is a long story, I will tell you in the morning," said William, "but tell me your troubles, I may be able to help you all," he smiled at Floppy.

Meanwhile Julia and I were sitting on our beds, discussing what to do next. After about fifteen minutes of useless talk we grew quiet, quite at a loss.

"Let's go and look for Floppy?" I said suddenly getting decisive and jumping up from the bed.

Julia looked at me, a worried look on her face, "Of course, I'll come with you, but Emma I doubt if we will find him. Why, we waited for him for ages and he didn't turn up."

I looked at her, impatiently, "get up Julia, anything is better than sitting here and worrying, we can hardly go to sleep!" For the second time that night, we went out of our room, and down the corridor. This time we took two torches and Julia, as a last minute afterthought, armed herself with her badminton racket, "just in case..." she said.

We walked slowly, trying to make as little noise as possible, which was difficult due to the wooden floors of the great old building. At some places the floor creaked ominously, making us stop, and look around in case anyone was following us. In this manner we looked for Floppy in all the common rooms, except the green room as we had already been in there, and the music rooms that were on the ground floor; needless to say there was no sign of him. We were now almost in the centre of the school, near the main entrance.

"Let's go back," pleaded Julia, pulling at my sleeve.

"In a moment," I whispered back.

"Emma," she said "I insist, it's too scary, walking around in the dark."

We were standing in a little visitor's room, the windows of which looked out at the front porch. I was casually looking out, as Julia was persuading me to give up the search for Floppy. My eyes caught sight of a light in the bushes that stood on the left side of porch.

"Come on," I sprinted out of the room, pulling the reluctant Julia with me.

"Where are we going now?" she almost wailed.

"Come on, be adventurous," I said.

"Emma, its cold, I refuse to go," said Julia stopping in her tracks, and almost stamping her feet. "Oh bother, we should have put on our coats," I murmured. I looked around the lobby and saw the coat stand next to the great front door; it had a few coats on it. Julia was following my eyes, as soon as she saw me looking at the coats, she shook her head vehemently.

"Oh, come on, we'll just take a quick look," I coaxed.

"At what? The garden? If those men are around they might just hit us over the head. One of these days your spirit of adventure will really get you into trouble...and me with you," she mumbled.

I wasn't listening to her, having grabbed the nearest coat, I was busy putting it on. Suddenly, I realized Julia was giggling. "What?" I asked.

Julia turned me towards the mantelpiece, above which was a colossal mirror. I too laughed; I was wearing a huge man's coat and swimming in it. "Oh bother," I said, getting out of it. I selected two other coats, this time more carefully, trying to match our sizes. We both hastily put them on, one was grey and the other brown, we then grabbed matching hats.

I turned the handle of the front door, thinking it would be locked, and we would have to use another exit. To my surprise, it was open. I peered out, at first glance I saw nothing unusual. A cold blast of air, greeted us as we stepped out. Quickly Julia stepped back indoors whispering imploringly, "I can't. Come back please." I looked at her for a second. "Wait here, I'll be back in a minute," I said and without stopping for any reply, I pulled the hat down on my face and went down the stairs that led into the school's main porch. It was quite dark outside as the moon was hidden in the clouds but I walked purposefully towards the bushes I had noticed from inside.

I skirted round the bushes; there was no sign of any light. In fact everything was quite as usual, I looked around carefully. I couldn't see anything suspicious. It was very cold, with a slight mist coming up. I pulled the belt of the coat tightly round me and pulled the hat down as far as it would go. It was on my way back, shivering in the freezing cold, that I had a great fright!

A figure appeared to jump out from the trees that stood to the left of me. At the sight of it, I froze; I just stared at it as it moved straight towards me. In my mind I knew I should run, but my legs just wouldn't move. The mist, now like a blanket around me, and the figure, approaching...nearer and nearer.

As it came, I realized it was a huge man, with a great coat and dark hat, he was purposefully walking towards me, it was only when he came within touching distance, that I turned from him, about to take to my heels, but just then, to my utter horror, he grabbed my hand, thrust something in it and hurried away.

I stood there, paralyzed with fear, staring at the running figure. I heard an engine start somewhere and the sound of a running car. I turned and ran back towards the porch and up the stairs where Julia was standing, her worried face relaxing as I came in. She pulled me into the building and pushed the heavy door shut behind her.

"You saw?" I asked.

"Saw what? She replied, "I couldn't see you, you went behind those bushes, I was dying of fear,"

"A man," I said impatiently, "came towards me."

"A man?" she said, I nodded. "What's this?" She asked pointing at my hand.

I looked down at my own hands. Automatically one hand was clutching a white narrow sheet of paper.

"He put it in my hands, Julia," I whispered. We looked at each other.

"My god!" said my timid friend.

Now that I was indoors and the door was shut, I was feeling more like myself. I managed to give Julia a half smile. She was looking petrified!

"Let's go back, I insist," said Julia.

"Alright," I replied, not very unwillingly. We took our coats off and put them and the hats back from where we had taken them. All the while I held on to the paper I had been given, we then made our way back to our rooms, luckily without any further incident.

Lights off time at Winwood Manor School was 9.30 p.m. sharp. The rule was strictly implemented. Hence everyone was pretty well equipped with torchlights: when we sneaked down the corridor and pushed the door of our room, the first thing we noticed was that the lamp was on.

"Didn't we put the lamp off?" I whispered to Julia, she hesitated, "I'm sure we did," she whispered back, "I can't understand it, if anyone noticed..." she stopped, staring ahead of her.

Now Julia was standing near the door she had just opened, thus facing the room, I, meanwhile, was a little behind her. We both looked into the room and got the fright of our lives. In the dimly lit little room, there seemed to have magically appeared two figures, instinctively I shrank towards Julia.

"Don't scream, don't scream for God's sake," said a familiar voice, I turned and gave a careful look at the figures.

"It's me girls," said one figure. "Oh god Floppy, you almost killed me with fright," I said forgetting to whisper, and pushing Julia into the room.

"You, miss Emma, die of fright? Whatever is the world coming to!" said Floppy.

"Hush" said Julia, "you will have everyone in here if you talk so loudly."

"Tonight, I could die of fright, I really could," I grinned.

"Hello," said the second figure drawing attention to his presence, perhaps feeling left out of things.

"You," I said, not too politely, recognizing William.

"Me," he said simply and waited. There was a pause, Julia was staring at William, who I might mention looked exceedingly handsome, even in the middle of the night. Floppy was looking nervously at me, and I was, well, confused.

"It's all right Emma," said Floppy, "I have told William our story."

I gave him a sharp look; it was obviously not too trusting. William caught my look and burst out laughing.

"Hush," said Julia blushing all the while, "not so loud, please." I gave Julia a contemptuous look, "Okay he's unusually handsome, but why go to pieces?" I thought to myself.

"Would you like to share your adventure with us?" asked the Prince in a meek voice.

I looked him up and down.

"How do we know, we can trust you?" I asked curtly.

"Emma," said Floppy "really!"

"It's okay," said William. Obviously, his being Mrs Weston's nephew was enough for Floppy. William looked at me reflectively, "You don't, you know, but it looks to me that you are in trouble and could do with a little adult help or else, what are you all going to do?" I couldn't argue with that, not after tonight's adventures. All of a sudden the fight went out of me and I sank down on my bed. With that action everyone in the room seemed to relax. Julia came and sat down beside me. Floppy sat on the small stiff chair in front of a little desk, on which was the little lamp, and William sat on the only arm chair in the room.

"Tell us," said William invitingly, "your story."

For the next ten minutes none of them said a word. I spoke softly, trying not to leave any of the details out.

I started with our looking for Floppy in the green common room and went on with the adventure in the dining room. Common sense told me that it was time we got someone's help, I personally would have preferred the Head but now that Floppy had taken William into his confidence, there was nothing to be done. I had the satisfaction of seeing them look quite shocked when I came to the part about the man thrusting the paper into my hand, the two men, younger and older both looked quite taken aback.

"That paper?" asking William pointing at my hand.

"Yes," I replied, looking down at my own hand, which was still automatically holding on to the paper.

"Well, what is it?" He asked.

"I don't know," I replied truthfully, as I hadn't got a chance to look at it.

He stretched his hand out for it and I gratefully handed it over. Glad now to have an older ally. He got up and walk towards the pathetic little lamp we had. We all got up and stood round as he bent down and held the paper up to the light. It was rather a dirty little paper, in fact, nothing but a scrap of paper. Printed on it were a few words 'THE HIDDEN CELLAR–1.15 a.m. SUNDAY'.

"What does it mean?" blurted Julia, the first to react.

William was turning the note in all directions and looking at it under the lamp's dim light.

Floppy had got up from his chair and was leaning on the table on which the lamp rested and looking intently at the note as William moved it around. At last William looked up at us. Floppy took the note from him and began examining it. "Held by dirty hands," he remarked, holding the paper up to the light.

"Not mine," I snapped.

"Relax," he said "wasn't talking of you. Your friend, who gave it to you!" he teased.

"You hideous character! He was certainly not my friend," I said rudely.

"Yes, wonder why he gave it to you?" mumbled William.

"Perhaps he mistook Emma for someone." Suddenly said Julia in a rare moment of enlightenment.

We all looked at her wonderingly "Yes, of course," I said excitedly "it was very dark and even misty. Must have mistaken me for someone."

"His real friend," said Floppy giving me a sly look "poor Emma."

"Funny!" I said.

"Yes, yes," reflected William. "The man was in the bushes, as you saw from inside. He was waiting for someone. You came out, so he thought you were that person and handed you the note and left. As simple as that. But how was he so sure, he must have been quite near you to thrust the note in your hand."

"May be she looks like the someone?" suggested Floppy. "You know, height, figure..."

"The coat!" I shouted suddenly.

They all stopped what they were saying and looked at me. "I told you, each of us put on a coat from the rack next to the main door. By sheer chance I must have put on the coat of the expected person!" I was looking at William as I spoke.

"Yes, and it fitted you, so you must be a similar shape and size," finished William.

"The plot thickens," said Floppy reflectively.

"It is all very strange," I said. "I mean, who are these people and why the sudden interest in our school. It's just a school after all, isn't it?"

I looked at William. "Yes, just a school. But it wasn't always a school, was a family home originally, then a nunnery, then a family home again. God knows, how many things have happened here," he was frowning as he spoke, clearly trying to sort something out in his mind."

"All this, so soon after you all came across the house in the woods, when you got lost...," he continued.

"Oh! Didn't I tell you?" I said excitedly. Everybody looked at me.

"Tell us what?" asked Floppy curtly.

"Listen carefully, Julia recognized one of the men in the dining room," I whispered.

"I recognized the voice," clarified Julia, again blushing.

William looked at her, speculatively.

"No, really," I said, "she's got a great sense for voices, can recognize anybody's voice, and imitate them too," I said, a little challenge in my voice.

William grinned, "Is that so?" He asked, clearly not convinced.

"Yes, really, you must believe that," I said, "It's very important that you do. For don't you see, one of the men in the dining room was the man with Marianne!"

As I said that, the smile suddenly vanished from William's face. For a minute he looked for some strange reason, furious. I was a little taken aback.

"And you forgot to tell us this?" said Floppy accusingly at that same moment.

I turned to him, "I'm sorry I forgot one point in all this madness." I looked back at William curiously, but he was back to his old self. The strange expression I had just seen, completely gone from his face.

"Mr Goddard?" he asked.

"Yes," I said simply.

"And this note, was it given to you by him?" He asked looking at the scrap of paper still in his hand, a sense of urgency in his voice.

"I don't know. How can I? We never saw the man," I replied almost apologetically.

"Hmm, THE HIDDEN CELLAR, We must find out what this means," he said softly.

"What about Edward?" I reminded them.

"Yes, we must bring him back," added Julia.

"You are all very sure he has gone there, the house in the woods?" William looked round us.

"Oh yes, no doubt about that," I said.

"You see, she was so very beautiful," added Julia, as if that explained it all.

William looked at Julia, a strange inexplicable expression on his face. He saw me looking at him, and immediately turned from me. There was a long pause, each of us perhaps thinking of the unusual situation, in our own ways.

"Floppy," I said "something just occurred to me, none of us have been to the Head as planned earlier."

"She isn't here," he replied.

"What do you mean?" I asked.

"She is not here," he replied. "Watch my lips N-O-T here."

"Has gone to a seminar at Greenwood Hall," (a neighboring school), explained William, hastily seeing me bristle up, "left this evening, in fact I saw her off."

Again there was a pause, as Julia and I digested this news.

"Well, then, we must rally about somehow," I said in my usual style, getting back into action mode, and walking up and down the little space we had, Julia looked at me, a little worried. "Emma, please don't come up with a crazy scheme," she said.

"She usually does that, does she?" William asked, bending towards her as he spoke, she blushed a bright red.

"We cannot sit here wondering what to do. Let's just do what we have to," I said, mostly to William.

"And what is that?" He asked, an amused look on his face, which I must say, irritated me exceedingly. "Go and look for Edward, of course!" I answered.

"Of course, why didn't I think of that," William grinned.

I gave him a look and turned to Floppy. "Come Floppy; get up, stop looking so dazed. Let's find Edward and then we'll think of the rest," I said.

"Should we tell Matron or Miss Lewis...?" trailed Julia's voice, meeker than ever.

"I'm not sure," I answered.

Floppy and I looked at each other then at William. "What do you advise?" Floppy asked him.

"I'll go with whatever Emma decides," said William in a docile voice looking at me, a twinkle in his eye.

"He's laughing at me," I thought to myself "best to ignore him."

"Well, Emma?" said Floppy.

"What? Oh, yes of course." I said.

"Yes, what?" he asked, most amused.

"Yes, of course, we must set off to look for Edward," I replied coldly, looking at Floppy, and trying to ignore William.

"On foot?" William asked.

"How else," I said, "hope you are a good walker, he must have gone in search of the house in the woods, you are coming aren't you?" I looked at William challengingly.

"I'll try to bear up," he said meekly.

"So we are not to take anyone into our confidence," said Floppy looking at us intently.

"This evening's events suggest that somehow the school is involved in something shady. Now someone from here could be, indeed must be, mixed up with these people or rather this gang, whatever we call them. I think it best to manage on our own right now," said William. He spoke seriously, we all looked at each other and nodded, seeing the sense in what he said.

"The question is, should Floppy and I go on our own, it is one o'clock at night," he said, looking at Julia and me "and it may not be very safe, in fact, quite the reverse..."

"Of course we will go," I interrupted rudely, "why should we be left out? Right Julia?"

"Oh Emma," said Julia resigned to her fate.

+ + +

7

It had been decided that we would all gear up for the outdoors, so to speak, and meet in the green common room in ten minutes. Thus, Julia and I once again left our cozy room to creep down the corridor and head to the green room. We were the first to arrive; followed in about five minutes, by Floppy, dressed in his brown coat and brown and black check hat. We waited silently for our new friend. He did not disappoint us. Wearing a black overcoat and matching boots, his thick blond hair in some disarray, he looked like the perfect picture of a romantic hero!

I glared at Julia who was staring at William. I do not think she even realized it really, most irritating! As soon as he entered we all stood up, ready to go. Floppy had our exit well planned. The boys sometimes went for walks in the grounds after lock up and so knew which door to use. We trooped down several passages, as noiselessly as possible. The door Floppy had in mind was precariously near the teachers' rooms. When we reached it, we discovered that it was locked. We looked at each other in dismay. "Now what?" I asked Floppy.

"We can try the door leading out of the piano room, that is Julia groaned, as the said room was a long walk away, back towards our rooms. We headed towards it and tried the door. This too, was locked.

"Now what?" I asked no one in particular.

"You went out earlier from the main door, didn't you?" William asked in a low voice.

"Yes, the great big one, that was open, I was quite shocked." I answered.

"Let's check it, whoever opened it may not have locked it as yet," he said.

We all went to the school's entrance. Once there, we strained our eyes and looked around. In the dark, we could see no one about. Floppy gestured to us to stop and listen; there was no unusual sound, so we went into the lobby, from where, earlier in the night, Julia and I had picked up the coats.

William tried the door, it was still unlocked. We exchanged meaningful glances. William stood to one side and gestured to us to go out. As the door opened, a cold blast of night air greeted us, Floppy slipped out first, followed by the unhappy Julia. Just as I was about to step outside, William stretched his arm and stopped me, "one moment Emma, can you tell me which coat you had put on?" he whispered, "I think it's very important."

I walked to the coat stand, the door shut behind me. William followed me. We both looked at the various coats hanging there.

"Look carefully, don't make a mistake," he cautioned.

There weren't too many coats. In fact only one grey one, I pointed to it. "That's the one," I said.

"Sure?" he asked, lifting it up, and examining it.

"Yes absolutely," I said.

Suddenly he looked excited. I looked sharply at him.

"What's the matter?" I asked.

"It's warm Emma, touch it," he whispered.

I touched the inner lining, just below the collar, with my hand. Sure enough it was warm; someone must have just taken it off. Instinctively I glanced around. We were both standing near the coat stand, the large mirror opposite us, it was dark. There was no sign of anyone else about. All the same, I shivered and moved closer to William. He was still examining the coat.

"No name," he said, "nothing in the pockets, let's go." He hung the coat back up on its hook, and went to the door. "Come on," he called softly to me. I was standing near the hat stand staring at it. He came back to me, and looked curiously at me.

"Is anything wrong?" he whispered.

"The hat, the grey one I wore with the coat. It isn't here," I said to him.

"Are you sure you hung it back?" he asked.

"Hundred percent, I was careful to put it where I had found it," I explained.

We looked at the hats that were on the stand, there was no grey hat.

"Well come on, Floppy and Julia must be freezing outside." He reminded me.

"Yes, we'd better go," I agreed, reluctantly. "Someone definitely went out after me. Now who could it be?" I whispered looking at him.

"Don't worry we'll find out," he said firmly, pulling me outside after him.

To our surprise, Floppy and Julia were not waiting outside the door on the top of the stairs as we expected. We stood still for a moment and looked around. It was now decidedly misty, the cold air felt pretty uncomfortable. I shivered involuntarily. William ran down the stairs, I followed him quickly. We went down, across the porch, along the drive, all the while, looking around for our friends.

"Floppy," I called softly, "Julia."

There was a sound 'psst....' I stopped and peered around in the darkness. 'psst....'

William too, must have heard it for he too had stopped.

"Here, we are," said a familiar voice. "In the bushes."

I looked around frantically, I couldn't make out which bushes he meant, there were so many, well shrouded in the darkness and mist.

"Come out, man," said William impatiently. "What's with hiding in the bushes?"

I gave a start as Floppy suddenly sprang out of the bushes, next to us, almost on top of us, he was that close.

"It's Julia," he said "she's too scared."

"What of, the cold? There's no one about," I said, "who in his right mind will come out on such a night as this?"

William looked at me and laughed, he said cajolingly, "Come out Julia, we'll look after you," Pushing some branches with her hands, Julia stepped out, she actually looked frightened. One look at her and I knew something was wrong.

"What's happened?" I asked.

"Oh Emma" she whispered "there is something going on here all right!"

"We were standing at the head of the stairs waiting for you two," explained Floppy glancing at Julia, "I saw something moving in those bushes," he pointed to his left and paused.

"Go on," prompted William, standing with his arms crossed, his head slightly bent towards Floppy.

"A light, I saw a light, like Emma said she had seen. It looked like a lantern being swayed, or it may have been the wind. I pulled Julia and we ducked behind the large flower pot outside the main door. In a minute the light disappeared. Then nothing, no one appeared. Absolutely nothing."

"A ghost, I'm sure it was a ghost," mumbled Julia.

William looked slightly taken aback, but didn't say anything. "I tried to pull the door, in order to go back indoors but it wouldn't budge from the outside. Then all of a sudden I felt that I should investigate the event instead of running away, so I moved towards where we had seen the light."

"I went with him," said Julia breathlessly.

"But there was no one about, absolutely no one, not a person, not a lantern, nothing," said Floppy. "But I swear I saw a light, it flashed from somewhere in the distance...around there..." he pointed in the direction of the orangery, which, of course, we couldn't see from where we were, "and then, it disappeared just like that!" He snapped his fingers.

"A ghost" chanted Julia.

William walked into the bushes Floppy had been talking about. We stood still, while he made a round and came back to us. "I can't see anything unusual. But we'll come back and check in the morning. Right now I suggest we carry on with our plan. Is that okay with everyone?" He was looking at Julia when he said the last sentence. To my surprise she nodded her assent. William glanced at me, my chin went up as if daring him to ask me, his eyes twinkled, "well I have at least one good news for you all," he said softly. We stood still, looking at him "it's about 'the house in the woods'," he continued.

"Well, what about it, it's where we are heading, isn't it?" I interrupted.

"Patience," he said to me, and turned to the others. "I know where it is," he looked around at us all.

"You know where it is?" I said angrily, "you know where it is and didn't tell us till now?" I said accusingly.

"How do you know it?" asked Floppy, a little excitedly, but making an effort to sound calm. Julia just stared at William.

"From your description, it sounds like the 'Old Dowager's House," he said in a flat voice.

"Old Dowager's House?" echoed Floppy.

"How dare you be so insensitive? You knew all along and didn't tell us," I stamped my foot.

He was looking and me, grinning in a most irritating manner, "now I know first-hand how school girls behave," he murmured, further irritating me.

"This is not fair. You know how worried we are about Edward and you're just fooling around," I accused him.

"No, I'm not. I'm taking you all there," he replied calmly.

"But you..." I started, ready to battle.

"Emma stop, its cold and getting late, can you continue this discussion some other time, some other place?" Floppy looked from me to William.

"Of course," I said coldly and lapsed into silence.

William was looking around at us, "listen, all of you," he said, his voice suddenly serious. "I know this house because I used to go with my friends and explore it when I was at school,"

Here we looked at him in surprise, as we had not known he'd been at Winwood Manor School.

"It is actually not very far once you know how to reach it, you must have been walking in circles when you got lost so you thought it to be very far." He paused, looking at us. None of us said anything. He waited for a minute, then he said simply, "shall we go?"

None of us showed any surprise when William took another path than the one we had been expecting. Quietly, we followed him. We cleared the school fence and got into the little lane outside, he led us to a motor car parked unobtrusively on the other side of the road. Julia nudged me as we got into the motor car; Floppy in the front with William, and Julia and I in the back seat. Floppy was visibly excited at the sight of the motor car and was openly marveling at it. Julia was too shocked with all the events to react to anything, whereas I was still chaffing at what I considered William's dictatorial way of functioning! The engine was started, we drove through the narrow lanes and then into smaller paths for about half an hour. I was almost dozing off; when I was jerked awake by the car suddenly coming to a halt. Looking out I saw we were in the forest; it was pitch dark and awfully quiet. I turned to Julia, she was fast asleep.

"We will park here, it's better not to go too close to the house," said our self appointed leader.

"Yes, the engine might be heard," agreed Floppy.

"Come on girls," said William getting out of the car with some difficulty; he had rather long legs.

I nudged Julia, not too gently. "Get up Julia, we're there," I said, close to her ear. She gave a start and opened her eyes.

"What, so soon?" she said. I was already out of the car, she quickly jumped out. We stood still for a moment, taking stock of our surroundings. They were pretty daunting, to say the least. I shivered, Julia grabbed my arm, "gosh!" she said, looking around.

We were standing in a little clearing. The car had been parked on one side, next to some trees. Ahead, what can only be called a narrow, uneven path, that lead further into the forest. We were surrounded by tall trees and darkness (and God knows how many wild animals!)

William had already started down the said path, Floppy closely following him, Julia and I almost ran to keep with them. We walked for about five to ten minutes. Then, abruptly, the boys came to a halt, William turned and gestured to us to be quiet, we crept ahead through some bushes and then suddenly, there it was, the mysterious house in the woods! The view we got of the house was from the east side, we could only seen the walls and the windows on that side. William seemed to know his way about and kept moving, slowly getting closer to the house. All of us following his lead.

Finally we reached the part of the wall that was closest to us. We walked along it till we reached a ground room window. The curtains were snugly drawn, we could see nothing. William tried to push open a window, it was locked. In this way, we circled the entire house. It was rather a large building and took a while, at some places we tripped over little side steps, once I almost fell on top of a potted plant; Julia grabbed me just in time.

"Nothing," Julia whispered to me.

"Seems deserted," I whispered back.

"Shhh" cautioned Floppy.

We were at the back of the house now. There was a large garden, in front of which about five or six stone steps led up to a balcony, which opened into a path that led up to a large door. It was really very pretty; the garden had huge trees forming a sort of square line around its boundaries. In one corner, there was what looked like a pond or something made of some sort of stone. I couldn't see from where we stood. William was trying all the windows patiently; Floppy was trying to peer into the house. I was looking around curiously.

"Where could Edward be, he doesn't seem to be here..." I thought to myself. I went up to William, "shall I whisper his name?" I asked.

He shook his head; his hand pushing at a window, we both gave a start as it swung open. Floppy and Julia came running up to us, Floppy excited, Julia looking shocked. William pushed the curtain a little, just enough to peep into the room. It wasn't a room at all, it was a narrow passage. William turned back, we all straightened up and stood in a circle.

"I'm going in," he said.

"Oh no," said Floppy instinctively, pushing his spectacles up on his nose.

I bent down and looked down into the passage again. It was dark and silent, not giving anything away.

"I'll come with you," I whispered.

"Oh no Emma, you cannot break into other people's homes, it's against the law," mumbled poor Julia.

"We have to go and search for Edward," I stated simply, "and anyway, it's a weird house, doesn't seem to belong to anyone."

"You all wait here," said William meaningfully.

"I will come with you, two is better than one...," I looked at him, then added coaxingly, "besides you may need help."

"I'll come too," said Floppy.

"You and Julia stay here," said William firmly, "if we don't come back in an hour, go back to school and get help. Do you understand Floppy? It will not be safe to stay here for long."

Floppy and William looked at each other, understandingly; Julia looked over her shoulder and shivered.

"Now go and wait," William looked around, "there, in those bushes," he pointed to one corner of the back garden. "That's where Emma and I will join you when we come out."

"Let Emma wait, I'll come with you," appealed Floppy.

"No, better not to leave girls alone," replied William after a minute's thought, "in fact I would much rather go on my own."

"Oh no," I said quickly, "I am determined to come with you, be sensible, it may be helpful."

"Stubborn, aren't you?" he mumbled.

"Very," I whispered back.

"Well come on then, let's not waste time," he grinned and turned to the window.

Floppy and Julia moved towards the bushes. William looked inside to make sure there was no one about, then he turned and watched till Floppy and Julia disappeared from sight. He climbed in first, with some difficulty as the window was narrow and low for so tall a person to squeeze through. Once he was inside, I nimbly jumped in.

I must say that, although I am a person who is always ready for an adventure and does not scare easily, I felt a distinct sense of apprehension as we moved further into the house. It was much larger than the impression it gave from the outside. There were several passages with doors opening into various rooms, most of the furniture covered by dust sheets. It did not look as if anybody was living in it, as we went about looking into various rooms we saw nothing unusual. After a while we become bolder and louder.

"The furniture looks pretty old," I murmured, aiming my torchlight at a large arm chair that was not covered by any sheet. William did not reply. He was slowly walking along the wooden floor boards and examining them with the help of his torchlight. I turned from him and looked around curiously; there was a large table and two chairs, in the room. I looked out of the window at the drive way. Suddenly it came to me. "Yes, of course!" I said.

"What is it?" asked William sharply.

"This room," I said gesturing round it. "It must have been in here that David saw the man and two women. You know, when we first came here..." my voice lowered "he said that one woman was covering the mouth of the other one."

William looked around. He walked to the table and directed the torch at it. I followed him.

"Look," he said, excitedly "at last some sign of life."

I looked at the table but saw nothing unusual. It was quite as dusty as all the rest of the visible furniture.

"Here, look here," he pointed to the edge of the table.

Then I realized what he meant. There were distinct finger marks along the edge of the table. Definitely someone had touched it recently. There was also a round mark further down the table as if something had been put on it and then taken away. The rest of the table top was covered with dust. We looked at each other, a little satisfied. "I was beginning to give up," he said, "but now we know someone has been here...come on."

We went out of the room and down a passage. We were now in the main foyer of the house. On one side was the large solid wooden front door, and on the other, an extremely ornate console table with a mirror hanging over it, next to it, a wooden staircase of baroque style. For a moment I just stared at the grand staircase.

"All this faded grandeur and Mr Goddard, just don't go together," I whispered to William.

"No, I don't think they do," he replied. "Shall we?" he gestured at the stairs and offered me his arm invitingly. Like a gentleman asking a lady for a dance. I giggled and put one foot on the stairs, it made a creaking sound. I stopped and looked up apprehensively, no, there was no other sound. Carefully we began to climb over the stairs.

The wall was lined with portraits of unknown people dressed in old fashioned clothes. I looked around me with wonder. Clearly this house belonged to some old family. Once on the landing upstairs, I looked down. "Gosh, it really is very grand," I thought to myself. The landing bifurcated into two directions. "Why don't you do one side and I, the other?" I whispered to William. He hesitated for a minute.

"It will save time and in any case I don't think there is anyone here, it is too quiet," I added.

He nodded, "I will wait for you here when I finish," he said and moved into the corridor on our left.

I went down the passage on my right. The rooms on either side of the passage were mostly bedrooms and bathrooms. I patiently crept into each and every room and looked around. Here too, there were dust sheets over the furniture. Two bedrooms had wooden four poster beds with faded curtains around them. There were beautiful old desks and large chairs. I looked around in wonder, almost forgetting the purpose of my visit. I was now standing in the largest bedroom which was at the end of the passage, it had a huge ornate four poster bed with old brocade curtains.

"Must be the master bedroom," I thought, looking around curiously. A mahogany side board had two large candlesticks on it, covered with cobwebs. An ornate fire place stood proudly in the centre of the wall, facing the bed, white sheets covered the furniture in front of the fire place. I stood almost mesmerized; here in this room was tremendous atmosphere, no doubt about it. I walked around slowly, carefully looking at each and every thing, as if searching for a clue.

Till today, I feel that something or some presence guided me in that room. Somehow I found myself pulling out drawers and looking inside them, which I had not done in any of the other rooms. Everything smelt musty, there were several faded papers, even dry flowers, in the drawers. By now I was scared; I looked over my shoulder at the cold, deserted room and shivered, but kept to my task "what am I looking for?" I asked myself "what can possibly be in these drawers?" I had reached one of the bedside tables, its cover had fallen to the floor next to it. My heartbeat raced as I pulled open its drawers. There were three drawers, all of which were empty. Disappointed, I moved to the other side. 'Curious,' I thought, for the dust sheet from this side table too was lying on the floor next to it. I looked over my shoulder, then back at the table. As expected these three drawers were empty too. Unconsciously, I sat down on the bed. Again, I looked around the room, frowning. "This room must have belonged to someone, someone must have lived here, slept on this bed..." I patted the mattress. Absentmindedly, I pushed the lowest drawer of the side table, near me as it was protruding slightly. I pushed it, in order to close it, but it wouldn't go any further "perhaps something is stuck behind it," I thought to myself. My heart was jumping wildly as I pulled the whole drawer out of its place, I sat on the floor and bent my head to look inside. It was dark. I directed my torch inside and sure enough there it was, the impediment, a yellowish paper. Without a moment's hesitation I pulled it out. My hand shaking with excitement or nervousness, I know not which. I straightened it with my hands. Breathlessly I looked at it, at first glance, it looked like a blank sheet of thick paper. I turned it around and froze. There in my hands was a photograph. A woman dressed in an old fashioned blouse and a large hat. The woman stood straight and was looking into the camera. I stared at her face, aghast. For the woman in the photograph dressed in the fashion of the generation gone by, was none other than our new acquaintance, Marianne! I fell back, on my knees onto the floor. It creaked painfully and that was enough for me. My bravado quite gone, I scampered to my feet and fled, out of the room down the corridor, towards the landing, straight into the shocked William's arms.

"What?" he said, automatically putting a reassuring arm, around me, "steady there, what's happened?"

For a moment I couldn't speak, I just clung on to the lapel of his coat. I was, I am ashamed to admit, in a panic. "Let's go, please," I whispered as soon as I could find my voice, glancing fearfully towards the direction I had come from.

"Yes of course, but what has caused you to be so frightened?" he asked in a soft kind voice.

I looked up at him and then silently handed him the photograph. He pushed me gently away from himself and looked down at the old fashioned photograph. Again I saw the strange expression on his face, it was difficult to describe.

"Why is he looking like that?" I thought to myself. I looked around nervously. I took two steps away from him "after all we don't know him at all! Gosh, there is no one here but me and him." I looked around wildly but no help came from anywhere, there was only darkness and silence in the strange old deserted house! At last he looked up from the picture in his hand.

"Emma," he said in a deep low voice, "I need to tell you something," again that intense, serious look, I was about to faint with terror.

"No, no, listen to me," I interrupted. He look surprised "that's Marianne, the girl we met," I blurted hysterically, somehow I wanted to keep talking, god knows what I feared that he might say to me.

"I know," he said "but listen carefully to what I am going to tell you," he continued.

At that very moment, there was tremendous crash. We stood absolutely still. Not moving, totally shocked. Then, there was silence. Just a C-R-A-S-H, then silence.

"It came from there," I said in an expressionless voice, pointing at the corridor from which I had just come running out.

He was already in the corridor, looking into each room as he went along. I stood where I was, staring after him. Then I heard his voice, calling my name urgently.

"Emma," he said "Emma, come here, quick," he shouted.

Somehow that voice brought me back to my senses. I shook myself and ran to where he was. The room, from which he was calling my name turned out to be a large and airy, bathroom. I had looked at it when I was exploring, which seemed so long ago now. It had a large washbasin, a mirror hanging over it, a rich heavily carved towel stand, a large wooden bath with a soap tray still on it, and a wooden screen in one corner. It was this wooden screen that had fallen down and must have made the noise we just heard. Silently I moved further into the room, the beautiful screen lay on the floor, exposing what had been hidden behind it: a huddled form, over which William was bent. I went towards him and received another shock. The huddled form was looking at us, and we at him. It was our friend Edward, with his mouth expertly gagged and his hands and feet tied up!

✦ ✦ ✦

8

Edward's Tale

Not content to let things be, Edward had made up his mind to try and do what he was sure the beautiful Marianne was in need of – rescue. He told us that his plan had really been very simple. He would steal out in the middle of the night and get to the old house in the forest. Unknown to us he had found out all about the house itself. It now seemed that almost everyone at school knew about it! He decided not to involve anyone as he thought he would be leading us into trouble. So he took a bag with some biscuits, a water bottle and a torch, some wire, a rope and a stick, wore his warmest coat, and set off, unseen by anyone. He didn't go by the forest path but the motor way, (as we had done) "this road was easier to follow although much longer," he said.

Cautiously he approached the house. It looked exactly the same as the last time he had been there – only a little sinister at first sight, as it was in total darkness. He moved stealthily, till he was right up to the walls. Then he felt his way along till he reached the back of the building. Like us, he tried every door and window. At last his hands found a window with a loose latch. He used a bit of wire, to undo the fastening, "it was easy," he said.

Once the window swung open, he jumped in without any hesitation at all. He walked through what seemed like countless rooms, but besides the wooden floor creaking occasionally under him, he heard nothing. Once his eyes got accustomed to the darkness he could see the outline of the rooms, with white dust sheets covering the furniture, quite well. Thus he reached the main entrance. As soon as he put one foot on the stairs, the wood groaned quite loudly, he stood still and looked over his shoulder. For a moment he could have sworn he saw a shadow in one doorway near the staircase. He paused, literally holding his breath, and staring hard all around, but could seen nothing.

"Come on," he told himself, "don't give up, there's nothing to fear." He moved up the staircase.

Once on the landing, he looked down, the moonlight showed him the main door with a large mirror and console table at its right, but no sign of any human life. He moved to his right and tip-toed past the rooms, most of which had shut doors. He put his ear to each door as he went by...still, nothing. Then it happened, a tiny movement, so soft, like the shuffling of a skirt. He moved back against the wall, and peered ahead of him; silence. The house had several dark, corridors; it was hard to decide which way to turn. He paused, blinked in the darkness and listened for any sound. Just then a hand gripped his arm, and pulled him into a room. He gave a start, "shhh" said a female voice.

"Please don't scream, I cannot harm you," the voice whispered urgently.

He stood still, his heart thumping loudly in his chest, he looked at the dark form next to him, it was much shorter than him. She moved to shut the door. He let her, for, he had recognized her in a second, yes it was her, Marianne!

At last he had found her! At that moment he felt no fear, just hugely protective of the person standing in the dark, next to him.

"Who are you?" she asked, her voice trembling.

"A friend...wait..." he said. He put his bag on the floor and took out his torch from his pocket and switched it on. They both blinked at the sudden light. For a moment they stared at each other; 'She's beautiful,' was all he could think.

She looked shocked, "it is you, you are...Edward, aren't you? You've come back to help me!" she whispered wonderingly.

He nodded, taking a big gulp, staring at her. She was dressed exactly the same as when they all had met her, her hair hanging loose, untidy and her face, he thought surprised, looked almost dirty, as if she hadn't washed it for a long time. As if sensing his thoughts she put up a hand and tried to smooth one lock on to one side of her face "I'm sorry, I am not fit to be seen," she stammered.

"No, no," he said reassuringly. Then before he could stop himself, "you're beautiful," as he blushed. "Thank god for the darkness, you idiot," he silently reprimanded himself.

She was not looking at him, but ahead towards the door.

He said gently, "listen, tell me now what is the matter, how are you here, you said this wasn't your house?"

"The funny thing is, I don't quite know what is happening," she whispered.

He looked curiously at her bent head; she looked up at him and suddenly smiled.

"I suppose I shall have to trust you, let me start at the beginning. You see...." She paused. "I think it has something to do with my grandmother," she blurted suddenly. Edward blinked at this disconnected information, but waited patiently for more.

Her large greyish blue eyes flashed. "Yes," she said, "yes it all started in grandmama's last days. She was taken ill, rather suddenly. I was away at Lady Cynthia's in the Peak District, she's grandmama's childhood friend, you see," she explained.

Edward nodded, Marianne went on, "they said she was taken ill and that I must come back at once. My companion, Mrs Hastings and I reached back home. To my surprise, I found not only grandmother extremely ill, but, a few hitherto unknown guests at our house. One of them was that man you saw, Mr Goddard."

"Go on," Edward whispered excitedly.

"At first I didn't notice them, as they were not the sort we usually entertained."

"Rather coarse and crude...I should say," added Edward, "not your sort," he mumbled, almost apologetically.

She half smiled but went on, as if she was just trying to piece things together, as she went. "Yes, funny sort of crowd, I thought. Like I said, at first I didn't notice them, we have a large house. You understand, people tend to get lost in it," she explained, "and then I was shocked to see, my usually strong and healthy grandmother, suddenly weak and frail.... One afternoon as I sat beside grandmama who lay asleep on her huge bed, Mrs Hastings whispered to me, 'strange visitors', she said."

"Whose guests were they then?" Edward asked.

"The old governess, it seemed that the gentleman was her brother and the lady his wife. They had come to stay for a week as they were touring the countryside. Grandmama had given permission, without even seeing them. You see, a lot of people stayed at our house. Often we did not know them, relatives of our staff or friend of a friend..."

Edward stared at Marianne's heart-shaped face, fascinated. The torchlight cast vivid shadows in the little room, it was an unreal situation, almost dreamlike. "Go on," he said, realizing she had become silent.

"Then one morning there was a knock on my door, Mrs Hastings stood there in the cold, long corridor in her maroon silk dressing gown, her face distraught, 'I'm sorry my dear, she's gone'." Marianne broke into a sob at this point.

Edward stared awkwardly, not knowing what to say to the unhappy girl.

"I say," he said, "don't be so sad," he mumbled "get a hold on yourself. What happened next?"

She looked up at him, a strange blank expression on her face, "that's just it," she said softly. "I put on some clothes and went to grandmama's room. The old governess, Miss Goddard, was there at the door. She said, she had arranged everything. Grandmama lay there her face a deathly white, a fixed glassy expression on her usually vivacious face...it was horrible." she sobbed softly, crumbling down onto the cold floor.

Edward crouched down next to her, with some difficulty as he was a large boy, and the room a small one, that too, filled with what looked like large pieces of furniture in the semi darkness. He patted her shoulder kindly with no idea what to say, but his manner communicated his sympathy to her, for she looked up at his face and gave a gallant half smile.

"I'll be fine," she murmured, through her tears.

"What happened next?" he asked urgently.

"The next day was to be the funeral. That very night I was about to go to bed, Miss Goddard burst into my bedroom. She was in a hysterical state. She said grandmama's lawyer wanted to see me urgently, and that Mrs Hastings and I were to go to him immediately."

Edward, aghast, looked at Marianne, who was looking ahead into the darkness.

"I went with her, Edward," she said slowly, turning towards him, she looked straight into his eyes. "I was mad to do as she said but Mrs Hastings and I followed her instructions without doubting her for a minute. We put on our street clothes and followed her outside. Later, I realized she had led us to a side door, (usually used to take the dogs out for their walks) and not the great door. The motor car too was not ours, and the chauffeur, we didn't so much as have a glimpse of him."

"Mr Goddard," gasped Edward. She nodded dumbly.

"We were driven for hours and hours in the dark, till we reached this house. By then I was getting a little suspicious, I asked for Sir Arkwright, grandmama's lawyer, as soon as we got out of the motor car, they said he would see us in the morning. Mrs Hastings and I looked at each other, we knew then that there was something terribly wrong."

"How long have you been here?" asked the shocked school boy.

"Almost a week now," she whispered, in a low voice, "I think..."

"But what do they want?" he asked.

"I don't quite know but they want me to sign some papers. Oh! Edward, you can't get someone's property like that, can you? I presume it must be grandmama's inheritance..." she seemed to be talking aloud to herself. "Can they get my inheritance if I sign a legal document, won't there be any questions?"

"I am not sure Marianne, but I hope you haven't signed anything," said the perplexed Edward.

"No, but they say they will keep us here, till I do. Oh! Edward, I think they are losing patience with me," she whispered hoarsely, her big eyes wide open, real fear in them.

He leaned forward and patted her hand, just then there was a slight sound outside, they both froze. Edward put the torchlight off, "quick get behind something," he said.

In a minute they were in pitch darkness. The two young people held their breath and listened. Someone was outside the door. Fascinated, they saw the door knob slowly turn, then the door opened a fraction. A tall form looked in, there was a tense moment, then to their relief, the intruder seemed satisfied and shut the door. They both breathed again, and crawled out from behind two large chairs.

"We'd better get out of here," whispered Edward.

"How? Mr Goddard always keeps watch, then there is another horrible man who brings us food," she said.

"We will wait till it is darker, and then go, I'm surprised you haven't tried to escape up to now," he glanced at her, then stared as she shoved her wrist in front of his face. There were red marks on both her wrist, which looked as if they were made by rough ropes. He took her hand in his and stared horrified at both her wrists.

"Oh my God!" he whispered.

"I tried once but they caught up with me. This was my punishment. Now they lock us up in one room every night. It is impossible to escape," her voice trailed off hopelessly.

Edward straightened, he pulled her up almost shaking her. "Come on, let's go," he said. "I'll get you out of this mess."

"Now?" she asked staring at him.

"Yes, I didn't see anyone about as I came up, it's quiet, let's make a dash for it," he smiled reassuringly down at the young girl in the strange, dark, stuffy room. He moved towards the door and put his hand on the door knob.

"Wait, I must get Mrs Hastings," she whispered.

He paused, "let's get you out and then I'll come back for her, or better still, I'll get help," he said, a note of excitement in his voice.

"No, no, poor thing, she has stood by me so loyally, I cannot desert her," she said, her voice surprisingly firm. Edward looked at her set expression, then stood back from the door. "Get her then," he said.

She turned before leaving the room. "You will wait here, won't you," she said looking imploringly up at him; "you won't go away?"

"No," he shook his head. "Come back here as soon as you can."

Without a word she slipped out of the room. He sat down on a chair and waited in the dark. It was very quiet, once he thought he heard foot steps outside but nothing happened and no one appeared. In about half an hour he got worried and started thinking of what he should do, if she didn't show up at all. Then he heard it, this time a definite sound right outside the door, he got up quickly, the door opened and Marianne's soft voice whispered his name.

"Quick lets run," she said.

Outside, he saw she was holding the hand of a frightened looking middle aged lady. No introductions were made, the threesome simply made their way downstairs, each clinging on to the wall or the staircase balustrade as they went along. By now it was almost pitch dark inside the house. They reached outside without seeing anything to alarm them, the cold crisp night air revived them! Feeling more confident, Edward led the two ladies back along the side of the house. Keeping as close as possible to its walls so that the weak moonlight wouldn't betray them. He was about to turn the corner and reach the front of the house from where he wanted to run towards the trees outside the boundaries of the house, when all at once a dark figure loomed up ahead of him. Before he could even pause, he felt a thud on his head. He fell down heavily and everything went blank. When he come round he was lying all tied up, on the bathroom floor with a stranger over him anxiously calling out to him.

✦ ✦ ✦

9

I must say, I had never really expected such 'happenings' as these. For a moment I was speechless, which all my friends will affirm, is the ultimate reaction from me, as I am never at a loss for words!

William and I un-gagged and untied the unfortunate Edward, as quickly as we could. Edward was bursting with his story, and began talking as soon as he was able to. There, on the cold bathroom floor, two shocked people crouched awkwardly and listened, without interrupting even once. I slowly got up, when he stopped talking. Then I looked over my shoulder fearfully. William was helping Edward up, who was touching his head gingerly.

"A bit lumpy old boy?" grinned William.

"Swollen like a tennis ball," said my friend ruefully.

"Never mind, you seem fine, will be fit as a fiddle soon," he said encouragingly.

"Let's get out of here," I interrupted. "Oh please, I can't take it anymore."

"You both go, I want to look round," said William, moving towards the bathroom door.

"No, no," I clutched his arm, tightly, "we're not going without you."

"Listen Emma, Marianne is in dreadful danger," said William, in a flat dull voice.

"We have done nothing for her as yet."

"I know but we should get help, this is out of our league," I implored, looking from one to the other, but I knew they were not going to listen to me.

"I think they must have gone, I've messed it up," said Edward, a sad note in his voice.

"You tried your best," said the other man, stepping out, back into the silent corridor. "Let's search the place...come on, no point in wasting time."

The house was almost entirely made up of little rooms, with lots of old furniture; we went from room to room, using our torchlights to look round.

"What are we looking for?" I whispered feeling tired and overwrought as we stood in the centre of a large bedroom, in front of a heavily curtained four poster bed.

"Signs, any signs of them," said William absentmindedly.

"Clues," whispered Edward into my ear.

William drew back the burgundy curtains that were around the bed, "look," he said. The bedspread was crumpled, and lying on it was a book. Quickly he grabbed it. Edward and I moved closer to look at it. Edward directed his torch on to it. It was a prettily done up book, with expensive leather binding, William flipped open a few pages, "a diary" he whispered "its a diary."

"Give it to me," I said.

"Let me see," said William, ignoring me and holding onto the precious diary. He was looking round the room. Now, we saw clear signs of life. An overturned side table lay on the floor, on the bed stand was a bowl of water and a large jug, a half burnt single candle stood pathetically on a large grand candle stand, and a plate with a stale piece of bread next to it.

"So we know," whispered William.

"They stayed here, in this room," said Edward wonderingly.

"There is nothing else here, let's go," suddenly said William harshly. Again I noticed a strange emotion in his voice. I glanced towards him; he was already out, into the corridor.

Dumbly, we followed him, down the stairs. This time no one cared if the wood creaked, as we were quite sure now that the house was empty. We searched the rooms downstairs but save for a few cigarette butts in one back room, found nothing of interest. I noticed William picked up one cigarette butt and put it in his pocket.

"The kitchen," I whispered suddenly. "We should look in there, if you live anywhere, even for a day, you need to use the kitchen."

"Of course," agreed Edward. The kitchen was in one corner of the house, we found it, after a five minute walk down yet another window-lined, long, cold corridor. I shivered as we finally reached the kitchen. At a glance we could see, this was where the abductors had based themselves. It was a large, old-fashioned kitchen with a huge cooking range, an oven standing against one wall. A heavy wooden square Victorian kitchen table was covered with bags of food; unwashed utensils lay all around, a tea kettle stood on one stove, as if someone had been about to make themselves a cup of tea.

"Filthy," I said instinctively.

William was on his knees, directing his torchlight on the floor, while Edward looked carefully at everything on the side board. I sat down on one of the chairs that stood round the kitchen table, resting my elbow on the table, my torch slipped onto the floor, I bent down to pick it up.

"What's this?" I said.

"What! what!" said both the men together.

"Where are you?" asked Edward urgently, "Emma?"

"Here," I called out; I could see both their legs from under the table.

"Where, where?" asked William, coming closer to the table and looking around wildly.

"Now Emma, don't play games, this is hardly the time for that," scolded Edward.

"I'm not playing games," said I, crawling out from under the table and shaking my head at them. "Would I, at this point?"

They were both grinning, as I sank back onto a chair.

"Look," I said and dropped a crumpled piece of paper on to the table. They both snatched at it.

"Careful," I warned.

Edward backed off and it was William who smoothened it out. I bent over the table to look at the paper eagerly, and almost fell off in shock, at what I saw, for written on this crumpled piece of paper was a now familiar line–THE HIDDEN CELLAR–1.15 a.m., SUNDAY. All three of us looked at each other.

Floppy and Julia almost fell on top of us as we emerged out of the house, "Oh thank god," whispered Julia, grasping my shoulder.

"You can't imagine what we saw," whispered Floppy excitedly to William, who turned towards him.

In the moonlight I saw William's face, it struck me that he looked very sad. "Why? What's the matter with him?..." I thought to myself.

"We saw two people," Julia squealed, pulling at my arm.

"You actually saw someone?" asked William, almost angrily.

"Yes, you see, we were worried about you two, so after a while we couldn't bear to be still. We decided to walk round the house and examine things from the outside, so to speak," mumbled Floppy.

"What did you see, man? Come to the point!" asked William taking Floppy by the shoulders and shaking him.

"Now, wait a minute," said Floppy trying to disengage himself from Williams hold, "we saw a man and a woman come out of the main door and simply walk away. We stood there helplessly, unable to do anything. We have been worried to death about you, not knowing what was happening inside, or if there were any more of THEM inside the house! Thank god Edward is with you," added Floppy, a little emotionally, glancing at Edward.

"How long ago did they appear?" interrupted William urgently.

"More than an hour, I should think," said Julia staring at him. "Who were they?"

William ran down the driveway and looked around, in all directions.

"They've got Marianne prisoner," whispered Edward.

We looked at each other; no one knew what to say, or what to do, there, in the darkness outside the mysterious house.

"The police, we should go to the police," I said at last, my voice sounding frightening in the silence. I looked at William who was pacing the driveway and looking, sometimes at the house and sometimes at the surrounding trees.

"You're right, we don't have a minute to loose, let's go, there is nothing we can do here," he said, suddenly galvanized into action by my voice.

Our subdued group made our way slowly towards where we had left William's car; we squeezed into the car and drove off in the direction of the school. Instead of taking a left turn towards the school from the main round-about, we took the right turn and drove right up to the police station. The high street was, well, shadowy, with only one tall lamp burning somewhere and not a soul in sight along the lane. Julia held on to my arm as we hesitatingly got out of the car, even the boys looked slightly shocked with this unexpected turn of events. I must add here that none of us had actually been inside a police station before. William wasn't looking at us, he was up the three stone steps that led to the door of the station, in a minute, and then through the door.

"Come on," I said to the others, gesturing towards the door.

"Do we have to?" whispered Julia fearfully.

"Of course, think of that poor girl, don't be a coward," I said, somewhat harshly.

We went up the stairs and into what was, to our surprise, a small room. Behind a large desk, on which burnt a solo lamp, was a chair on which the Constable on duty seemed to be dozing. Next to him, bent over his chair, our friend William was shaking his shoulder and trying to rouse him. The poor Constable looked positively astonished as he sprang up from his chair muttering something unintelligible.

"Huh...ah...huh," he murmured looked around, blinking in the dimly lit room.

He looked at us, then he turned to William, for some reason he took a dislike to our tall friend.

"Now, now," He said pushing William away, towards the rest of us. "That's better," he said, as we all stood in a line opposite him, staring at him. He was a fat, rather short man with a round pink face and a pince-nez hanging from his coat pocket. "Now what have we here?" he said in a pompous voice, putting up his pince-nez and observing us through it.

There was plump Julia, clinging onto my arm, there was tall and thin me with short bob hair, followed by short and thin Floppy with his glasses halfway down his nose, next to the large Edward, followed by the tall and, well, handsome young man, William. Looking back I think it must have been William's sheer handsomeness that put Constable Wotley's back up, for he took an instant, firm dislike of him. I learnt later that Constable Wotley was a poet who thought of himself as very good looking, except for his weight problem, which he attributed to his 'ma', who 'won't stop feeding me, miss.' You see, in time we became good friends, Constable Wotley and I.

Coming back to that moment though, we spent a confused half an hour trying to tell him our story, but quite frankly, we made absolutely no headway. He looked from one to the other, blinked and shook his head. He even went up to William and Edward and sniffed, close to them, obviously suspecting them of being drunk. William looked furious, I moved quickly towards him at this point.

"What are you about man?" he shouted. "Can't you take down a report?"

The Constable looked pompously at him, "now, now, calm down. Can it be that you all have dreamt this up between yourselves? Winwood School, you say..., indeed, I often do... between us," he smiled, somewhat confidingly at us. "You know, beautiful girl kidnapped by villains, me to the rescue." He looked patronizingly round at us, like a teacher trying to be indulgent to his students.

"Oh God," muttered William, literally pulling at his own hair, until it stood upright on his head. Floppy grinned at me, I moved towards the Constable.

"You appear to me to be a very intelligent young man "I said loudly and shamelessly, to the utter shock of my friends, who looked curiously at me. "Now, if you will let me explain, I am confident you will know just what to advise us." I walked him back, behind his desk.

"Yes, yes...to be sure," he mumbled as he had no choice but to walk backwards and finally sit down in his chair. I perched myself on the table, next to him, and began chattily, "you see, there really is a young girl." He looked up at me, about to say something. "Forget what she looks like," I said firmly, putting up my hand. "It is sufficient to realize that this young girl has been carried away by villains. And you," I pointed at his chest dramatically, "must help her, for we," I gestured to the group behind the desk, "have failed pathetically in our attempt to do so." My last comment met its target, he sat up and took his pen from the table.

"Perhaps I should write it all down," he murmured, "then perhaps..."

"Yes," I said "you are right, it will take too long to write out, you can do that later, I will help you. Let us mobilize forces, isn't that what you were going to say...?"

I heard a smothered giggle behind my back, but dared not look.

"Yes, yes, precisely my thoughts young lady." said the Constable.

"Of course, sensible man," I said jumping up from the table. "Are you going to ring up...whoever...?" my voice drifted off as I had no idea who this 'whoever' could be.

"Yes, yes, we must call the Sergeant in," he said picking up the telephone and starting to dial automatically.

"He had to dial twice as there was no response from the other side. In a small village like ours, people regard post 10 p.m. to be the middle of the night.

Finally someone answered, followed by a longish wait. Poor Constable Wotley looked quite nervous as he explained to his Sergeant that a group of young people, that included the foreign Prince from the school yonder, had arrived with a strange story about another kidnapped young lady, and "Sir, what was I to do?"

"No, sir, of course I am not," said the Constable...there was a pause, then. "No, no, it is true, sir, they are standing in front of me as I speak, I see them clearly, it is dark to be sure, but... you can talk to them if you like," he said, there was another pause.

"Yes, very good Sir," he replaced the receiver and looked round at us.

"Thought I was intoxicated, fancy that, me drunk on duty!" he sounded affronted.

I shook my head disbelievingly.

"Precisely," he said, pleased with my unspoken sympathy.

"Will come to the station directly," he informed us.

"Let's all sit down and wait for him," I said.

"Yes, yes of course, please do," said the poor Constable, now putty in my hands.

"You poor man," I said perching myself on the table again and beginning to chat, do you have to sit here all night and every night?"

I could hear one or two groans from behind me, but ignored them, better to make friends with the Constable, might be useful to us, I thought.

Whatever Constable Wotley was, his Sergeant was not. At least so far as appearances went. The policeman, who appeared within a short wait of about ten minutes, was a thin rather ugly man, with a longish face and an almost triangular chin. What struck us after a few minutes, though, was his twinkling blue eyes, that appeared to dance as he looked round at us. He seemed to seize us up in five minutes. His manner as he questioned us was neither friendly nor unfriendly, very businesslike. He asked for our story, looking straight at William in a marked manner, that left no room for any interruptions.

William related our story quickly and clearly, leaving no detail out, starting with our finding the Dowager House, meeting Marianne, getting back to school, the men Julia and I actually saw in the dining hall, the men Floppy and William saw in the common room and so on. I had the satisfaction of seeing the impassive looking Sergeant blink when William told him of the note that was thrust in my hand. William's voice went on softly as he told the Sergeant of our second trip to the Dowager House, my finding the old photograph and, finally, the rescue of Edward. He paused, "I think you should hear Edward's story from him," he said. The Sergeant turned to

Edward. "Well?" he said, as Edward stared ahead quietly, as if in a trance.

I nudged Edward, "Come on, it's your turn," I whispered.

"Oh Yes...of course," he mumbled. Blushing a bright red, he related his part of the adventure. He spoke haltingly but did not stop till he reached the part when he was struck down outside the house.

There was a long silence as he finished his tale. In that little office in the Police Station, all of us stood, rather cramped, trying to take in all that had happened. Nobody minded the cold draft coming through, from the open door, or even noticed then, that the first light of day break could be seen. We were roused from our thoughts by the Sergeant's voice, "and where are these notes you speak of?" he asked. William put his hand in his pocket and pulled them out. The Sergeant took them and looked curiously at them.

"Envelope," he said turning to Constable Wotley. He then placed the notes carefully into the envelope, the Constable humbly handed it to him, and then turned back to us.

"There is a photograph you say?" He asked.

"Yes," I answered, "in the car I'll go and get it."

The cold fresh early morning air felt strange as William and I went to the motor car. We didn't speak a word to each other, he waited while I found the picture. He simply took it from my hand and went back inside the station. I followed him.

Everybody crowded round the Sergeant as he looked at the photograph. Julia, Edward and Floppy looked shocked as they had not seen it. I looked at it curiously, not afraid now in the company of my friends. Everybody stared, quite startled, at the beautiful girl, in the picture.

"The girl, you say?" asked the Sergeant, looking at me.

"Yes..." I answered doubtfully, staring at the obviously old yellow toned photograph.

"Around seventeen–eighteen years of age?" He enquired sarcastically.

"Yes," I looked at him helplessly, my voice sounded ridiculous, even to my own ears.

"Spitting image of her...," said Edward wonderingly.

"Sergeant, May I have a word with you," suddenly said William.

"Certainly," replied the sergeant.

"Outside, if you please," said our new friend, authoritatively.

The two men went out. The rest of us looked questioningly at each other, wondering what was it that William wanted to talk about in private with the Sergeant. They came back in about ten minutes.

"Now, look here everybody," said the Sergeant as he came in, "you l have told me everything, now go back to school and get some rest. I will come back later in the day and we will discuss what is to be done."

I stared at the man, there was a marked change in his manner, no patronizing patience anymore but an obvious note of seriousness. I looked curiously from him to William. "There is something here, that I don't quite understand," I thought to myself as we made our way out, into the car and silently back to school.

✦ ✦ ✦

10

We drove up boldly to the main gates of the school, too tired to even think of any clandestine entrance, much to the shock of the gate keeper, who stared open-mouthed, at our strange group squeezed into William's small motor car. The burly Mr Cleve moved forward, almost angrily, but William held up his hand and barked out only one word, 'later' and drove on. He parked the car in front of the great door and we all got out. The door was still unbolted, as we had left it.

Daylight was creeping in, but as yet there appeared to be nobody around. "To your rooms every one, and we will see you in a while," said William authoritatively and strode in the direction of the Head's rooms without waiting for any reply. I stared at his retreating back frowning. Julia nudged me weakly.

"Come on," she urged.

"Let's go," added Floppy.

We made our weary way along the silent corridors back to our respective rooms, each person lost in his or her own thoughts. Surprisingly no one woke us up the next morning. I opened my eyes and jumped at the sight of the time for my bed side clock showed "eleven o'clock, I'm dead!" I screamed, springing up.

Julia was still asleep and equally frightened when she woke. Hurriedly we got dressed and made our way to the green common room as breakfast at this hour, we knew, was out of the question.

The school appeared surprisingly normal. We looked around fearfully, half expecting the school mates that we passed by, to interrogate us, but nothing. "Could it be that we are un-discovered..." I thought to myself suspiciously as we walked down the corridor.

"I'm starving," said Julia.

"Julia, how can you think of food at this point?" I said, as I made my way to the corner of the room, and sat down on a colourful floral sofa. Julia sank down heavily on it, plucking at a nearby cushion.

"Oh God, I'm famished," she moaned, holding the cushion to her stomach and bending over it.

There were only two other girls sitting in the room, one was Mabel, a largish, pink faced girl who was always laughing and spoke in a loud booming voice and the other was serious-faced Elinor, who was her best friend. The two looked up as we entered and waved a greeting.

"Fancy a game of cards?" yelled Mabel cheerfully.

"Not now," groaned Julia.

"Why, whatever's the matter?" yelled Mabel again, now looking curiously at Julia's bent posture, "sick?"

"No, no," I answered, trying to sound casual.

"I'm so hungry," again groaned poor Julia.

Mabel got up and walked towards us, "ate less at breakfast?" she said sympathetically, as she herself had a large appetite.

"Worse," answered Julia, looking up at Mabel, "No breakfast!"

I stared at Julia, trying hard to catch her eye but she was beyond caution, clearly food was the only thing on her mind. Mabel leaned on the top of an armchair covered in old burgundy velvet, and looked at us curiously.

"Why?" she asked simply in her usual blunt manner.

"Overslept," I butted in quickly, "missed breakfast."

"Matron didn't wake you?" went on Mabel, "seems rather odd!"

Elinor got up and joined us; she sat down on the chair over which Mabel was leaning. She put her hand in her pocket and took out two cookies, which she silently offered Julia.

"Oh thank you," said Julia taking them and handing one to me grudgingly. I shook my head, she proceeded to gobble both.

"Emma...Emma!" repeated Mabel.

"Yes, what is it?" I answered, trying to bring my attention to her, for I was miles away.

"What are you thinking of?" she asked me obviously extremely curious now.

"Nothing," I snapped back.

"You two are up to something," blurted the good Mabel, moving closer towards me. "Now come on, out with it, are you in trouble?"

I looked at Julia, who was lying slumped on the sofa, a faraway look in her eyes. "No guesses about her thoughts," I murmured to myself.

"It's just a game," I blurted, my mind wildly trying to cook up an instant story. I knew Mabel; she was too smart to be put off easily.

"We were trying to cook up an adventure for ourselves... imaginary of course," I said. Mabel's, red face became redder.

"What sort?" she asked.

"Ummm," I hesitated, my mind, I am ashamed to admit, racing through all sorts of untruths I could get away with.

"Secret doors," suddenly said Julia, loudly and clearly.

"Secret doors? That's fantastic," screamed Mabel.

I looked at Julia in horror. There was a moment of silence. I looked at Mabel; she was very suspicious now, her eyes darting instantly from Julia to me.

"You mean, you know of some secret doors here, at Winwood's?" asked Elinor in her usual soft way.

"Come on why the secrecy?" went on Mabel, relentlessly.

"No, no," I said hurriedly, "just been playing a game, between ourselves, you know."

"A game?" repeated Mabel, "searching for hidden doors!" Her voice was gradually getting louder with excitement.

"Can we join you?" asked Elinor gently, looking straight at me.

"Oh my goodness!" I thought and stared back at her, horrified.

"But of course we will," said Mabel, her face beaming around at all of us; "and a jolly time we will have of it," she rubbed her hands together.

At that moment David burst into the common room and ran around it two times making, the sound of a fire engine before coming to a halt in front of me.

"Hello sister dear!" He greeted me.

"Well!" I said "and where have you been?"

"Where have you been more like?" said the abominable boy.

I could feel Mabel and Elinor's gaze on me. I tried to sound casual "just entertaining ourselves by playing a game."

"We are joining in," said the relentless Mabel.

"What game?" asked David looking up at her with his twinkling blue eyes. "We are going to hunt for secret doors," said Mabel in a dramatic voice."

"Ooo!" yelled my brother.

"There must be many here," added Elinor, stealthily looking over her shoulder, "it's such an old building."

"May I join in?" asked David. "Will get Jimmy to help, he's awfully good at sniffing things out, will be capital!" he said gleefully. And off he went, his little feet making an unbelievable noise on the wooden floor as he galloped out.

"Great," mumbled Mabel moving towards the door, "when shall we start?" "Now's a good time," said Elinor springing up from her chair.

Mabel turned back to me, one hand on the door knob "Listen lets meet up here after lunch and compare notes, all right?" Without waiting for a reply, they both hurried out, I stared in dismay at the door as it banged shut behind them.

✦ ✦ ✦

11

We stood in a straight line outside the Head's study door. No one said a word. Edward, Floppy, Julia and I, red faced and scared. The wooden door opened and Maria, Mrs Weston's old faithful secretary appeared. Maria was short and stocky, she wore a brown tweed skirt and plain brown jumper that had buttons down the front, she always wore brogues, 'good sensible walking shoes' and had her grey hair in a tight knot at the back of her head. Besides the severity of her appearance, Maria usually had a smile and sometimes even a cookie or two for some of us whom she liked but today she looked extremely serious and I thought, slightly worried.

"Come in children," she said, simply, standing back as we trooped in. She shut the door silently behind us and stood by it.

The room was as it always was, cheerful and neat. Mrs Weston sat behind her desk, William stood near the long French windows, that were shut on this occasion, leaning his shoulder against a glass pane, looking out into the rose garden. Sitting on one of the chairs in front of Mrs Weston was the Sergeant we had met the day before, saying something in a low voice to the Head. He stopped abruptly as we all lined up behind his chair, facing Mrs Weston. She looked at us, thoughtfully through her glasses, then sat back and pulled up a sleeve of her grey jumper; she appeared to be in a quandary.

"Well, a nice little problem you have brought for me," she said at last, her eyes passing over all of us.

The Sergeant leaned his elbow on the antique wooden study table, and turned his head towards us. Julia and Edward stood very straight, their heads bent down, I looked curiously at William. Mrs Weston followed my gaze and almost smiled. Hastily I looked away.

"I have never believed that there is any good in crying over spilt milk," she said suddenly in a loud clear voice. "Why you children went out the other day, and somehow ended up with this," she gestured towards the Sergeant and paused "situation, I think we can discuss later. I have heard the whole story in detail and what is the pressing issue here, to my mind, is what has become of that poor girl you talk of. The Sergeant is here to ask you certain questions, hoping to find a bit more about what actually happened, since your first coming upon the Dowager House. Please do not be alarmed, there is nothing to be afraid of." She stood up and walked round her desk. "I will not be far, have to see to a few things," she said to the sergeant. "Please call me if you need me," so saying she walked out followed by Maria, softly closing the door behind them.

The Sergeant stood up and moved towards Mrs Weston's Chair. He gestured to us to sit down. Julia and I sat down on the two chairs opposite him. The boys moved closer to us. William stayed where he was.

"Well now," said the Sergeant "let me introduce myself to you all. My name is Sergeant Milford; I am here to help you sort this out." He looked round at us; his manner like it had been the day before – very businesslike.

"What we have here I think is a neat case of kidnapping," he paused; a thrill of fear went down my spine as I heard him put it to us so bluntly.

"This girl, Marianne, and her companion have been held in the house in the woods, for a few days at least." He looked intently at us, "you all have interacted with her and heard her speak of her plight."

"She was terrified," interrupted Edward rather fiercely.

William made a slight movement, I looked at him but he was looking out into the rose garden.

"Tell me the story from the start, I should like to hear it again," said Sergeant Milford. Again I noticed William move restlessly.

All at once it was as if a storm broke loose, all of us began talking almost simultaneously, as if relieved to put our thoughts into words. The Sergeant's blue eyes twinkled as he held up his hand.

"Now, now, slowly, if you please," he said firmly, "I don't want to miss anything."

So again we went through the whole story, from our first seeing the Dowager House, to Edward's heroic attempt to rescue Marianne single handedly, right up to our meeting with Constable Wotley and finally with the Sergeant himself.

Gradually our voices petered down, there was silence. The Sergeant leaned back on his chair. William straightened and moved towards the fire place. He stood with a hand on the mantel piece above staring down at the empty grate.

"Let us examine the evidence," said the Sergeant, his voice sounded very loud in the little room.

"Please, sir," he stretched a hand towards William.

This seemed to distract William from his curious mood; he bent towards the floor and picked up a small brown hold-all, which must have been standing behind one of the large armchairs that stood in front of the fire place. William put the hold all on top of the Head's table and opened its buckle. We all looked at him, as if hypnotized. We stared as he put his hand in and took out a plain envelope, then another and then a dairy, which looked very familiar to me. Slowly he opened one envelope and unfolded the dirty piece of paper, then ditto for the others. I stared at these three objects before us, the diary and the two dirty scraps of paper. "THE HIDDEN CELLAR–1:15 a.m. SUNDAY," read Sergeant Milford in a clear loud voice. We all stared at the notes, a thrill of excitement shot through me. "What if.... Can it be something to do with the school," I thought to myself.

At the same time Sergeant Milford said, looking round at our little group, "there must be cellars here...I wonder."

"I've thought of that, had a look round last night but there seems to be nothing unusual here," said William.

"Hmm..." mumbled the Sergeant deep in thought, "all the same, I would like to have a look round, if I may."

"Of course," said William, moving towards the door, they both went out in search of the head. The rest of us, thus dismissed, trooped out.

That afternoon, I sat in my favourite little common room alone. I wanted to think. It was raining heavily and had become quite dark. I curled up in an old armchair and pondered over the situation. One thing I was sure of was that William knew more than he was letting on, but try as I might I couldn't in honesty, mistrust him. He was definitely not one of them! Yet there were people who appeared to walk around the school at night, a secret doorway in the dining room, known to them! God! And then the cellars. Why should they be of any interest to anyone except the staff of Winwood school who stored supplies there. I was completely mystified. I kept thinking of astonishing possibilities, it was completely quiet, save for the rain beating against the window panes. Then I heard it, the same sound, the one we had heard in the forest, something like a human sneeze. In a flash, I was out of my chair and opening the door that led into the corridor outside. Frantically I looked out and saw a shadowy figure walking at the far end. "A man definitely," I thought. Boldly, I followed him. As it was still afternoon the lights were not yet on, it was hard to get any idea who he was, I would have to get closer. He didn't seem to be in a hurry, he was wearing outdoor rubber boots and a wide brimmed hat, could be one of the gardeners I thought. He turned two corners with me walking behind him; we were now near the dining hall. He then stopped abruptly, I ducked behind a large plant, just in time, as he turned and peered all around. I stared and stared as I recognized the head gardener Mr Peters. As if to confuse me further, just then he sneezed again, and at the same time turned and walked into the dining room. Recklessly I followed him; I peeped into the room and saw him walk to the far end of the room. Within seconds I saw the gap appear in the wall and Mr Peters calmly walk through it. I stared as the wall slowly closed, as if eating him up! I turned and, to my horror, collided into somebody, who must have been standing right behind me.

"Oh!" I screamed.

"Steady," said a infuriatingly calm voice.

"You! Thank God!" I said as I recognized William.

"Luckily for you, I could have been anyone," he added meaningfully, giving me a look. "You really must be very careful if you want to be a detective," he mumbled, looking down at my white face a little kindly.

I pointed to the far end of the dining room, "you saw?"

"Yes," he said simply.

"What does it mean?" I asked him.

"That man, works here?" asked William.

"Yes, oh, you aren't to know are you, sorry, yes, yes, he is Mr Peters, the head gardener, been here ages." I shook my head in disbelief, still staring at the end of the dining room.

"Sure?" asked William.

"Completely," I answered my voice stronger now I had got over the initial shock.

"Come," he said "we will achieve nothing further here."

"No," I pulled at his arm, "let's wait till he comes out."

He paused for a minute, "you think..."

"Yes, let's not leave just yet," I urged. I pulled him into the dining room. He looked amused as I dropped to my knees and crawled under one of the wooden tables and gestured to him to follow. To my surprise he walked off towards the far end of the room. I stared as I saw him stop near the wall and begin to examine it. Quickly, I scampered up and ran to join him.

"What are you doing?" I asked breathlessly.

"Looking for the latch," he whispered, "must be here somewhere."

"Yes," I whispered back running my hands over the part of the wall where I had seen the men standing. "Somewhere here," I whispered. William was running his fingers over the carvings on the wall; a border of flowers in gold, framed the white wall. He was pressing various points of the border, I did the same. Suddenly I heard it, the click, we both stared as the wall opened up, right in front of our eyes, "what was it?"

"Don't know," I answered softly.

"Which of us opened it?" he asked.

"Could be either," I answered, "never mind, now what? Shall we go in?"

"Brave girl," he smiled down at me, then stared thoughtfully into the darkness in front of us. He looked at his watch, "getting to tea time, won't everybody be gathering in here?"

"Yes at four o'clock," I answered.

He hesitated.

"Oh come on, let's have a look," I urged. Impulsively, I put one foot through the gap on the wall.

"No Emma, wait," he cautioned, trying to pull me back, but it was too late I was through the secret door. The gallant William had no choice but to follow me. We found ourselves in a small sort of enclosure, if it could be called as such. The door through which we came in, was still open.

"Must be a way to shut it from here," said William softly.

"Here, look, this iron handle," I pointed to it. "Shall we pull it?"

"Wait, we need a light," he said.

"Oh yes," I whispered disappointed, "I don't have one, shall we have to leave?" William pulled out something from his coat pocket.

"I think this will do," he switched on a small torch and looked at me. "Ready?"

I nodded casually, trying my best not to show how scared I actually was. He pulled the handle, there was a creaking sound, and the wall slowly came together again, "beautiful" said William as we saw the dining room disappear from our sight. "Don't look so shocked," he said. "Haven't you heard of secret doors, many of the old houses and palaces have them, used for hiding places at various times in the past."

"I have read about them but have never seen one, let alone been through one," I whispered.

"I've seen one exactly like this one, in fact it is quite remarkable, must have been built in the same period, could be the 1700s." He was pointing the light around us as he spoke, curiously looking around.

There was really not much to see, just dark greyish-black stone walls and a narrow passage leading out to heaven knows where. He moved towards it slowly, carefully following the light, and I walked close behind, one hand on the grimy old wall for support.

"Careful, steps," he warned me, we climbed down about ten to fifteen small, narrow steps and found ourselves in another little enclosure. I shivered, as it was quite cold in here. We could see yet another little passage leading out of it and went through. Again we found ourselves walking into an enclosure, this one was slightly larger and not as empty as the others had been, for when we directed our little light around we saw something kept in one corner. I grasped William's arm as he move closer to it.

"Let's go," I urged, pulling at his arm, suddenly frightened.

"Shhh," he said, pulling his arm free from my grasp. "You stay back," he pushed me into the passage we had just come in from. "Let me have a look, don't move," he ordered. Automatically, I stood where he put me and stared as he stealthily moved towards what now looked like a heap of something in the far corner of the little space we were standing in.

I strained my eyes to see, as William went closer and closer to the heap, but it was dark and he was a broad man, all I could see was his back bending over something.

"My God, stay there Emma," he barked an order at me, and within seconds disappeared down the passage that went out the opposite direction. I stood there in the pitch darkness completely paralyzed with fear. The cold stone walls on either side of me seemed to close up as the tiny light disappeared with William.

"Oh my God!" I screamed in my mind, "where's he gone, suppose he doesn't come back, suppose they get him, I'll die in here all alone...."

My heart thumped wildly in my chest, I could almost hear it in the silence around me. I stood like that for what seemed like hours and hours. My eyes fixed in the direction my friend had gone from, as if I was frozen. At last I saw the small light approaching and his familiar voice, "it's me, I'm back Emma, don't be scared," he said softly.

"William, oh thank God," I almost sobbed and moved towards him.

"Stay there Emma," he said curtly.

"Why, what's the matter?" my voice sounded strange to my own ears.

"There's something unpleasant here, better for you not to see it," he answered.

By now I was next to him, pulling at his arm. "Show me," I whispered.

"It's pretty horrid, don't bother," he said roughly, "let's go."

By now I was too curious to listen to reason. "No, I won't go without seeing it." I stamped my foot.

"Stupid girl," he said rudely, "don't be childish."

"William, I will see whatever it is. Shine the torch on it please." I insisted in my most grown up voice. In a minute I was to regret it, for when the light stopped on the heap, I saw what was actually there. A man lay there, in an awkward position, a horrible startled expression on his white face. A wide brimmed outdoor hat lay on the floor next to him, marked with what couldn't be anything but human blood.

"Oh no," I screamed, clinging on to William "Mr Peters!"

"Satisfied," he grunted, at the same time leading me away from the gruesome sight. I sobbed openly as he almost pulled me along the path we had come from, up the few steps, finally, we reached the dining room wall.

"Get a hold on yourself, child," he said.

He pulled at the iron handle, for a moment I panicked, "suppose it doesn't open," I said hoarsely.

He didn't reply, something clicked and the wall slowly opened.

The dining room was bustling with tea time activity, the sounds suddenly died out as people noticed the wall behind the tea tables opening up and two people standing on the other side of it. There was a loud clatter, as someone dropped something.

Calmly, William stepped out of the secret passage and turned to help me; I wiped my eyes quickly and took his help to get out, blinking at the sudden light. There was complete silence as we looked at the occupants of the dining room, and they at us.

As my eyes accustomed themselves to the bright lights of the room I looked around. The room was not even filled to its half capacity, as it was term break, but all the children who were at school were there as no one liked to miss tea! On my right was Mabel looking shocked, next to her Elinor staring with her mouth open, her spoon stuck halfway on route to its destination! Behind them I noticed Edward had stood up and was hesitating as to whether he should come up to us or not, one hand on the back of his chair and the other clutching his napkin.

One or two attendants standing behind the tea tables looked shocked. I looked around to see if any mistresses were around; I saw Mrs Lewis sitting at a table in one corner just looking at us, next to her stood the French teacher, a plate in her hand, again looking aghast in our direction.

Suddenly someone pushed a chair back noisily, jumped up and ran between the tables towards us. It was my brother David, he must have just noticed us, perhaps he had been too busy eating to look up sooner!

"Wow, fantastic," he said breathlessly coming to a halt in front of the hidden door, and looking at it delightedly. "You actually found a hidden door, and I thought it was only a game," he said innocently. His movements seemed to revive the others and all of a sudden the whole room seemed to fill up with voices. Everyone seemed to speak at the same time, till Mrs Lewis finally came forward, clapped her hands and called everyone to order.

I noticed William talking to one of the kitchen attendants who brought a chair forward. William pulled it in front of the hidden door and sat down on it, as if guarding the secret chamber. The kitchen attendant then hurried out of the dining room, almost running.

"Emma, Emma, you found it, you won!" said David jumping up and down.

"Yes, she won, didn't she?" said William coolly.

I looked at him, he gave me a meaningful look and continued. "Emma found the secret door, just now you know."

"Wow," cooed David, curiously trying to look through the open wall.

"It's so dark, and I can't see anything, can I go in?" David looked at William.

"Not now, perhaps later, let us first make sure if it is safe to go in," replied the other, very much in control of the situation.

"But you both just came out of there," reasoned the little boy, his big eyes looking beseechingly into William's eyes.

"Yes but we found it by accident and came out very quickly as it is very dark and dirty in there," explained William patiently.

David went to the edge of the Wall and stared at the dark hole, so to speak, completely fascinated. William didn't stop him; the others too seemed to accept William's explanation and nodded to each other wonderingly, enjoying the excitement.

Mabel came towards us, red faced, "You beat us to it, Emma, quite a find," she remarked, looking curiously at me.

"Yes," I replied dully not knowing what to say.

"Emma's very clever," added William, giving me another look. I tried to rouse myself, but only succeeded in giving a feeble smile, still seeing Mr Peters's horrid form in front of my eyes.

"Mrs Lewis," said William, getting up and, turning to the teacher who was now standing next to him, "so sorry to disrupt tea," he said formally.

She stared at him, completely at a loss for words; then said automatically, "it's quite all right," then blushed.

"You too," I thought to myself "does he have that affect on all women, all ages!?Really!"

At that moment Sergeant Milford strode in through the main entrance of the dining room, followed by Constable Wotlely. Everyone turned to look at them, again there was silence in the room.

"Perhaps tea can be served elsewhere," suggested William looking pointedly at Mrs Lewis.

"Oh, is that advisable?" she said looking trustingly at him, then, "of course certainly, everyone let us go to the flower room, we can have tea there, let us leave these gentlemen here," she said a little hesitatingly.

Everyone moved slowly to their feet looking confusedly at each other. "Come on," she urged and moved towards the door, people began to follow automatically. The kitchen attendants began to pick up the serving bowls and follow the rest. I noticed that Mabel and Madame Gustave were the last to leave. We waited in silence till the room was completely empty, only then did William begin to talk to Sergeant Milford. He spoke quickly and clearly relating events exactly in the order in which they had happened. The Sergeant, in his usual style, did not interrupt once; only when William stopped talking did he ask just one question, "quite dead?"

"Absolutely," said William.

The Sergeant turned to me. "Poor child, you go and have a lie down," he said looking at me kindly. "You have been very brave, we will talk later." Gratefully I moved towards the door of the dining room.

"Emma, wait," said William. "You'd better take this along."

I turned back and stared as William pulled out David from behind his chair. He must have hidden there when everyone began to move out.

"Oh God," I clutched my hair, embarrassed.

David looked completely thrilled, totally unconcerned with the three men looking down at him.

"Now young man," said the Sergeant, bending down towards him, "what you have just heard is only a story and it is to be kept to yourself, all right?"

"Of course," said the little boy.

William went down on his knees next to David. "It is a secret between Emma, Sergeant Milford, Constable Wotley, yourself and I...can you keep a secret?"

"Oh yes, on my honor," promised David, now a little subdued looking at the three men. I went up to him and took his hand.

"I will explain everything to him," I reassured the others, who looked quite worried. Only the Sergeant gave a half smile in reply as David and I turned and left the room.

Our scruples were of no matter, as the totally unexpected case of Mr Peters spread over the school like wild fire. A huge contingent of policemen arrived in the school; you could never go anywhere without running into one or another of them. They walked around, polite but expressionless. Now and then, some important looking people could be seen walking to and fro from the Head's office or the dining hall. It was a strange time for Winwood Manor School. Floppy's father was the first parent to pay us a visit. Surprisingly, while many elected to take their children away for a while, he was not in the least rattled. He merely expressed his concern about the events to The Head and had a little chat with his heir. Then, He gave a large thump on Floppy's back, waved at us all and cheerfully drove away.

No one remained unaffected by these developments. I could see that even the most blood thirsty of our school mates were a little dazed by this gruesome event. The dining hall was cordoned off; all meals were shifted to the flower room, a somewhat smaller and less formal room. In a way it was nicer, as we crowded round, and the sheer closeness of everyone gave us all some support.

✦ ✦ ✦

12

"Oh, I wish it would stop raining," I said pulling at a curtain sash and looking out of the window."

"Hmmm," murmured Julia in reply from where she sat on the sofa.

The grounds outside seemed almost flooded with the rain water, and still it came down heavily, beating against the window panes. Although it was three thirty in the afternoon, it was already quite dark and we had switched on two lamps in the room, one on a side-table next to Julia, and the other on a corner table in front of which David sat, busily drawing something. I turned from the window and looked into the room, then looked out again.

"Settle down Emma, do," said Julia.

"How can I when there are so many unanswered questions?" I replied.

"Yes, but the police must be making some headway..." mumbled Julia.

I looked at her impatiently; she was so different from me. I could never be content to let matters just be.

"Elinor's parents came and took her away today," said Julia, suddenly sitting up, "did you know?"

"Yes, so did several others. Mrs Weston has written to everyone about the murder," I replied.

"The murder," repeated Julia, her voice full of awe.

There was a huge banging on the door, we both jumped. Edward popped his face in through the door, "sorry you didn't hear us, can we join you?"

"Oh, do," I replied raising my voice as the rain was making a terrific sound as it beat against the window panes.

"Edward threw himself on the burgundy armchair next to the sofa on which Julia slouched. Floppy walked in behind him, slowly, looking deep in thought.

"Any news?" I asked them.

"Apparently Mr Peters was hit on the back of his head by a heavy instrument like a shovel or something..." said Edward.

"Urggh!" said Julia.

"Poor Emma...couldn't have been a pleasant sight," said Edward looking at me sympathetically.

"Someone must have been waiting there, inside, for him. No one went in after him and by the time we found the secret door and went in, he was quite dead," I mumbled.

"The question is why?" Floppy spoke for the first time. "Why should anyone want to do away with a poor gardener who has been working some twenty years in a school?"

I looked at Floppy. "Do you think he was following us about in the forest that day? That sound of the sneeze?"

"Oh, quite definitely, you heard it when you began to follow him to the dining room, you must have recognized it or else you wouldn't have run after the sound!" said Floppy slowly, as if trying to piece the story together.

"So he was a snoop," declared Edward, "but why was he following us about? Doesn't make sense," he said, shrugging his shoulders.

"Perhaps he was up to something else in the forest and we were in his way..." I said. Everyone looked towards me. "May be he snooped about a lot and came across something to do with the intruders we all saw in the school...," I paused and looked around.

"And he found out too much!" whispered Julia, her eyes looking into mine meaningfully.

We all looked at each other. "Yes, this must be it. Couldn't be any other reason. Mr Peters was certainly mixed up with the 'Gang', shall we say, and they shut him up!" rounded up, Floppy.

"He must have been the one to let them into the school..." murmured Julia.

"Their contact here..." finished Edward.

"Yet.... How did he manage that? Even if he did...I mean, I have always thought that nothing here goes unnoticed by the Head..." I said, haltingly. Floppy and I looked at each other.

"I too have been thinking along those lines.... Look at it this way, the main door which is always shut, is open...people are walking around without a care!" Floppy looked at me steadily as he spoke.

"Mrs Weston. Could it be? She is a very private person to be sure, and none of us knows anything about her personal life.... Come to think of it, she has been away a lot in the past few weeks," I mumbled, thinking aloud.

"Leaving the coast clear?" Floppy whispered.

Just then, there was a loud knock on the door that made us all jump. Mrs Weston's secretary, Maria, appeared in the doorway. We looked at each other, almost guiltily.

"Oh good, you are here all together," she said looking round at us, as she walked briskly into the room. "Mrs Weston wants you all to come to her study."

"Now?" I asked.

"Now," she said firmly and turned away as if to go. "You too," she adding turning around and pointing to David, who was still busy with his drawing.

We all trooped out and followed Maria all the way to the Head's, now familiar, study. David still clutching his drawing and looking preoccupied.

Mrs Weston sat behind her desk writing something. She looked up as we quietly entered the room. "Come on in," she said pleasantly and continued writing.

We stood in front of the desk and watched. There was a knock on the door. Maria opened it to admit William and a complete stranger. He was an old, large, darkish man with a rugged face, we all looked curiously at him. Mrs Weston stood up and the stranger went up to shake hands with her.

"Retired Detective Inspector Crawley," introduced William. "Scotland Yard."

We all exchanged glances, completely thrilled, a real life Inspector from Scotland Yard! So what if he was retired.

"These are the children that first came across the intruders," said the Head gesturing towards us.

"Is that so? Exciting, what?" said the large Inspector to us. None of us said anything; he looked at us searchingly for a moment then moved to an armchair in front of the fire place.

"May I?" he asked Mrs Weston politely before sitting down on it.

"Come around all of you, I have come to tell you a little story." We must have looked rather surprised, as his face broke into a smile and he said, "Come on then, it's a very extraordinary story, I promise you." Mrs Weston moved to the armchair opposite the Inspector and sat down on it. Julia, David and I then sat down on the carpet next to her, while Edward and Floppy stood next to the Inspector's armchair. William stood with his shoulder leaving against the chimney piece, he looked as if he was miles away, lost in his own thoughts.

The Inspector began his story. "I was a young man of fifteen helping out one summer in our family law firm in a little village called Chiltern Common. It was a beautiful place, very quiet and small, you know the kind where, everybody knows everybody." He paused looking round at us. "All the 'old' families were our clients. I often had to fill out mundane forms on behalf of someone or other and take them along to the relevant client's house for his or her signature. One such house was Golden Oaks. It was, by far, the largest and the grandest house in the area. It had a beautiful winding drive-way surrounded by well kept grounds. The gardens were admired for miles around and the house itself was a delight to look at. It always took me a few minutes to adjust my eyes when the butler opened the door. The huge twinkling chandelier cast a golden light all over the entrance highlighting the ceiling with its beautiful carvings. Large paintings by most of the popular masters hung almost anywhere as if they were the most casual things, antique furniture of the best quality was arranged artistically all over the house. Here I have a confession to make; regarding my enthusiasm for the house."

I looked curiously at him, for his face had reddened a bit. He smiled, a little self consciously and went on, "the family that lived at Golden Oaks was a small one. It comprised four people, a mother, Lady Cecilia, her son Trevor, his wife Victoria and their son Thomas."

"Ah," I thought to myself as I noticed his blush when he said "Victoria." I nudged Julia, who gave a silent giggle.

"Lady Victoria was a woman of astonishing beauty, she fully took your breath away," he said smiling round at us. We all moved closer to him, getting more interested as he went on with the story.

"Yes, young lady," he said suddenly looking straight at me, "I was fully smitten by her, I must admit." Everyone broke into broad smiles here.

"I cannot describe how wonderful she was, a woman of average height with a neat figure. She walked gracefully, spoke in a soft musical voice, dressed in the best of clothes, threw the best parties that were very famous in the entire county..." His voice seemed to trail off as if he had gone back in time.

Julia and I exchanged glances, I looked towards William, he was fiddling with a small clock, that was standing on the mantel piece.

"She had an oval face, large blue eyes, and dark hair, a small delicate mouth that would break into a warm welcoming smile...." Again his voice trailed off.

"Oh, please, Inspector don't stop," said Julia involuntarily, then blushed as everyone looked at her.

"Something in her manner made you want to protect her. She gave the impression of a delicate doll. Well, I have said quite enough about her, you all can see that she was a special person. Her husband, Trevor, was a tall, muscular young man. He was fair with light grey eyes and light hair. He adored her, they used to say, every wish of hers was his command."

"Gosh!" whispered Julia, clearly enjoying herself hugely.

"Yes," said the Detective Inspector, "a handsome couple, as the world said back then. She was beautiful, he was rich, and had immense property. Lady Cecilia was a white haired graceful old lady; she looked frail but was remarkably sharp in all business dealings. It was her who I had to see most of the times I visited Golden Oaks, as she went through each and every paper that had to do with her family, no matter how trivial it was. His Lordship kept to himself, only raising a hand in greeting if he saw me passing by. He was usually in weather-beaten outdoor clothes, taking a tour of his grounds, talking to his tenants, or going fishing or hunting with friends. I came across young Thomas quite a lot in those days, he would be peeping out from some nook or corner of the great old house trying to catch my eye, always looking for a play mate. I often obliged him for a bit, enjoying running around playing hide and seek almost as much as he did. In fact it was he who told me about the ghost!"

"Ghost!" I said, before I could stop myself, thrilled.

"Yes, young lady, I dare say you modern people do not believe in them," the Inspector looked round at our little group searchingly, shrugged, then went on.

"One afternoon I had an invitation for tea in the school room from Thomas. Of course I went, as back then, any excuse to visit Golden Oaks worked for me. So there we were, Thomas, his governess, a Mrs Mamble, and myself.

"What did he say?" interrupted Julia impulsively.

"Patience, child," said Inspector Crawley, "we sat round the tea table eating scones and cake, it was getting dark and someone brought in some candles. In those days many houses still used candles for light. We played some board games for a while and then I got up to go. It was then that Thomas began to be difficult, perhaps he did not want me to leave, but he suddenly started saying that he wishes to take Humphrey, (that is, myself) to the Queen's Chamber. Mrs Mamble said no, that was not possible but he would not listen, like most children who take a fancy to something, he held on to his wish in a loud and stubborn manner."

"Like my brother here," I said, putting my arm around David's shoulders, who grinned at me good-naturedly.

The Inspector's eyes twinkled at David, "Yes, a regular fit he threw, young Thomas. His mother had to be called in. I tried to leave several times but he held on to my hand. 'No', he said 'Humphrey and I will go and see if the ghost is there, Humphrey will like it!'

"That comment caught my attention and I looked down at the little boy, quite taken aback. This was the first I had heard of any ghost to do with Golden Oaks. Just then lady Victoria hurried in, she must have been expecting dinner guests as she was in full evening dress, with her hair piled high on her head, a pale blue dress, with sapphires clasped round her neck and hanging from her ears. She looked spectacular, like a princess. I don't mind admitting I couldn't take my eyes off her. She was on her knees bending next to her son, talking softly into his ear, trying to sooth him down. 'But please, mama, say I may Humphrey will look after me, will you not?' I was most embarrassed as I did not want her to think that I was the troublemaker. I stood there, miserably self conscious, in a bit she looked up at me with a most understanding smile, that completely disarmed me, at that moment I could have done anything for her, even gone to war." The Inspector sighed, then went on. "She said 'oh very well only a peek, mind you, but you must let me come too'. She got up from the floor and led her son out of the door, 'come along Mr Crawley, and meet our ghost', she said in jest, looking over her shoulder as she left the school room. I followed as if in a dream.

"We walked down what seemed like endless passages, past a great number of doors, Thomas, ran ahead almost jumping with excitement. I was struck by how well kept the house was, we were now in the oldest part of the house but everything was polished and cared for, 'such a large house must take a lot of work to keep it so immaculate,' I thought to myself.

"At last we took a turn into a narrow little passage with a wooden arch in dark wood. The arch was so elaborate, it dwarfed the entrance of the passage. I looked around wonderingly. Here both mother and son stopped and turned, beckoning to me. I hurried up to them, we stood in front of a large wooden door.

" 'This is called the Queen's Chamber, it was built in honor of Queen Elizabeth I, who was scheduled to pay our ancestors a visit, she never made it then but the room was prepared nevertheless, come.'

"The great wooden door creaked as I pushed it open and held it for them, it was heavy as it slipped from my hand and swung back with a slight sound which made us jump. I turned to look around me, now quite as excited as little Thomas. It was a large room, very much Elizabethan in décor. In the centre stood the most ornate wooden bed, I have ever seen. It was not too broad, was very tall; in fact had four steps leading up to it. Heavy velvet burgundy curtains hung on all four corners, that were trimmed with golden ropes. A majestic crest was carved on to the front panel, truly fit for a queen. Indeed, no one else would dare sleep in it, I thought looking at it in awe. A large, imposing, fire place stood against one wall, with two straight backed chairs in front of it, an old rug in front of them. In this room, unlike the other parts of the house, the upholstery was quite faded, in fact the fire screen on one side was positively tattered! Long windows lined one side of the room; they had dark criss-cross bars across them with iron handles. The curtains that came all the way down from the high ceiling matched the bed, and were likewise faded in colour, their gold trimmings hanging loose from several points.

"Lady Victoria was standing near a tall, narrow table, trying to light the candles that stood in a stand on it. I hurried to help her, she handed me the matches gratefully and moved off. Thomas was looking out of the windows at the grounds outside. My task executed I turned to look for Her Ladyship but couldn't see her anywhere; my heart missed it's first beat. 'Thomas, where is your mama?' I asked anxiously.

" 'Oh, must be here,' said the boy who was kneeling at a casement, staring at something outside.

" 'Humphrey, see, it has started raining,' he said.

"I turned from him and called out 'Ma' am, where are you?'

"I looked round the room carefully and saw a tall screen in one corner. It was covered with a dull golden fabric, framed in gold. Going closer to it, I noticed that it half concealed the entrance of a room. I went towards it and peeped in, Lady

Victoria was standing in front of a full length looking glass, she was looking at herself curiously. For a moment, I stood transfixed, utterly mesmerized by her beauty. This corner was a sort of small dressing room with dark wooden paneling on all three sides that went up to the ceiling. There was no light in the room, the candles I had just lit provided a little glow in the room, through their reflection in the mirror and in that light I saw the beautiful lady Victoria standing tall and staring at her own reflection, as if for the first time. All was silent, the little boy sat at the casement still looking out, and I kept staring at the young woman who stood as if hypnotized in front of the looking glass. It was then that I felt it, a feeling of great fear, I felt a shiver as if suddenly it had grown very cold, I looked over my shoulder, the golden screen blocked half my view of the room, Thomas was looking out, his head now resting on his arms. I turned back and looked at Lady Victoria, my eyes met hers, and I froze. Her expression had changed. Her face was white; her eyes meeting mine in the mirror were full of a nameless fear. She didn't speak a word, I looked around wildly, there was someone in the room, watching us, I was convinced. I could see nothing, but the terrifying coldness remained. I saw Lady Victoria's hand go up and feel her own throat, then she gave a tiny cry and slumped down on the floor. I panicked; first I moved towards her, then paused and called out to the little boy. Fearing, I do not till this day, know why, for his safety. I went towards Thomas, he had jumped up from where he had been sitting and was looking curiously at me.

" 'Listen Thomas, your mother...' my voice trailed off, for at that moment, the door was flung open, Lord Trevor stood at the entrance. He too, like his wife was in full evening dress. He stood there looking thunderous.

" 'What is the meaning of this Thomas? You know I dislike your coming to this room?' he scolded loudly, walking into the room.

" 'Mamma said it was quite all right,' said the boy softly standing still, not daring to look up at his father.

" 'Excuse me, your Lordship,' I tried to interrupt at last.

" 'And you are?' he asked me, looking at me, having obviously forgotten me.

" 'Her Ladyship,' " I whispered, pointing to the screen. Never have I seen a man move faster, in a minute he was out of my sight.

" 'Come here, man!' he called out.

"I ran up to the little chamber. Lord Trevor was kneeling on the floor, holding his wife in his arms, looked desperate.

" 'What's happened here?' he asked me sharply.

" 'Nothing, Sir, we just entered about five to ten minutes ago, Her Ladyship was standing there in front of the mirror and seems to have fainted, I was just going to fetch help... when,' I stammered out.

" 'Go, fetch some water!' he shouted. I ran, glad to be of some help. When I came back to the room I saw he had brought her to the bed, and laid her on it. He was sitting next to her, her head was on his shoulder and her arms around his neck. Thomas stood next to them. Silently I handed over the glass, he put it to her lips, she looked up at me gratefully her eyes looking into mine, a silent message in them.

" 'All right my dear?' said his Lordship.

" 'Oh yes Trevor, let us go now, I do so dislike this bed,' she made a grimace and tried to get up. He smiled for the first time that night, got up and pulled her up. 'Come,' he said to Thomas and myself, quietly we followed. I held the door open for everyone, then hesitated before shutting it 'just a minute, the candles', I said.

" 'Better blow them out man, for no servant is going to enter this room now that it's dark,' laughed the Lord of the manor. I must have looked dismayed, for he paused, 'come, I will hold the door,' he said moving to do so. Lady Victoria waited with Thomas, I was silently grateful, as the thought of going into that room alone was terrifying. I walked up straight to where the candles stood and was just about to blow, when something caught my eye. A slight movement, again near the golden screen, as if someone just went past it into the chamber within. I shivered, my heart thumped loudly. I turned instinctively to Lord Trevor, pointing at the screen, but he wasn't looking my way. I hesitated for a minute then hastily blew the candles and ran out, towards the others.

"We walked back to the school room, the elders quiet and the little boy chattering away, apologizing to me on behalf of the ghost for not showing up! 'Don't worry dear Humphrey, next time you may be lucky,' he said squeezing my hand, then added as a consolation, 'but mamma fainted, that was exciting was it not?' he looked up at me; I smiled down at him, he obviously thought I was disappointed, he pulled me towards him, I bent down. 'perhaps she fainted from fright, at the thought of the ghost,' he whispered into my ear, 'she is really quite timid, I should not have taken her there. I do not think I will take her there again.' He looked protectively at his mother's back, as she walked ahead, her arm drawn through her Husband's. Mrs Mamble was standing outside the school room, her worn face looking plainly worried, wringing her hands together, and I suspected, muttering a prayer. Her charge was handed to her and she bore him off quickly, the little rascal winked at me before demurely following her. I turned to take my leave of lord Trevor and Lady Victoria, muttering something about being sorry for Thomas wanting to show me the room, they were very gracious and kind. I could not help expressing the hope that Her Ladyship was feeling well now. She put her hand out, I took it in mine shyly. She smiled at me and said softly, 'Come tomorrow and have tea with me, I will explain it all to you, Mr Crawley, will you?'

"I blushed Scarlett, simply nodding, my consent; she turned, again taking her husband's arm. I stood there watching them as they walked off down the grand gallery lined with their ancestor's portraits. I can't express to you all, he said, looking round at us, "what a beautiful picture they made! it was only when they were well out of my sight, that I turned and went on my way, exiting from a more informal side entrance. Lamps were lit along the drive that led up to the house, the main entrance looked grand, with the footmen standing around in their formal livery, greeting guests that were getting out of carriages. I watched for a while and then made my way home." Inspector Crawley paused here, as if lost in the past. Julia and I looked at each other completely fascinated.

Everyone waited patiently, even Mrs Weston sitting with her legs crossed, her head on the back of the armchair. After some five minutes, he began to speak again. "I reached Golden Oaks the next day, a tad too early I am afraid. The butler guided me to a small room on the ground floor, and requested me to wait. It was a charming room, very much a woman's room...a lot of flowers, two beautiful screens in two corners of the room, a large mirror on top of the fire place, a little stool in front of the same. A comfortable sofa was placed against the wall, its upholstery matched the curtains and were both of a cheerful floral design. There was a painting of a mother and her baby hanging over the sofa. I was standing in front of it, admiring the artist's work when I heard a soft step behind me and turned around. Lady Victoria, looking fresh faced and seemingly recovered from last afternoon's experience, came towards me, smiling, holding out her hand. I took it and bent over it in the fashion then prevalent of greeting ladies.

" 'Come Mr Crawley, sit down,' she gestured to a comfortable looking chair placed next to the sofa, and herself sat down on the sofa. 'Tea, I think,' she said smiling and rang a little bell that was on the table in front of her. In a second, mysteriously, a servant appeared on the door. 'My lady,' he said. 'Tea please, John', she said and he withdrew as silently as he had come.

" 'Well, Mr Crawley,'" she turned to me, 'yesterday was a strange day, was it not?'

" 'Oh yes,' I stammered, 'quite shocking,' I said, wringing my fingers, feverishly. She began to talk in her soft, musical voice.

" 'A long time ago someone came to stay at Golden Oaks, she was brought by the then owner of the house. It is said she was a poor relative, she was of impeccable family but had no fortune. A woman of great beauty called Mary. It was her beauty that caught the Lord's eye, she stayed in that room for many months,' her voice drifted off as the tea was brought in. I waited patiently, looking intently at my story teller. She poured out a cup and handed it to me, I took it from her declining to eat anything. 'Please go on,' I said.

" 'Oh! Yes, of course you want to know, well, this beauty was promised marriage by the Lord of the manor, but when the time came he let her down. One night when he had gone to London on a so-called business trip, news was brought to her that he had contracted a marriage with a lady of great fortune. Poor Mary was distraught. It is said she cried and cried for two whole days. She stood at the casement in her room and looked at the drive hoping to see her Lord and learn that it was all a great mistake. It is said that she would walk around the house, in a pale ivory lace dress, with her long black hair streaming behind her back. Then at long last, one day, he returned, bringing with him his bride! There was a scene, she knew it was over. He, it is said, still promised to look after her. Money, he said, made him marry someone else. That very night Mary took her own life in the Queen's Chamber, and ever since she is seen, sometimes walking down a corridor, but mostly in her own room crying for her Lord,' her voice trailed into silence.

"Suddenly she bent towards me and looked into my eyes. 'you felt her presence did you not, Mr Crawley'.

" 'Yes,' I answered simply,' 'someone was certainly there,' I mumbled.

" 'I felt her there, for the first time, believe me, never before have I seen her. I have heard of her but never seen her. Yesterday, she was there,' she said, her voice, rather fierce. I looked helplessly at her, I could not refute her, but my mind searched for a logical explanation. 'Ghosts' surely do not exist! Yet, I have to admit, I had felt a presence in that room, I knew I had, despite being a logical person. It was then that she told me something which I believed no matter how fantastic it would seem to anyone else. 'Mr Crawley, there is one other thing I have not told to anyone, not even to Trevor, for he will be desperately worried. You know when you saw me standing in front of the mirror...?' I looked at her, now quite frightened, she nodded understandingly, her own face, white and tense. 'I did not see my own reflection in the mirror...but that of a total stranger!' I gasped and put my tea cup on the table, my hand went out and held hers instinctively. Tears filled her eyes. 'Yes, it was a woman, in a pale lace dress with black hair streaming behind her. Her large eyes staring tragically into the mirror,' Lady Victoria began to sob quietly. Her head bent down as she sobbed and I held her hand tightly trying to console her. At length, she looked up sadly into my eyes. 'Oh Mr Crawley, you haven't heard the worst yet. I looked at her in alarm, her beautiful eyes still full of tears, looked sadly into mine, as she went on softly, 'it is said in our family that whenever such a thing happens, it brings great personal tragedy to the one who sees Mary in the mirror..., 'My God' I gasped again, 'How can that be?'

" 'That is the reason why no woman from the family is encouraged to enter that room, I myself went in for the first time, Trevor is most particular.'

" 'Yes, he was furious when he entered the room,' I affirmed.

" 'He would be,' she went on, 'in the history of our family, two Ladies of the Manor saw Mary in this way and terrible tragedies happened to them.' Her voice broke and tears streamed down her lovely face.

" 'No, no, don't think that dear Lady Victoria. It is too fantastic to be true. Nothing bad will happen to you. You have just had a bad fright that is all,' I soothed her softly.

" 'I admit I felt a presence in the room, you felt it too, perhaps you saw it or perhaps it was a sort of suggestion, but other than the fright, what could it possibly do to you? No, do not believe in this story, even for a minute.' I went on in this strain for quite a while till I could see she felt better, yet when I walked home I felt a nagging nameless fear at the back of my mind."

"Gosh!" said Julia, her big round eyes looking shocked. There was a silence as everyone digested this strange story.

"Did anything bad happen?" suddenly asked David, a worried expression on his little face.

Inspector Crawley turned a weary face to the little boy. "At first nothing happened. I went back to my college after the summer was over. The family at Golden Oaks went on with their daily affairs. Now and then when I came down to see my family, I would visit and take tea with Lady Victoria and Thomas. The strange experience we had shared became a sort of bond between us and we were friends. Although she did not talk about the Queen's Chamber, I was convinced that the cheer had gone out of her eyes, she was desperately worried about the 'family curse' as it was called. I would try to raise her spirits by telling her funny anecdotes from college, sometimes I was bold enough to broach the topic of the Queen's chamber, I would explain to her in a rational manner how an old story can work us up into believing almost anything no matter how strange. The image she thought she saw in the mirror was actually her own imagination, because of the power of suggestion, things like that. Often I had the satisfaction of seeing her spirits lift after we had talked.." Again his voice drifted off as if he was back at Golden Oaks, talking and drinking tea with Lady Victoria.

"But, did anything bad happen?" again interrupted David, frowning.

"Not for a while, dear boy, not for a while..." He moved forward on his chair. "It was Lord Trevor. He had gone to purchase a necklace for Her Ladyship, to be given on her birthday...an unexpected accident on his way back...he did not survive. He was only thirty years of age."

"My God!" I said.

"Still, nothing to prove it had anything to do with the curse," said Floppy reasonably.

"No, none whatsoever, except that it happened exactly one year from our visit to the Queen's Chamber, it was in the month of February the same day, the 15th...one year later," murmured the Inspector.

"Poor Lady Victoria," said Julia, a tear in her eye.

"Yes, she was heartbroken, try as I might I could not convince her it had nothing to do with the curse. The incident in the Queen's Chamber completely changed her life, she became obsessive about it, the house was shut down and she, Lady Cecilia and Thomas left to live in some other property far from Golden Oaks."

"Did you see them again?" I asked.

"Oh yes, I visited whenever I got a chance. You see, I was the only one to whom she could openly talk about her fears, no one else would believe her," he said.

"They would probably think she had lost her mind," murmured Floppy, "no offense, Sir," he added hastily.

"Yes, Yes, exactly so" mumbled the Inspector. Again there was silence in the room. After about five minutes Inspector Crawley shrugged his shoulders and looked round at us all.

"I suppose you are all wondering what this story has to do with you all and the trouble you are having here." He looked intently at us, "shall I tell you Lord Trevor's full name? That I think will explain the connection to you."

We looked at him completely mystified. Suddenly his voice became loud and formal, "Lord Trevor's full name was Lord Trevor McMillan Christopher Winwood."

There was a hush in the room, save for the crackle of the fire. Never have I seen a bunch of people so completely at a loss of words, as we were at that moment. Only William and Mrs Weston looked as if they were aware of this beforehand.

The long silence that followed this announcement was broken by Mrs Weston, "and children" she said softly, "that was not the end of Lady Victoria's troubles." She looked at the Inspector as if asking him to go on. He was looking quietly into the fire, as if searching for answers in it. It was now pitch dark outside. The only light in the room was provided by the fire, in the chimney. Then William spoke for the first time, "Sir," he said gently.

"Oh yes," sighed the Inspector, "so sorry children, I was miles away, where were we?"

"What happened after that?" I plucked up courage and asked him, "were they happy in their new life?"

"Happy! Oh no, there was no question of happiness for Lady Victoria after the death of Lord Trevor and the fear of the curse hanging like a sword over her head, so to speak. Yet for some years it was all right, Lady Cecelia lived a long life and they were friends, the two of them. In fact it was Lady Cecelia who told me about the fate of the necklace," he stopped again.

Shocked, I looked up at him, this was the most strange story I had ever heard. "Necklace?" I blurted and before I could stop myself, then I said, "I'm so sorry excuse me."

Inspector Crawley looked at me. "Of course you are amazed. Is it not an extraordinary tale? Now listen carefully everyone, come closer," he said glancing round at us all. There, in Mrs Weston's dark study, all of us children moved closer to the white haired Inspector's chair and crowded round his feet, we looked up at him, with undivided attention.

"Haven't any of you wondered what happened to the necklace Lord Trevor had bought in London for his wife's birthday? Let me first tell you that it was a priceless antique. It is said to be made of rubies and emeralds of the best quality, with a large tear-drop diamond at the centre, created by one of the foremost jewelry houses of the land. The necklace was bought in an auction and had a history attached to it, it seems that it was worn by royalty at sometime or other, but I know nothing about such matters, sorry girls," he said apologetically addressing the last sentence to Julia and me...

"Oh, please, do go on?" I said. "Well, Lady Victoria would have none of it, in fact when it was placed in her hands by Lord Trevor's secretary after the accident; she flung it away and burst into tears. 'Oh no, no, throw it away what use is it to me now, it is bad luck, it has taken Trevor away,' She wailed. All this was told to me by Lady Cecilia on one of my visits to them in the new house, somewhere in the Lake District near Derbyshire. I still remember, I was standing in the entrance handing my hat to Briggs, the butler, when a lady's maid came running down the wooden staircase that was opposite the main door through which I had entered. 'If you please, Sir,' she said breathlessly, 'Lady Cecilia would like a word with you, if you could step this way..' I was quite surprised as the Dowager lady had never sought my company in the past few months, but obediently I went. I was guided to a large formal drawing room, where Her Ladyship sat, in state, on a most ornate chair that resembled a throne, her foot on a little stool, a frilly handkerchief hanging from one bejeweled hand. I went up to her and took the hand she held out to me and kissed it, she gestured to a chair placed strategically next to her. I sat down, almost on the edge of it, my eyes directed towards the floor, so nervous was I in the company of this grand lady. For grand she was, the type that can never be seen again in our modern times, a strong women with regal manners, perfectly turned out at all times, extremely dignified, a chip of the old block as my grandmother would have said.

" 'Mr Crawley,' she said after we had exchanged pleasantries, 'there is something I wish to tell you, you have proven yourself, these last years, a loyal friend to the Winwood family, standing by us through our troubles.' I tried to mumble something, which sounded like 'not at all', She silenced me with a wave of the handkerchief.

" 'There is something I would like to tell you in confidence, but we have to wait for someone else to join us, till then let us have something to drink, some sherry perhaps?'. I nodded and promptly two beautiful crystal glasses were carried in on a silver platter by Briggs himself. The sherry was poured out, I had only just taken my first sip when Briggs announced the second visitor. To my surprise it was my cousin, John

Arkwright, a lawyer by profession, who briskly walked in and greeted Lady Cecilia. 'Well,' said Her Ladyship after a glass of sherry had been offered and accepted by John, 'you both must be wondering why I have asked you in here, but there is something I need to tell you as friends of the Winwood family. John of course is our family lawyer, (as his father has been before him), so knows of all our legal affairs. Those do not concern us today. It is another matter that has to be told. I am an old woman, I do not think I have long to go, indeed without my son, life is more of a trial to me than anything else. I shall be glad to give it up.' Again I tried to say something but was waved into silence. John gave me a half smile. Lady Cecilia's eyes twinkled at us before she continued. There is this necklace of great monetary worth. In fact it is, I have been informed by experts, an antique of astonishing value. It was purchased some years ago by my son for his wife, unfortunately he met with a fatal accident. Lady Victoria refused to touch it and in fact threw it way, after which it was rescued and handed over to me by a loyal employee. I tried then and later to convince Lady Victoria of the blamelessness of the necklace but my daughter-in-law, you both must realize has become very superstitious after losing her husband. She insisted on disposing it of. I tried to sell it but to do so would have attracted a lot of attention As the necklace is a well known one, Lady Victoria would come to know. She, you see, wanted nothing of it, even the money from its sale! If I sold it clandestinely, we would not get its full value, which is not acceptable to me, as you both know quite well.' John and I smiled at the quaint old lady, how shrewd she was with money matters, we knew very well and had met her wrath many times. Even the waste of a few shillings in the transaction of any of their business matters.

" 'So, gentlemen, I came up with a plan. Last May I set out to visit all the houses that our family own. It was a long and tiring business but very rewarding. Something my son had attended to every once in a while, I met all our family retainers and listened to their grievances and,' she stressed "attended to them." Again John and I smiled. 'Well, in the course of this journey, I hid the necklace in one of our properties.' Here we both look up at her, quite shocked.

"She looked at us, almost victoriously, glad at getting a reaction from her audience! 'Yes,' you both have heard right,' she said in an amused voice. 'But, really Lady Cecilia', interrupted John, as your family lawyer I cannot advise such a step.' She put up her hand. 'Now, now, don't get excited Mr Arkwright it is done and cannot be undone. You advise most conscientiously but I choose to do things my way.'.

" 'But really Madam, what are bank vaults for?' said poor John.

" 'I prefer to distribute my assets, thank you,' she stated. 'Now hear this, this envelope,' she picked up a large white envelope and waved it at us, 'has in it a map which explains the exact location.' I stared at the white haired old lady, I must admit, completely shocked. She continued without paying any attention to my surprise or poor John's interruptions.

" 'This envelope is to be handed over to any descendant of the Winwood family who is in dire need of financial aid. It is not to be given out in any normal situation, only in an emergency. Consider it as a sort of emergency fund, mind' she pointed a finger at us, 'the need to open it may not arise for several generations, God willing, and you two young men can pass it on to the legal representatives of our family down your line. There I have said my bit.' She looked from one to the other of us.

" 'But really Your Ladyship...,' tried John, once again, 'I cannot advise this...this is most irregular!'

"The wicked old lady chuckled, I realized then that she was enjoying herself hugely, this act was bringing a sense of drama and excitement into her rather dull life, she felt a sort of high from it. She looked challengingly at us. Argument, to my mind, was useless; I attempted none but quietly accepted my role as a guardian of the Winwood necklace, resolving in my mind to honor Lady Cecilia's trust."

Inspector Crawley paused his recital, we all looked steadfastly at him, each person, i think, equally amazed as we listened to each new twist in this story.

"What happened next?" asked David breaking the silence in an uncharacteristically soft voice. "Well, young man," said the Inspector looking at him, "the months passed by, we all went on with our day-to-day lives. Towards the end of the year, lady Cecilia was taken ill, she died within ten days. I went to see her, along with John; she was alert to the last.

"I remember the occasion, Lady Victoria was reading to her, sitting by her bed, when John and I walked into the majestic room. Of course, formally announced by the Dowager Lady's maid, (Lady Cecilia maintained strict formalities to the last) Lady Victoria looked up towards the door; the sharp old Lady on the bed caught the movement. 'Who is it?' she whispered hoarsely. 'Mr Arkwright and Mr Crawley,' said Lady Victoria. 'Ah! Come to pay me a visit, let them come in, near me,' she said, thumping her bed with one hand. We stood there smiling bashfully like two schoolboys as she looked sternly at us.

" 'Frittering away your time, are you? You both should be at work,' she scolded, then suddenly she beckoned to John and he bent low towards her, she whispered something in his ear.

" 'Everything will be as you wish it, Your ladyship need not worry,' said my cousin as he straightened up. She smiled contentedly, "you are very regular," she said looking pointedly in my direction, "still it is good, my daughter-in-law needs the company. She looked from Lady Victoria, who was standing on the other side of the bed, opposite us, to me, a sly look on her face. Then in her signature style waved a hand, thus dismissing us. I left the room in some confusion, convinced Lady Cecilia knew of my secret regard for her daughter-in law. I looked timidly at Lady Victoria but she smiled serenely, giving nothing away as we took leave of her. Lady Cecilia died in her sleep that night. It was to me like the passing of an era, a way of life, Lady Victoria organized a beautiful funeral, full of pomp and show, as befitted the Dowager Lady."

The inspector again lapsed into silence, William made an impatient movement and prompted softly, "Sir, should you not tell them about the immediate events that have brought you here?"

"Yes, of course, am I rambling about the past?" the Inspector looked around apologetically.

"No, No please, tell us everything," I said to him.

He smiled, "I will try and shorten the rest, you see you could not begin to understand without hearing the whole story." After a pause he began again, "three weeks ago I was called to Lady Victoria's bedside; she had suddenly been taken ill. She seemed to have a premonition of her own end, as she insisted I look into all the family affairs and summon John, now Sir Arkwright. I did as she bid, (as I always have since knowing her), but I thought she was being too morbid; I even teased her saying that she did after all resemble her mother-in-law somewhat. She was terribly worried about her young granddaughter who lived with her, Marianne, who was young Thomas's only child and thus her only living relative."

There was an audible gasp in the room at the word "Marianne."

"But, Inspector," interrupted Mrs Weston, "what happened to her son, Thomas? Where was he?"

"Oh did I not tell you, young Thomas and his wife were killed in an accident, some ten years ago. They were on holiday somewhere in the French Riviera. When the accident happened, their little girl survived. Lady Victoria had to travel all the way to get the child home. Oh, and for those of you who are interested, the accident happened on the same day as Lord Trevor's had, February the 15th, that day of doom as it was for the Winwood family!"

There was a stunned silence in the room. Even Floppy the scientist looked taken aback. Nobody said a word; there was nothing we could say.

"Inspector Lanyon came to meet me one day, regarding Lady Victoria," said the Chief Inspector, gesturing towards William! We all looked, shocked, at William, David was the only one who jumped up gleefully and ran to William pulling at his hand.

"A policeman, my friend William!" he said proudly. William smiled at the little boy and ruffled his hair, then looked up apologetically round at the rest of us.

"Sorry, but I had instructions to work under cover," he said. "You see, we suspected foul play in the illness of Lady Victoria," blurted William from where he stood, near the fire place, as if losing patience. "So we set out interviewing all the people who had visited her in the months preceding her death. The family doctor was suspicious and had called for an investigation."

'So you are not Mrs Weston's nephew!" I said almost accusingly.

"He is not," answered the Head, "you see the police sent officers to all the properties belonging to the Winwood family. William was sent here as my nephew, they thought it would look quite natural to anyone scrutinizing the place, and of course we did not want to worry the children or the staff..."

"Hmm," murmured Floppy, "this explains the whole thing about the strange events that have been taking place here."

"Lady Victoria passed away on the 20th of April," continued William, "and her only grandchild Marianne disappeared mysteriously on that day itself. Traces of a poison, Atropine, was discovered in the autopsy, which proved the doctor's suspicion. Meanwhile, the search for Marianne proved fruitless, until you all came along with your discovery of the house in the woods and the mysterious events in your school."

"So those men in the school, what are they after?" asked Julia.

"The necklace stupid," said David loudly. We all looked slightly uncomfortable as the child simply put his finger on the crux of the matter.

"What else does the Inspector mean!" completed David, with an air of finality.

The Chief Inspector smiled, "I suppose this young man is right, somehow the story of the necklace leaked and these people are after it...I have been wondering about that..."

"Marianne has been kidnapped by the same lot, oh poor thing," said Julia.

We all lapsed into silence trying to digest this extraordinary story. Presently Mrs Weston got up, glancing at her wrist watch, "Its very late children, you must be exceedingly hungry, I have arranged for a little meal for all of us, come." She led the way out of her study, we all followed, a little slowly, as we had been sitting for a long time. As I left the room, I turned back and looked over my shoulder, Inspector Crawley was still sitting in his chair, his head bent down, William was bent over him, one hand on his senior's shoulder "Sir please, come and have something to eat."

✦ ✦ ✦

13

The next day was bright and sunny. I had spent the entire night going through the story we had been told and sorting it out in my head. As soon as I could, I headed out to the orangery, taking care to avoid everyone, as I wanted to be alone. There were two or three perplexing questions: Why was Lady Victoria poisoned after all these years and of course, by whom? What possibly, could Marianne's abductors get by holding her prisoner? And who was the woman, whose grey coat had been worn by me and led the 'gang' to mistake me for her? I had searched in vain for the owner of the grey coat, but it stayed where I had left it, and no one had claimed it until now. I sat down on a small garden stool resting my back on a pillar inside the orangery, the sky was blue and clear, the plants around me gleamed, baking in the sunshine, like I was. I was almost dozing off, when I heard a murmur of voices.

A woman's voice said, "it is now very difficult as the police are everywhere. Why did you have to do away with Peters?"

"He was a fool getting greedier and greedier, we had to shut him up," said a gruff male voice.

"I cannot help you now, it is too dangerous," said the woman.

"Oh really," said the man, making those two words sound extremely menacing, like a threat. I felt a shiver go down my spine, I dared not move. Breathlessly, I waited for more.

After a moment's silence, the man said, "in any case, I doubt if the goods are hidden here or we would have found them. Peters knew the old place pretty well. You all have searched quite thoroughly."

"What do you want from me then, let me go," she whispered.

"You will keep an eye on the police investigation. Ask innocent questions of the children, especially those four, including the foreign boy. They are forever interfering, a nosy lot," barked the man.

My heart was pounding in my chest, I could hardly breathe as I heard us four mentioned so casually by a member of the 'gang'.

"Keep your ears open and report any development in the usual way," said the man, harshly. There was the sound of soft footsteps and then silence. For a moment I sat there, like a statue, then impulsively I sprang up and looked around. At first, I saw nothing, then I noticed a slight movement to the right of the orangery where there was a thick undergrowth. I moved towards it, half running, half walking. I peeped through the bushes, and saw a figure walking slowly ahead. The figure was wearing the same grey coat I had worn when I had been mistaken for a member of the 'gang'! It was obviously a woman. More determined than ever to see who she was I kept following her. It was easy as she did not turn round even once. She went up the stone steps and towards one of the side doors that led into the school, I hid behind the balustrade but kept my eyes on her.

She pushed open the long heavy door and turned; just for a moment, as if to check if there was anyone watching, that moment was enough for me. In a second I recognized the familiar face of Madame Gustave, our popular French mistress!

"My God," I thought to myself, staring at the door as it slowly shut behind Madame Gustave. Suddenly I was scared. I turned and ran, I wanted to get to my friends and did not want to look around anymore, I just ran towards our usual balcony. Just before I reached it, a hand shot out and grabbed my arm, I was pulled into a little arcade. "Oh!" I whispered breathlessly.

'Don't scream for heaven's sake!" said a familiar voice in my ear. I felt a huge sense of relief as I recognized William. I leaned against a grey stone wall, rubbing my arm.

"Do you want to give me a heart attack?" I whispered angrily.

"No, but what's with you? Why are you running as if the hounds are behind you?" He asked.

"I saw something," I whispered my irritation vanishing as the memory of what I had just discovered came back.

He looked at me inquiringly; I paused, then said abruptly, "it was the woman who owns the grey coat."

Luckily he caught on, asking no questions, just raising an eyebrow "and?" he enquired.

"Madame Gustave," I blurted out "I saw her talking to a man in the orangery, and followed her till I recognized her. Oh, and William, she spoke in a perfect accent, she isn't French at all!"

"Good work," he said, "I have been wondering about the grey coat, this is excellent. Now listen to me, do not tell anyone about this. Let's keep an eye on her and follow where she leads."

I nodded, seeing the sense in what he said. I repeated the conversation I had heard in the orangery, he listened quietly, but did not say anything, merely asking me to go back to the others and to keep an eye on the French mistress.

As I resumed my walk, this time more staidly, I met one more person. Just under the balcony where my friends and I sat every afternoon was a familiar uniformed figure, pacing up and down, his helmet glowing in the sunshine, Sergeant Wotley.

"Hello!" I greeted him.

"Miss Emma," he nodded.

I stopped; "well," I said, "any developments?"

"Kind of you to ask, Miss," he replied, his plump face going red, "this beautiful day is so inspiring."

I looked at him frowning, not understanding him.

"Just composed something," he went on, "if you would care to listen," without waiting for a reply he plunged into his recital, his voice, dramatic and loud.

"The sky is blue and bright,
but it still gives me a fright,
for something is not quite right,
we must put together all our might,
to put an end to the young lady's plight!"

I stared at Sergeant Wotley, completely speechless. He was looking at me, waiting for a response. I gulped, "very good, quite remarkable!"

"Thank you Miss, thank you," he said, his voice full of pride "clever, though I say it myself."

"Very good," I mumbled politely, as I saw he was waiting for more praise. "There is another poem I am working at..." he went on encouraged by my response "it is of a tragic style."

"Yes, yes, would love to hear it, but later as Ms. Lewis has just sent for me," I muttered hastily and ran up the stairs. Once indoors, I stopped and gave way to my laughter.

"Oh God!" I said holding my stomach, as David walked up, looking curiously at me. "Are you having a fit Emma?" he asked in a matter-of-fact voice.

"Oh no," I replied, still laughing.

"You certainly look peculiar," he said.

"Want to hear a poem?" I asked him, and repeated the Sergeant's poem. We both went into peals of laughter.

Back in my room, I thought over things again, to my mind, the first thing we needed to do was rescue Marianne, never mind the necklace. The question was how; was not the police sufficient for that? They must be doing their best, we were only amateurs after all. How could we hope to achieve what they had not...I was sitting on the chair staring in front moodily, my mind unable to accept this blank on Marianne's whereabouts. I wished Julia was there to talk things over with but she had gone on a visit to her aunt's for a few days. The quiet was broken by a distinct scratching sound coming from the long French windows that led out to the balcony, in a second I was on my feet and peering out, it was Einstein, our school dog, a large white terrier. He went on poking at the door, I kept staring at him; that night too, there had been a sound, we had actually seen a man running off, Mr Peters, I thought now. I tried to open the door, it was locked, I went out of the room and round the back of this side of the building and finally reached our balcony. I ran up the three stairs. I joined Einstein, he sniffed around me and seemed glad of the company. I looked around, a broken chair and five or six potted plants standing in the corner was all that was there. Slowly I walked along the row of pots looking down at them, nothing unusual. I bent down and looked more carefully, "what could there be here," I thought to myself, then I saw it, just like that! I was so excited, I could hardly breathe, for as I poked at the plants with a stick that I found lying on the ground, one by one, I found that the stick did not go far in one, that the floor was hard, in fact solid. There was an artificial base in one pot. I was on my knees looking at it, Einstein next to me, with his tongue out, panting, as if waiting to play. I picked up the pot and hurried back along the wall of the building looking fearfully around me. Einstein running along next to me perhaps, expecting me to throw the plant for him to fetch!

"Sorry Einstein not today," I whispered, "got work to do." Leaving the disappointed dog outside I went inside shutting the long heavy door as silently as I possibly could. Stealthily I made my way to my room. Only when I was safely inside did I breathe easy. I pushed the plant under the bed where I had hidden things on earlier occasions, and left the room. I was very clear, I must get William to look at the plant. That man whoever he was, that we had seen earlier through the window, must have placed this in the middle of the other plants. Why? There must be a reason. I ran down the corridor and bumped into David, for once I did not scream at him but caught him by his collar as he did not seem to be in a mood to stop.

"Let go Emma, I'm busy," he said, trying to wriggle out of my grasp.

"No, stop, I need you to do something for me," I said softly.

"Later," he said.

"Now," I said.

"What's cooking?" he asked suddenly, pausing in his wriggling and staring at me, "did Sergeant Wotley tell you another poem?"

"No, no, go and fetch William, for me, now, please there's a dear."

"What's in it for me?" he asked, business-like suddenly, still looking ready to run if released a moment. I thought quickly, "my new fountain pen, it's yours."

"On your word?" he asked.

I crossed my heart, "Okay," he said promptly, "where do you want him?"

I laughed at his style of putting it, "in my room, get him there quickly," I replied.

David ran off and I made my way back to my room.

I did not have to wait for long, within ten minutes there was a knock on the door, I opened it quickly and William and David entered, I shut the door behind them.

"The fountain pen," said David getting to the point at once.

I went to the desk and took it out of the drawer. David put it in his pocket.

William was looking amused at us, "Is that what I suspect it is, bribery?"

David grinned; I turned to him and said unceremoniously, "now get out."

"But I want to hear your conversation," said the incorrigible little boy, happily perching himself on my bed.

"Certainly not, off you go," I said, pushing him towards the door.

"Well?" said William, as I turned from shutting the door behind the reluctant David. "What is the matter, why the urgency to see me, didn't know I was so popular with you," he asked, laughing.

I did not reply, simply getting on my knees and pulling the plant out from under the bed and placing it on the worn carpet. "I wanted you to have a look at this," I said.

He sat down on the carpet, "A plant...a rather dirty, muddy pot," he said looking carefully at it. "Where did you find it?"

I gestured towards our balcony, and quickly told him of how I had come across the plant. He took it in his hands and turned it around. Then pulled at the leaves, nothing unusual. He put it upside down and shook it, the plant fell out. I bent forward, put my hands on the dark base and pressed it, nothing happened, then I tried to pull at it, something gave, it was like a lid, crudely made. A tiny little cavity appeared in the mud, William put his hand in and pulled something out. A paper, a rather dirty, folded, piece of paper. We opened it. It was large sheet, a little yellowish, looked like a map. We sat back on the carpet and looked at it. "Most ingenious," said William, looking at the hiding place, "wonder who put it there?"

"Mr Peters, I think," I replied, telling him of our earlier experience of seeing someone run from our balcony.

"Hmm maybe this is what the men in the green common room were looking for that day..." he murmured.

"Yes, perhaps Peters found it and put it there for someone to take," I said.

"Only they could not, as there are so many policemen around now," he concluded.

We looked at the map, it was full of vertical and horizontal lines, some figures were scripted on it but it was not easy to decipher. At last William got up, "I'll take it to the office and get an expert to look at it. Lord knows we may have something there," he said, folding it up.

"Wait a minute," I said. "Won't it take a long time?" He looked at me inquiringly "Floppy...let's get Floppy to look at it," I said breathlessly. "We don't have so much time." we exchanged glances perfectly understanding each other in that moment.

"Where will he be?" he asked me curtly.

"I will go and find him," I said.

"Meanwhile," he said, "I will put this back from where you brought it, someone might come looking for it." he picked up the plant from the carpet.

"Wait a minute," I said," taking a paper from my drawer.

"What are you doing?' he asked coming up to my desk.

"Why not send them on a fool's errand!" I said purposefully sitting down and beginning to draw a line on the paper.

"You go, get Floppy, I'll do it," he said pulling me up from the chair, "and with pleasure," he laughed. I went out of the room.

I found Floppy with Edward in the Billiard room, at first they were very annoyed at my disrupting their game, it took me quite a while to explain to them what I wanted Floppy for. When we finally reached my room, it was empty, almost half an hour later William joined us. Immediately he pulled the map out of his pocket placed it on the desk; everyone crowded round. Now, how can one decipher a map which could be leading from almost anywhere to anywhere? No title, no labels, just several lines leading here and there...very confusing.

Edward and I exchanged disappointed glances. Floppy kept looking at it, he turned it upside down and looked at it through the light of the lamp.

"Let's go to the library," he said suddenly, beginning to leave the room.

"No, stay," said William "it will attract too much attention, I don't want anyone seeing us pouring over a map, as I have just put a bogus one outside," he grinned.

"Well then," said Floppy hesitatingly. "I need a couple of books."

"I'll go," volunteered Edward "what books do you need?"

Floppy smiled, "I do not remember names old man, just the face of the volumes. Will go and get them, won't be long."

He came back with a handful of dark heavy volumes and thankfully handed them to Edward as soon as he entered the room. Edward put them on the desk and Floppy sat down in front of the desk. We all looked curiously at him as he went through the books, only William picked up one or two and looked at them. They appeared to be rather old publications on buildings over the last centuries, quite technical, full of diagrams and measurements, just the kind Floppy enjoyed! I picked up the map, now lying on my bed and idly looked at it. Call it sheer luck or the angle at which it was lying, but this time as I looked at it, I knew what it was. It was an old architect's drawing of the orangery. The very one where I had overheard the French mistress talking to a stranger.

"Gosh!" I said, "it couldn't be!" Everyone turned to me, "What? What?" asked Edward impatiently.

"I think this depicts the orangery!" I said jerking my hand in that direction.

Floppy took it from my hand and looked at it, "it's true, that's brilliant Emma!" he said, clearly thrilled.

Just then there was a knock on the door, we all looked up alarmed, I opened the door cautiously a uniformed policeman stood outside. "Come in officer," William said from behind me. "Constable Smith Sir, you asked for me," said the visitor, stepping into the already crowded room.

"You have become quite a socialite Emma," whispered Edward. I made a face at him.

William was playing host, and gestured for the Constable to have a seat. "Anywhere you find room," he added, laughing.

"Sorry it's rather a small room," I said apologetically.

The new entrant did not reply, simply reddened and sat upright on the corner of the arm chair Edward vacated for him. He was a tall thin young man with spectacles, a very serious expression on his long face, which closely resembled a fish.

"Now smith, I have been told you are somewhat of an expert with old maps and things?" started William.

"Sir, studying them is my specialty," replied the officer.

"Well here, have a look at this," William handed him our map.

Expressionlessly, the young officer, who I had already nicknamed 'The Fish', looked at the map and examined it. He took out a magnifying glass from his pocket and looked at the map through it, we all stared at him. Presently he looked up, again expressionless, he said, "in my opinion it is genuine, made sometime in the eighteenth century. Would even be this property, will need to see more evidence," he spoke like a telegraph.

"We think we know what it represents, we'd like you to help us reach it," said William.

"Sir," said The Fish and lapsed into silence, his mouth slightly open, exactly like a fish. For a moment even William looked at him in surprise, it was really quite funny. Then he shrugged and looked around. "Shall we say tonight, after eleven o'clock, we all meet in the orangey?"

Everyone nodded. The Fish continued looking ahead, his mouth a little open. William said, "You too, Constable." The Fish's expression did not change he simply said "Sir" again and continued looking ahead. William turned from the door, which he had been about to open, looking slightly perplexed, and whispered to me, "what's with him?"

"He's your man," I whispered back..."the expert!"

"Come on then Constable, let's leave this young lady alone," said William a little irritably, trying to rouse the Constable who remained seated, even as everyone else left the room.

"Sir!" said the fish and walked out of my room, very erect, leaving William who was holding the door for everyone, looking bemused after him.

Several arrangements were made that evening, for instance the number of policemen patrolling the school grounds was doubled. Edward later told me it was to warn off anyone spying on the place, William was not taking any chances. Madame Gustave was sent on an errand to little Meadows, a nearby town. Of Mrs Weston, there seemed to be no sign, which puzzled me exceedingly. I wondered about it as I made my way to the orangery. It was a dark cloudy night, rather chilly and in fact a little foggy. I was not sure if I should seek Matron's permission, or indeed, inform anyone of my plans. Nobody was around. The policemen outside saw me but did not attempt to stop me or even ask any questions. When I reached the orangery, it was quite dark, one or two policemen in their dark uniforms stood by with lanterns, they gave me quite a start. As my eyes accustomed themselves to the light, I recognized Floppy standing to one side, holding a thick book and talking to William. He seemed to be pointing something out. The Fish stood next to them, a paper in his hand, his expression, as always, extremely expressionless. William turned to him and said something, The Fish bent down and looked at the book in Floppy's hand, he nodded. Someone touched my arm, I gave a start. "It's only me, Emma. Fantastic isn't it, look at the atmosphere. Great of William to let us in on it, he's a chum," whispered Edward.

"What are they doing?" I asked.

"I believe Floppy's found something, he's been pouring over those books all day," he answered, looking at the little group excitedly. We stood there, a little to one side in the dark and waited. Far away, was the school building, dimly visible in the dark. After a few minutes William and his group seemed to reach some agreement. Floppy put his book down on a wrought iron table that always stood in one corner of the orangery. William called one of the policemen who came forward with some very long sticks, looking closer, we realized that they were scales. They started measuring the ground. Floppy and The Fish then got into action. They went up and down the orangery, each taking no notice of anybody. After a bit, I saw Floppy getting down on his knees, he began crawling all over, The Fish too went down on his knees. It was a strange sight, there in the dark foggy night, in the little orangery. Two policemen, one of whom I now recognized as Constable Wotley, held up lanterns. Edward and I stood in one corner just watching, Inspector William stood next to the entrance, also watching, and the other two figures crawled all over the floor. After a while, Floppy stopped, and went to the table where he had put the book, he said something to The Fish, who got up and joined him. They spread the map and the book on the floor, and crouched down. Floppy gestured for light, Constable Wotley went up to them and put his lantern on the floor. William too walked up to them and joined them on the floor, he pointed to something on the map, then he pointed to the table next to them, they looked at the book, Floppy turned it sideways. I looked at Edward "Gosh," I whispered, "this is so terribly exciting, wonder what they are looking for?"

"Could be that the necklace is buried here," he whispered back. I shivered with the thrill of it.

The three men had got up from the cold floor and were trying to move the table, it seemed stuck. William called to the two policemen, who set down the lanterns at once, there was semi-darkness.

"Emma," said William impatiently.

"Of course, sorry," I said rushing forward. Edward and I picked up the lanterns, and stood near the little group, again they tried to lift the heavy iron table. It would not budge.

"May be it's hammered down, I have always seen it in this corner," I said hesitatingly. No one replied. The Fish bent down and looked at the legs of the table. William looked around impatiently, "listen Wotley, go and get some saws or something," he said.

"Yes, Sir" said Constable Wotley, "where from, Sir?"

William looked at him angrily, "What do you mean where from? Can't you find it yourself, use you ingenuity man!"

I smothered a smile; "perhaps in the gardening shed," I said timidly glancing at William's disgruntled face. "Shall I go?" I asked. He nodded, I turned to go and heard William say "Constable Wotley, go on, accompany the young lady, what are you standing there for?"

"Of course sir, sorry Sir, I was just thinking," murmured the Constable.

"Well, don't bother," barked William. The Constable and I hurried out.

As I knew the school grounds, inside out, finding the gardening shed was no problem, even in the dark moonless night. The shed was unlocked so we quickly went inside, the Constable waved the lantern about, we quickly picked up two saws and two long forks and hurried back to the others.

Slightly panting, we arrived in the orangery and handed the appliances. William took the forks, and handed one to The Fish, he directed the other two policemen to take the saws. Then he began to pound the floor under the table, the others followed his lead.

Edward and I held the lanterns for them and Floppy stood by, lost in his own thoughts, slightly bending towards the ground. Suddenly he said, rather loudly, "wait, stop!" Everyone paused and looked at him, a little alarmed.

"What is it?" asked William. Floppy did not answer but to everyone's surprise, crawled under the table. He turned back, "light, please." Hurriedly, I went up to him and placed the lantern I was holding on the ground, under the table. In doing so, I saw his face, I had never seen him look so excited, his face was red and his eyes gleamed, he was frantically plucking at a tile on the floor with his fingers. In a minute William joined him under the tables, "this is it," whispered Floppy breathlessly! "I'm quite sure of it...look," he traced his finger in a sort of square, I moved closer at first I saw nothing different, then I saw what he meant, here was a dull faded border in the shape of a square on one tile from which he had dusted some mud off with his fingers, it was hardly visible, but now as I stared at the tile I saw what he was talking of. Everyone was on their fours, peering at the ground. "Okay, stand back everyone," ordered William. Floppy too, moved off a bit, though still staring at the tile, as if he would lose it if he so much as moved his eyes an inch.

Without a word, William and The Fish placed their hands on two sides of the tile, they struggled a bit, but in five minutes it was off. They moved to look at the ground under the tile, William dusted some earth off, then pressed his hands on the ground, he looked back at us, grinning. We moved closer, he took up the fork and banged it on the ground, it made a loud sound, as it struck metal. We stared in amazement as Floppy and The Fish moved closer. For a while we could not see too well, as the three men blocked the view as they worked. After about two or three minutes, William called out, we moved closer, peering down, there was in one corner, a round iron ring, like an old door handle. We stared, he said, "come on, pull." All four men placed a hand on the ring, slightly falling over each other, trying to balance themselves with their free hands. "Now," said William softly. At fist nothing happened but after two or three tries, the trap door opened up and all of us looked shocked at the darkness below!

"Fantastic," said Floppy, rubbing his hands together, "just as the book said."

"Beautiful," said The Fish bending towards it, his face, blank.

Edward and I exchanged awed glances, completely thrilled.

"Now, Sir?" enquired The Fish of William, who was standing next to the open trap door, looking down at it.

"Well, if it is the one Floppy identified, there should be a tunnel, we had best go in," he replied.

"Sir," said The Fish, moving forward.

"Wait," said William softly.

"Constable Wotley stay here and keep an eye on this door, if we do not show up for long, send in a search party. Mind, do not go to sleep!"

"Sir, you do me an injustice," said Constable Wotley, his face reddening.

"The Constable may find inspiration and compose something brilliant, he is a poet, you know," I couldn't help saying, somewhat wickedly. Constable Wotley's chest visibly swelled, and he looked around at the others in a superior fashion. William gave me a look, The Fish continued to look expressionless, only Edward giggled. After a pause, William looked at me discouragingly and said, "it may not be safe."

"No, do not even try it, I'm coming too!" I answered perfectly comprehending his look.

"But my dear Emma, it may not be safe or pleasant, bound to be dirty and stuffy in there," he pointed underground.

"I'm coming," I said putting up my chin.

He shrugged and turned to the others, "I will go in, followed by Constable Smith then Emma, Floppy and Edward can come in last. All right?" we all nodded. "Constable Wotley will take care of this end, admirably, I'm sure," he continued. Constable Wotley did not look the least bit mollified with this praise.

"I think we should take these along," muttered The Fish, picking up a gardening fork, "might need them.

I picked one up too, Edward took a saw. I noticed Floppy placing his precious books carefully on the table.

I looked around, it was quite dark and cold, the two lanterns cast strange shadows of the trees and plants around. William switched on a torch and took the first step into the ground, so to speak. The Fish followed close behind, it was quite a sight I must say, to see them both disappear under the ground!

"Emma," said Floppy.

"Of course," I murmured and put my foot on the stairs that led under the ground, absolutely thrilled with the excitement of it.

I went down a narrow flight of stone steps, then had to stop, as I almost walked into The Fish. There was hardly room to stand, even as we all stood in a single file. Then The Fish moved ahead, I followed close behind, there was not much to describe here, it was very dark with only the light of a torch, the passage was a very narrow one with cold stone walls on either side. I kept one hand on the wall for support as I walked. The ground was not very smooth. "Wonder who must have been here last," I said, my voice echoing a little. No one answered, and the silence was a little eerie. We walked on, it was a long passage and I started to feel a little claustrophobic. "Gosh, will it never end?" I whispered. Again no one replied, "men!" I thought to myself. Now I was walking, peering at the stone walls, trying to imagine who must have walked along here before us, when I collided into The Fish. "Sorry," I mumbled and tried to peer over The Fish's shoulder to see what was happening ahead. William was waving his torch around. I looked in amazement at a small flight of steps. William flashed the torch up the stairs, they led up to a little, dark door, with a round iron handle. By now we were all huddled together, staring as the torchlight shone on the old iron door handle, and then as it went down the narrow dark stairs. We looked at William, as if waiting for instructions. "Well, Smith, shall we?" said William softly.

"Yes Sir," said The Fish.

"Now, or shall we get more manpower? Can't say what will be there on the other side," murmured, William apparently thinking aloud.

"No one expecting us sir, should be all right. I can take two men, you can handle two. Cannot be more, from what we know," said the astonishing Fish.

I looked at Edward and Floppy, but it was too dark to see their reactions. "Well lets do it," said William. "Anyway let's try the door, wonder, how long ago it was last opened."

"A long time ago Sir, going by the grime, the gang has not been in here," said The Fish as he touched the wall and followed William up the stairs. I went up behind him. William was running his hands on the door, he directed the torchlight all over it, was a solid old door, made of oak wood. There was a little gap between the door and the panel but no light or sound came through. The Fish put his ear on it and moved back, shaking his head.

"Nothing?" asked William.

"Beautiful thick wood, Sir," said the Fish admiringly, "you will never see the likes of this today." I suppressed a giggle, so the fish was enthusiastic about wooden doors!

"Very very old, Sir, could be somewhere in the 1600's. Beautiful..." he went on, running one hand on the door.

"All right Smith, lets give it a shove," said William straightening up. They put their shoulders to the door and pushed, nothing happened. "It's been shut a long time Sir," murmured The Fish, "won't be that easy,"

"Edward," called William, Edward put his saw down against the wall and went up, to join them, so did Floppy, I stood and watched as they all pushed at the door together. Then Floppy said, "wait a minute." He took the torch from me and directed it at the gap between the door and its panel.

"Hold it," he said to Edward, "Emma, fork," he whispered. They all stood back as he pushed at the gap between the door and the panel, it was stuck. "Must be a lot of dirt, push at it" he said to Edward, moving back, "I'm not strong enough." Floppy kept the light directed at the door.

They worked at it for quite a while, trying different tactics; I stood back in the dark and watched their dark forms in the dim light. Suddenly, I heard William say, "I think it's happening... come on" he said, "together." They all lunged at the door, this time there was a creaking sound and I saw their dimly lit forms fall through, onto the "other side." Quickly, I ran up the stairs and joined them. The torch was in William's hands again and he was directing it around, we found ourselves in a tiny chamber. A small dusty wooden table stood in one corner, again, there were narrow stairs leading up to, not a door this time, but a trap door!

William went up carefully, the stairs were quite narrow, he stood up straight and pulled at the handle of the trap-door, "not so easy," he grimaced. Everyone moved forward to help, which was not an easy task as there was hardly space enough for two men to stand. I could see their outlines falling over each other, pulling at the round ring that was attached to the trap door.

"Stop!" said William, "let's count to three, then we pull," he said.

Someone said, "too eager, aren't we?" William counted out, "one, two, three," they pulled, no luck, the trap door remained shut.

"Please, be careful," I said instinctively, my voice sounding strange to my own ears as it echoed a little in this part of the secret tunnel. I moved a little up the stairs. "If the door opens you might fall backwards off the stairs," I cautioned.

"One, two, three," counted William. They all seemed to move together and pull with all their might. This time I saw them fall back almost collectively, half, as I had thought, off the narrow staircase. I saw them scrambling back up, the door had flapped open. I ran up to them. We all stared up at the darkness beyond.

At this point, I must admit to feeling a sense of fear, it was so dark and dreary inside the tunnel, very uncomfortable. On the other hand, the others, I felt, seemed to be excited, and ready to tackle whatever lay ahead.

"Shall we?" whispered William "Yes Sir," The Fish answered, in a matter-of-fact voice.

"Wait a minute, let's take our weapons," urged Floppy.

"Cautious Floppy," murmured William. Edward took the torch and went down the stairs I watched in wonder, my heart literally in my mouth as he disappeared through the door we had come in from, leaving us in pitch darkness for a few minutes. It was horrifically frightening, my mind raced through all sorts of dark possibilities that could happen to us quite easily in this secret tunnel.

"You alright Emma?" I heard Williams voice, "Not scared are you?" he said.

"No, no," I gulped.

"I'm back," said Edward, trying to hold one saw and two forks, as well as the torch. I breathed a sigh of relief and went forward eagerly to help him. The weapons were distributed, and we followed our leader and struggled through the trap-door, one by one. William and The Fish literally hauling me and Floppy up! We found ourselves in another small room. Like the previous one, this too, was dark and rather airless! I am quite sure no one had been in this place for years and years, our torchlight showed us the dust around which lay quite undistributed. There were also a strong musty smell and several cobwebs hanging everywhere. A similar narrow flight of steps stood in one corner, we shone the light over it. This staircase led up to a narrow wooden door, again with a round iron handle. We stood huddled together just under the staircase, staring at the door.

"This must be it," said William softly.

"Should lead somewhere," agreed The Fish.

We all understood what he meant, by 'somewhere,' I looked curiously at the door. "Well, let's go" said William, climbing up the stairs, slowly we followed, and stood in a line, one behind the other on different levels of the stairs, waiting for instructions. Again William and The Fish began working on the door, Edward moved to help. This door had hardly any gap from the panel around it; in fact it was difficult to distinguish the door from the surrounding wall except for its location, which was on top of the stairs. There was a sort of round protruding knob, and nothing else, so they could do little else but pull at it. This they did with all their might. Surprisingly, I saw the three fall back, almost immediately. A glow of light could be seen somewhere ahead. William scrambled up to his feet and went forward, The Fish, close behind, a fork held tight in his hand.

I heard a squeal, someone said "Oh God," a female voice.

I followed Edward in through the narrow opening, for that is what it was, and blinked at what met my eyes. A large room, a cellar obviously, a lantern on the dirty floor, and two forms, huddled together in a corner, my heart beat loudly, I grasped Edward's arm and shrunk behind him instinctively. One minute, William was standing ahead of all of us and looking around, and the next minute, he seemed to have lost his senses! He lunged forward, towards the two figures that were still in the corner. Like a madman, he was pulling at them, they shrank from him, holding on to each other, they were obviously petrified.

"Look at me, please look at me," he entreated.

"Oh, no," wailed one soft voice, "please go away." The female then sank on the ground sobbing. I stared at William, he had turned towards the other woman. "It's me, Mrs Potts, don't you recognize me!" he entreated. The woman turned her face up to him at last, "Oh heavens, the Lord be praised!" she said and put her arms around his neck. She turned to the female still sobbing on the floor. At the same time William went down on his knees, he put his arms around the pathetic creature lying down crying on the dirty floor. They stayed like that for a long time, we stood around them, as if frozen, staring at them.

"Oh, my darling," murmured William. "Oh my poor darling."

Gradually the sobs subsided, but they sat there on the floor, William, holding Marianne, for it was none other, tightly to his chest. We stood around helplessly, everyone shocked with this sudden event, except for myself, somehow I felt had known from some time that William had a deeper connection with this case than it appeared. His strange brooding looks from time to time had alerted me, the very mention of Marianne, seemingly a stranger, made him so sad and angry at the same time, hardly a normal reaction.

"I'm here sweetheart," he said softly, "look at me, please." She did not move, and pushed him away, she stayed there curled up on the floor, but she was not crying any more. The other lady bent down and put her hand on Marianne's head.

"My dear, it is William, he is here! Please, get a hold on yourself."

Still Marianne lay there. To my surprise, I saw Edward move forward and get on the floor next to the poor girl. He lay down and put his face in front of hers, she hid her face in her hands. He pulled her hands off her face, "Remember me Marianne," he said, his voice sounding shy but firm.

Would surprises never cease?

I actually saw a movement. At the sound of his voice, she lifted her face and looked at him.

She whispered, "You!"

"Yes, your friend, Edward" he said, softly.

"You came back again," she said incredulously.

"Yes, of course, I promised to help you didn't I? You did not believe me?!" He pretended to be offended, there was the sound of awkward laughter.

"Come, get up," he continued, trying to struggle to a sitting position. Slowly she looked towards us. Floppy and I moved forward and went down on our knees next to them, "My friends, Emma and Floppy" said Edward, "you remember them from the first time we met?"

She stared uncomprehendingly at us. Then she turned at last towards William, who was looking intently, and almost fiercely, at her. I saw her face in the light of the lantern, never before had I seen such a change in a girl's expression. From a deep emptiness, there came a soft glow into her eyes, they looked at each other, those two, in the dark cellar, with us crowded around them and strange shadows on the walls. Then he moved forward and took her in his arms, her arms slowly crept up round his neck and she started sobbing again. This time, he let her, she went on and on, poor thing!

"Let her cry her heart out.... Lord bless me, I cannot believe it, we had almost given up all hope of getting out," said her companion. "Dear boy," she put a hand on Edwards arm, "You were so brave to come to us as you did."

"But Mrs Potts, how did you get into this mess? I cannot believe it," said William, almost scolding.

"Isn't your name Mrs Hastings?" asked Edward, shyly.

"It is, to be sure, but Mrs Potts is Marianne's name for me, don't please ask me why," said the lady smiling at Edward.

"Really you walked right into a trap," went on William.

"So we did, I cannot think how, all I can say is I am sorry not to have taken better care of Marianne," said the good lady, humbly." "It was all so sudden, Her Ladyship leaving us..."

"Listen," I interrupted her. Everyone tensed up. "What?" asked William.

"A sound, Sir," said The Fish, speaking for the first time. "I heard it too."

"Shhh" said William, even Marianne looked up and stopped crying, but still held on to William.

For a moment we heard nothing, then, we all heard it together, a distinct sound, as if someone was walking on some creaking wooden stairs. "Quickly hide everyone," ordered William, disengaging himself from Marianne, who now refused to let go of him.

"Come on Sweetheart," he looked down at her, "I'll be right here. I want you to pretend nothing's happened," he coaxed her. "Do you understand? I want to catch the scoundrels."

She nodded, then said after a moment, "You will not go away?"

He looked at her, his eyes giving his feelings away. "Do you think I will? No, I will be here, behind you," he said. Mrs Hastings smiled at them both happily, as we all moved back into the shadows of the cellar, looking for somewhere to hide. Hiding ourselves proved easier than we thought as there were several old boxes and other things around, which we had not noticed at first as if they had been pushed back to make room in the centre of the cellar. I saw what looked like some old furniture, a large book case or something, which was covered with a sheet. I went and stood behind it. Marianne and Mrs Hastings sat down on the floor, everyone hid themselves in the dark. It was quite efficiently done!

"It must be very late now," I thought, "no wonder I am sleepy, in spite of this fantastic situation." I glanced at my wrist watch but it was too dark to read the time.

"What's the time?" I whispered. No one answered for a moment, "time anyone?" I asked again, "Everyone, listen!" I heard Floppy's voice from somewhere close to me.

"Do you all realize today is Sunday?" He whispered excitedly.

There was silence everyone waited for him to go on.

"The time is 1 a.m. ring any bells, anyone?," then he said, in a deliberate manner, "Secret Cellar–Sunday 1.15!"

"This is it," said William, his voice sounding excited.

"What is it?" I heard Marianne's voice, just then there was a sound of footsteps, we all held our breath. The cellar was in semi darkness, save for the weak light of the lantern on the floor near Marianne and Mrs Hastings. I almost jumped, as a door opened from somewhere quite close to me, someone entered the room.

The person walked forward, a man, he ignored the two women sitting on the floor. Purposefully he dragged what looked like a table from one side, towards the centre of the room, then came quite close to me. At that point I thought that we would definitely be discovered, but he walked past and dragged two chairs forward to join the table. He then left the room. There was silence, No one spoke.

The silence was broken some five minutes later, by loud footsteps and the murmur of voices. The same door was opened once more, and a little group of people entered. I stared, fascinated, two men, one tall and burly, the other shorter and thinner, they carried a lantern, each. It was not the lantern that I was looking at, but their faces, for each wore a black mask over his countenance with slits for their eyes and mouths. I almost shrieked at the sight of the black masked faces. They looked so menacing in the dimly lit room, only the thought that the others were present with me, bucked me up at that moment! Two women, clad in dark skirts and coats walked in behind them, each wearing similar masks on her face, they all went and stood next to the table. No one spoke for a few minutes.

"Well?" said a female voice, after a long silence. "We are all here, Sunday 1.15 in the cellar, though some of us were not informed of it in time!."

No one replied. "Well, come on, someone say something, why have we been summoned?" the same voice went on, "with no consideration for our convenience! I have a job, you know, it's not so easy for me to get out like the rest of you."

"Shut up," said a gruff male voice, rudely. "We have all done our bit, now it is up to the Boss to force the information out of her," he said, jerking a thumb towards the two women on the floor.

"She's not been too friendly, has she?" One woman walked towards Marianne, I stared horrified as she kicked Marianne, who simply clung to Mrs Hastings and did not utter a word. The masked women stared down at the prisoners. There was silence. I wondered how William was feeling, seeing his beloved being ill treated like this.

The woman walked back to the table, she started drumming her fingers on it, "we should have been sharing the spoils today, since there are no spoils to share, why call us here, a waste of time!" she grumbled. Suddenly there was a movement, the shorter of the two men lunged at her, he grabbed her hair and pulled her head back. She screamed with pain. He held her like that for a moment. Then pointed a finger in her face. "You shut up," he said in a loud, uncouth voice. "Mr Goddard!" I thought recognizing that loathsome voice in a second. He released the woman with force, basically throwing her to the floor. No one went forward to help her. The other woman, in fact, chose that moment to sit down on one of the chairs.

The grumbling woman raised herself from the floor, and sat down on the other chair, rubbing the back of her head with one hand. Again there was silence.

"Good Evening," said a voice from somewhere behind me.

A voice neither male nor female! I must say that this was the most frightening moment of my life. I felt that the voice was the coldest, the most devoid of expressions, a voice with no identity, no apparent feelings. It cast a chill in the room. The four people visibly tensed. The two women stood up at once. No one came into the room. I think the person must be standing in the same doorway, from which the others had entered.

"So we are all assembled," said the voice. "You all know that thus far we have not been successful. In fact, if caught, we shall all be charged with kidnap as well as murder!" There was a pause.

"I can explain," said the voice I had identified as Mr Goddard's.

"There is no need to do that," coldly replied the voice from the doorway, "murder was not in our plans, it clutters things up so."

I stared round eyed into the darkness behind me, then turned towards the four crooks round the table.

"General, Sir," again began Mr Goddard meekly "Peters had begun to get too greedy."

"Perhaps the old woman would have been more useful than her granddaughter here," boomed the strange voice from the doorway. I felt a chill down my spine as all four crooks turned their eyes on poor Marianne. Silently I said a prayer of thanks to God for getting us to Marianne at this hour.

"You villains!" suddenly screamed Marianne, scrambling up to her feet and running forward towards the voice. She didn't get too far as the two women grabbed her and flung her onto the floor. Mrs Hastings rushed to her and cradled Marianne in her arms.

"Oh Mrs Potts, poor grandmama," sobbed Marianne. She turned towards the crooks fiercely and screamed. "What it is you want from us?"

"Ah! now we are getting somewhere," said the creepy voice from the dark.

"We want you to give us the original floor plans of all your properties, simple," there was a pause, "you are to sign a sheet of paper."

Marianne looked completely confused, "that paper, what does it say?"

"Nothing, save giving us full authority to carry on a study in all the said properties. With the purpose of, shall we say... archeological research?" Came a slow and measured response.

"But, why? what can you gain from it?" screamed the hapless young girl.

"Oh, so you plead innocent!" said the voice, now a little sarcastically, but still silky smooth.

Marianne stared into the darkness, I looked at the four members of the gang, they stood still, as if waiting for orders.

"I have something to say," interrupted the burly man in a rough and coarse voice. "As I have done what I was hired to, I want to be paid."

"You will be paid when we get to our goal and not a minute before," said 'the general' in a cold, yet shrill voice.

"You lot will reach the gallows more like," mumbled the large man.

"Hold your tongue," warned Mr Goddard.

"No, let him," said the silky voice, "let us hear the serpent."

"I am beginning to doubt the existence of any jewel, it's to fantastic anyway..." mumbled the tall man, his voice a little subdued now, "what's your game?."

"The necklace must be found. Till that happens, you all continue to do as I tell you to," said the strange voice from the dark, "you will be paid after the task is accomplished, not a minute before."

"Not on your life," blurted the burly man. "I've got a wife and child, don't want to be put away for murder. You pay me now...wasn't told nothing about doing people in...I want out."

"You sure about that?" said unnatural voice, extremely politely.

The burly man moved a step forward, "You pay me now," he repeated fiercely moving threateningly towards the voice.

"Of course, if it is your wish," said 'the General'. A shot rang out, the burly man buckled over and fell with a thud onto the cold hard floor. There was a stunned silence.

"Now, you lot, let's get on with the meeting," said the voice.

"Sir," gulped Mr Goddard. "What are your orders?"

"She will sign the paper now," said the voice ominously.

Marianne stared as Mr Goddard took out a paper from the front pocket of his coat and slowly walked towards her. He held it out to her with a pen in his other hand.

"She needs help!" said the mysterious voice softly. The two women went to Marianne and dragged her to her feet. Mrs Hastings tried valiantly to push them away.

"No, no," resisted the brave girl, "I won't."

Mr Goddard's hand moved as if to strike her, at that very moment there was a loud noise of a man cursing, someone lunged out of the darkness and grabbed Mr Goddard by the throat; he fell onto the floor, completely taken unawares. A commotion now occurred, as several people came into the centre of the cellar and a regular fight was soon under way. The two women crooks showing themselves to be well trained fighters! Goddard had struggled to his feet and was making his way to the door. I saw The Fish lunging at his feet, but he tripped over an upturned chair and Goddard disappeared into the darkness. The Fish got up and ran after him. I heard their footsteps as they ran up the steps. I then moved out, for the first time, from my hiding place, towards the door, and made as if to follow them, thinking wildly of some way of being helpful.

"Okay, everyone, lets see what we have here," I heard William's loud voice. I stopped and looked back at everyone. They were crowded together in the centre of the room, around the wooden table, now lying on the floor at a strange angle. William was holding on to one woman, and Edward held onto the other, with Floppy's assistance. Both prisoners were struggling like wild cats. "Okay, calm down, you two," said William in the professional voice of a policeman. "Floppy, remove their masks." Floppy moved forward and pulled at one woman's mask, we all stared curiously at the unattractive face of a complete stranger. Floppy turned towards the other woman, who gave a defiant laugh as her mask slipped away, the familiar face of the French teacher appeared. "My God!" Floppy said involuntarily, "you, I can't believe it!." She gave us a contemptuous look, but did not say a word.

"Okay, I think there is nothing more to be achieved here," said William looking around. "There was a sound of hurrying footsteps, we all looked towards the dark doorway and in a moment heard The Fish's voice, quite breathless.

"Got away," he said, "tried to get them, but there was a motor car waiting, they jumped in, and drove off. Got the car number though."

"Good work, there was not much chance of getting hold of them, anyway," said his senior reassuringly. We watched fascinated, as The Fish proceeded to take out a pair of hand cuffs from his pocket, he put them on the hands of the woman held by Edward, he then proceeded to do the same to William's prisoner. As soon as he did so William moved towards Marianne who stood somewhere near his right. He did not say anything to her, just looked at her and took her hand, he then turned back towards the rest of us.

"Move, gang," he ordered, his voice changed, suddenly sounding strong and happy.

"Which way Sir?" Asked The Fish in a fascinatingly everyday voice, standing in the middle of the shadowy cellar, holding on to the astonishing French Mistress, and gesturing with his head towards the secret door. "Shall we go through the secret doorway, or the other one?"

"Let's take the stairs up and see where we are," said William walking with Marianne towards the dark doorway. Once there, he stood back and waited, Fish went through with his prisoner, followed by Edward and the second woman, then Floppy and I went through, supporting Mrs Hastings, who walked with difficulty in the middle of us. William and Marianne came in at the end. I looked over my shoulder and saw him almost carrying her up the stairs.

"I know this place," suddenly Edwards voice, shattered the silence, "Listen everyone, it's the old Dowager's house." And so it was, here we were back to where it had all started. The stairs opened up onto a small room, again the door most cleverly concealed on the other side, merging with the wall, with, this time, not even a handle to give it away! Moving out of the room we found ourselves in the main foyer of the dowager house, on one side of us was the staircase and on the other the grand front door. We stood irresolutely, not knowing where to go, sort of huddled together, the two crooks in the middle. William moved ahead, still holding onto his "fair burden." He pulled open the front door and we all dumbly followed him out. It was a cold moonless night, we moved behind William, everyone quite familiar with the geography of the garden, not at all daunted by the darkness around us. If I close my eyes I can still hear the sound of our footsteps on the gravel and then the wet grass. The Fish said "steady now" in a low, deep voice, to his prisoner as they walked. By now Floppy was helping Edward hold on to the other prisoner. It was quite a slow procession, what with Marianne and Mrs Hastings quite stiff after their long imprisonment, and the crooks trying their best to struggle out of their captors hold, so to speak. I gave a start as the sound of a shrill whistle broke the silence.

"God, help us," screamed Mrs Hastings, her nerves quite gone, poor dear.

"It's only me, ma'am," said The Fish hurriedly, "sorry to startle you?"

"You ass," said William, quite informally, "could have warned us."

"Sorry, Sir, just occurred to me to check if anyone's around," he said, a slight tremor in his voice for the first time. "We had deployed our officers all over the forest and school."

"Well, next time warn us before screeching," said his Boss.

"Right sir," said The Fish, there was a pause, "Now sir, I will be screeching again," he said politely, then belted out a deafeningly shrill whistle.

"I'm disappointed officer, could you not do any better," said William sarcastically, we all giggled in spite of our situation.

"Shhh, listen" whispered Marianne suddenly.

"What's the matter?" asked William gently.

"Shhh!" She said, again.

We all stood still and listened; and sure enough, we heard it; there, again it came, an answering whistle!

"Sir," said The Fish formally, "May I?"

"Whistle away, man, to you heart's content," replied William. I put my palms on my ears as there followed a chorus of whistles back and forth for the next minute or so. Then the welcome sound of heavy footsteps getting nearer and nearer, till, at last, the sight of a weak little light from someone's lantern, and finally the appearance of two strong looking policemen. Thus was our exit once again from the old Dowager house.

✦ ✦ ✦

14

The next morning was bright and cold, David and I wrapped ourselves well, and went for a walk in the school grounds. I related the events of the night to him softly as we walked, sorting them out in my own head as I spoke.

"Gosh," he said. "Its getting better and better," he paused, "I want to see Marianne."

"I'm sure you will run into her, now that she is here," I replied.

"Hmmm, do you think the Boss crook will be caught soon?" he asked.

I shrugged my shoulders, we sat down on a stone bench side by side, I put my arm round David.

"So the necklace has still not been found," he said, putting things in perspective, as was his style.

"No, no they have not found it, that we know definitely," I answered.

"No one knows where it is hidden?" He asked. I shook my head.

"The old woman hid it," he said softly, "she was smart."

"Yes," I answered.

"Somewhere safe," he went on.

"No doubt," I said.

"Hmm, somewhere, where no one was likely to find it, where no one, who was not a Winwood, would easily get to it..." he continued.

I looked down at him, my attention caught.

"That is why the gang is searching in Marianne's family properties..." he said.

"True, true," I responded.

"So the old lady hid the necklace very well, no one has found it as yet, even the crooks," he repeated in his childish voice. "Emma, if you were her, where would you hide it?" he looked up at my face.

"Where would I hide..." I repeated, slowly.

He nodded, "where you would think people were most likely not to find it? Where it would remain safe...somewhere people were least likely to look."

"Hmm, how should I know?" I said slowly, then I paused, something occurred to me.

"David," I said, jumping up, "you are so clever, I think, I've got it, come on, we need to find William."

Without a word he got up and followed me as I ran back to the school building. William and Marianne were sitting on a bench, on a balcony, I saw them from a distance as we approached the building. Breathlessly, we ran up the stone steps towards them.

"I need to talk to you," I blurted out, gasping for breath.

"Of course," smiled William, not moving from his seat, his long legs stretched in front of him.

I looked around fearfully, "no, not here, let us go to a more private place," I whispered. At this he looked curiously at me, Marianne got up and put her hand on my arm.

"What is it, something's happened?" she asked.

I looked at her, she looked quite spectacular now that she was washed and rested. She had on a simple long grey skirt and a white blouse with a frill around her throat, her hair was washed and held together by a red ribbon. My eyes met Williams' for a minute; he looked, well, so proud of her!

"Emma?" she asked softly.

"We think we've got it," suddenly said David.

Marianne looked down at him a little surprised, then she bent down beside him and put her, hand out, "Haven't we met before?" She said.

"I am David," he said.

"I remember, you thought I was a ghost," she said.

"Yes," he nodded, but added as a sort of consolation, "but a very pretty one."

William sprang up laughing and picked up David, he swung him in the air and gave him a hug. Marianne laughed looking at them. I was the only serious one.

"Listen all of you, we need to talk," I said, feeling like a wet blanket.

"What of?" smiled William looking down at me.

"You seem to have forgotten the problem at hand," I said, he frowned, looking at me.

Marianne put her hand on his arm. "We had, actually," she whispered, a shadow coming over her face.

"No, don't look like that," I could not help saying, "its not that bad, except that the problem must be solved, we cannot just leave it be." I looked from one to the other of them.

"My friend Emma," said William shaking his head at me, he turned to Marianne, "Emma is never one to run away, she will get to the bottom of the mystery, it must be solved...and we must do as she directs, come on." He took Marianne and David by a hand each, and looked at me, "lead on," he said exaggeratedly, I made a face at him but led them inside. I decided to take them to a little room on the first floor, to which we sometimes went for piano practice, as it was in a corner and was somewhat secluded. Once everyone was seated, I found it hard to get William's attention, having found Marianne and handed the two women crooks to the police he seemed to have lost interest in everything else. He was in a playful mood and kept making light of my comments, smiling at Marianne and talking to David. David encouraged him by laughing boisterously at his comments!

"Come on William, be serious," I urged.

"Yes, ma'am, of course, let's hear your story," he said, making a mock serious face.

"William," David nudged his shoulder, "Come on swing me up again, please," David tried to climb up on Williams knees, I looked at them, William made as if to get up from the chair on which he was sitting but to my surprise it was Marianne who brought order into our little meeting.

"Now you two," she said suddenly. They both looked at her obviously surprised at her uncharacteristic tone. She smiled. "That's quite enough of fooling around, we must hear what Emma has to say. It is important; I can see that." Her voice was soft but firm.

William looked at her, his eyes brimming with laughter, his eyebrows raised.

"Now, William, stop it," she said frowning at him.

David was looking from one to the other curiously.

Then to the embarrassment of all present my darling little brother said loud and clear in a matter of fact voice, "William, isn't she so beautiful, are you going to marry her?"

Marianne turned red and looked away in confusion, I stared at David speechless for a minute, William stared at Marianne, she continued blushing looking down, he then slowly lowered his gaze to David and ruffled his hair. "You think I should?"

"Yes, certainly, she is so very beautiful, and I like her a lot too. If you don't want to marry her, I will. That is, when I grow up."

We all burst into laughter, Marianne looked at David, shaking her head, tears of laughter running down her cheeks.

"Its settled then, old chap, it will have to be me, or else poor Marianne will have to wait a long time," said William to David.

"Perhaps that would be better," replied my incorrigible brother, a little regretfully glancing at the lovely Marianne, who stared at him, a little shocked.

"All right, now listen to me," I interrupted. Everyone turned to me. "Its about the necklace, I have an idea about where it could be hidden.

"Well?" said William, his eyebrows raised, his attention caught.

"It was David, he asked me where I would have hidden it, if I wanted no one to find it, and suddenly an idea occurred to me..."

About an hour after this discussion, we were all piled into two motor cars, speeding away into the country. David and I sat with Marianne. William drove the car with Edward beside him. Floppy and Julia, who was back from her aunt's, sat with Constable Wotley and sergeant Milford in the other motor car. I wondered for a moment, as we went past the school gate, what Matron and the others thought of our going out. But no one had said anything to us or indeed tried to stop us. Matron and Mrs Lewis in fact, stood at the great door looking thoughtful and worried as we drove off. William must have given them an explanation of our curious movements and the sudden appearance of Marianne and Mrs Hastings. Maria and Mrs Lewis had certainly looked taken aback at the sight of the two women yesterday. One of them had actually let out a cry and dropped a file she had been holding!

We drove north, stopping only once for a quick lunch at a rather pretty public house. It was called, strangely enough. "The Cock's Scream." Marianne, on further acquaintance turned out to be a good conversationalist, she chatted with me throughout the drive telling me about her beloved grandmama and analyzing the strange sadness which had always surrounded her. She had never been told of the necklace or the story surrounding it. For once I was the listener, fascinated with details of this lovely young girl's life and of course, of her recent ordeal, some of which we had all been witness to. William didn't say much, only asking us all to step into the inn and order our meals. We were all pretty quiet through the meal. William played host and was, I must say, very attentive to all of us, including the two policemen.

I couldn't help observing the unspoken communication between him and Marianne, their eyes spoke to each other even when each of them was talking to someone else. Quite romantic, really! Julia, sitting next to me, must have noticed it too, for I heard her sigh several times. Poor Julia, her first crush! She was quite broken hearted.

After lunch we drove for about three to four hours, it started getting darker and colder. The woods looking denser as we moved deeper into the beautiful countryside. The roads got narrower, the villages getting few and far between. By now we had all lapsed into silence, there was just the sound of the motor car engine groaning along. I looked out of the window curiously as we drove, a little scared and a little excited as we neared our destination.

Suddenly we stopped. I looked outside, we were in front of a rather discouraging looking, colossal gate, flanked by two large pillars on either side, followed by high stones walls. I was the first to reach the gate. I shivered as the chilly air hit me. It had been quite cozy inside the car with all the windows rolled up. William slowly got out of the motor car; Edward close behind him.

"Ho there!" called William, "anyone here?"

There was silence. We all stood holding the gate, trying to peer in. At the same time the other motorcar drove up and stopped just behind us. Sergeant Milford quickly joined us, Constable Wotley followed, at a slightly slower pace, as it took him a while to squeeze himself out from behind the steering wheel of the motor car he had been driving. We all stood there, still holding on to the gate and looking around. "No, William, see, it's locked." I heard Edwards voice. "Ho there!" said William, again.

"No one about Sir, not a living soul," said Constable Wotley, a little viciously.

"Ahoy there," called Sergeant Milford loudly, getting slightly nautical.

At this point, Marianne got out of the motorcar. Seeing her, Floppy and Julia too stepped out. They joined us in front of the gate.

"There seems to be a little lodge on that side, can you see it?" said Marianne softly, going up to William. She pointed to the right, "perhaps the gatekeeper is asleep."

At the same time there was a slight movement in the bushes, on the other side of the gate.

"Oh!" squealed Julia, grabbing my arm involuntarily.

A large form of a man holding a lantern appeared through the bushes. Silently we all stared, as the shadowy outline approached us, then stopped just short of the gate.

"Who are you? What do you want?" boomed a heavily accented voice.

"We are friends," replied William making an effort at sounding placating. The man waved his lantern towards us, I squinted my eyes at the sudden light.

"Friends of whom?" the man asked in a gruff voice after a pause, "I know of no friends, what is your game?"

"Friends of the family," said William, gesturing towards the house.

"There is no family anymore, they are all gone, dead, cursed!" came the unexpected reply. A chill went through me.

"I have had enough of you reporters trying to come here and poke around," he said. We looked at each other meaningfully. "They have all gone, God bless them, and I will guard what is theirs till my last breath. So go..." he almost shouted at us, "Go, or I will set the dogs on you," he turned and started walking away.

"Please," suddenly said a soft, now familiar voice. The man paused but did not come back to us.

"Please listen, I am Marianne Winwood, the granddaughter of Lady Victoria," she said, a tremor in her voice.

"And why should I believe you? You could be lying, as others have been doing these last months, trying to get in and poke around our estate, God knows why!" came the gruff reply.

"Again, the reference to people trying to poke around; so, I must be right," I thought wonderingly, "I hope we aren't too late!"

"Come here," Marianne's voice had changed. It was of command, a Lady ordering a member of her staff. I looked at her, but could not see her face, as she was looking inside the gate. I stared fascinated as the man automatically walked forward.

"Closer, come here," she commanded. He walked up to her and stood still as if waiting for further instructions.

"Look at me," she told him. "Come on, hold your light up."

He did as she ordered and peered at her face. Suddenly he let out a terrible scream and dropped his lantern, himself falling down on his knees and burying his face in his hands.

"Oh no, she walks, oh I knew how it would be," he swayed forwards and backwards on his haunches, wailing all the while.

For a moment I think, Marianne was too astonished to say anything. Then I heard her. "Get up immediately and get a hold of yourself. I am not Lady Victoria but Lady Marianne, her granddaughter and your mistress. Open the gate at once and let us in," the huge form of the gatekeeper struggled slowly to its feet.

"Pick up the light," she said, her voice softer now. "Do you want to set the grounds on fire?"

The gatekeeper peered at her, and shook his head, disbelievingly, "God bless my soul."

"Come on, get a hold on yourself," William said impatiently, unable to control himself any longer.

"Get the keys to the lock," said Marianne kindly, nudging the man along, so to speak.

"Yes, my Lady," he said breathlessly. Putting one hand in his coat pocket, he pulled out noisily a rather large ring with a multitude of heavy looking keys hanging from it. He paused for a moment, the lantern in one hand and the keys in the other, simply looking at Marianne.

"Put the light down and open the gate," she said calmly. He came forward and did as she ordered. William pushed the heavy gate just sufficiently to get through. We did so – the gatekeeper staring at us, still a little suspiciously, as we passed him.

"Now lock it again good man," Marianne told him, her small delicate figure looking tiny next to his huge form.

"Wait a minute," said William. "I think we should get the cars inside, it could be a long walk up to the house."

"Yes, it is to be sure, from what I've heard," said Marianne, "Open the gates," she turned to the gatekeeper, "and let us get the motor cars in."

The gatekeeper had been staring at her as if making sure, she was who she claimed to be. Apparently he was satisfied as he meekly did as she ordered. All the men had to help push the gates open as there was quite an undergrowth around and underneath the gate.

"Need a bit of cleaning up here," said The Fish, looking at the ground.

"Nobody come for years and years, there was no call to clean up," mumbled the gate keeper, a little sullenly.

"No one's blaming you," said Marianne quickly, "But maybe you could look into it now."

"Of course, m'lady, if you wish it," said the man, "That is to say, certainly milady," he broke off in confusion, blushing from ear to ear. "Whatever you say."

William grinned. "Et tu." he said softly, looking at the gatekeeper and then at his sweetheart. "Are we all to fall under your spell," he whispered to Marianne.

"William!" scolded Marianne, looking embarrassed.

"Come on get back into the motor cars," said William, laughing at her discomfiture. We all did as we were told. As soon as the cars were in through the gates, the gatekeeper rushed to push back the gates. All the men got out again to help him. Then William gestured to them to get back into the motorcars, I looked over my shoulder through the glass from the back seat of the car. William was talking to the gatekeeper, the man listened quietly. He now seemed to have accepted William as someone in authority for I saw him nod a couple of times quite respectfully, quite a change from his earlier hostile attitude.

William opened the door of the car and got in, behind the wheel. The motor car roared into action. I looked outside, now really excited. So this was the great estate called Golden Oaks, a place where Marianne's ancestors had lived happily till tragedy struck them. I glanced at Marianne in the dark. She was looking out of the window. The winding drive showed clear signs of neglect. In fact, it was as if we were driving through a forest. Tall trees with overgrown branches and tall grass was what I saw on either side. They made the atmosphere extremely dark and oppressive. To top it all, it seemed to be a moonless night. I shivered involuntarily, as I thought of the strange story Inspector Crawley had told us. In this light as I looked out, it did not seem to be such an impossible tale. The car slowed down, ahead somewhere was a weak yellow light. Around it towered the outline of a colossal building, dark and foreboding. Its tall towers warning outsiders to keep away, as it were. We went closer and closer to the house. Suddenly we were inside a sort of courtyard. The first car grinded to a stop. As the engines were switched off, for a moment there was complete silence. Nothing, not even a dog barking. Then, I heard a sound, I started, and looked around alarmed then realized it came from Marianne. I looked towards her in the dark. William got out of the car. He stood outside and looked around. There was a flight of steps leading up to a large door flanked by two large high pillars. A small lantern had been placed on a ledge that went up along the stairs, the only sign of life that I could see. I looked behind at the other car, no one got out, clearly waiting for orders. William went up the stairs alone. He looked around and then raised his arm, to pull at an old fashioned bell hanging from above. Suddenly he stopped, and rapped on the door instead. I stared, fascinated, as the grand door was opened almost immediately, as if someone had been expecting us.

A ray of light could be seen as the door slowly opened. William stood there, for a moment talking to someone, then disappeared inside.

"Brave man," I thought to myself, "I would not go in there alone."

After what seemed to be ages, he reappeared and walked slowly towards us. He seemed a little subdued as he opened Marianne's door and held a hand out to her. Dumbly she got out. He ignored the rest of us. I watched them both, as they walked up the stairs and then went into the house. We waited there, in the motorcars, in the dark, in absolute silence. The cold night seemed dark and mysterious around us. The old house loomed up over us, casting strange shadows around its surroundings. I looked up at it and shivered, a sense of sadness filled me. At last the door opened, just a fraction. William's tall form appeared, beckoning us. Immediately, The Fish got out, everyone else followed. We moved up the stairs slowly, our footsteps sounding loud and noisy, rather like an army going into battle, I thought. The mood was sombre, as we approached the door, which was still only slightly ajar. One by one, we went through the great door and stood on the other side of it. The door swung shut behind Edward, who was the last to enter.

✦ ✦ ✦

15

We found ourselves in a very large and exceedingly grand foyer. Straight ahead was a wide, dark staircase, leading upstairs. The floor was made of tiles of pale marble, in the centre was a round, antique table, on top of which was a colossal flower vase. I noticed someone had put fresh flowers in the vase, so we were expected here at least! Several pretty chairs stood against the wall under elaborately framed paintings. I glanced at the ceiling, here was a prime example of expert craftsmanship, there was a depiction of a scene from the Bible, it was clearly done by a master, and hanging down, rather low over the round table, in front of the great door, was the largest chandelier I have ever seen. It was partially covered in a white muslin cloth. The light around us was provided by two candle sticks that stood on a console table that was placed in front of a mirror that stretched from the ceiling to the floor along one wall. "All this in dim light, imagine what this great entrance must have looked like when dressed up in all it s glory!" I thought to myself, completely mesmerized. I looked towards Marianne, the mistress of all this! She was standing next to a chair on which sat, the oldest man I have ever seen. I looked at him curiously. He was dressed in an old fashioned butler's livery, his shriveled form, a little bent. Marianne's hand was on his shoulder, her head bent slightly towards him, as if straining to hear what he was saying.

Everybody stood silently, waiting, not knowing for what. Marianne, not taking any notice of us, continued talking to the old man. At one point she sat down on the floor, next to his chair and put her hand over his. The old man swayed, and buried his face in his hands. He was sobbing. We stood by awkwardly, not knowing what to do. Marianne had tears running down her face. We could not hear what the old man was saying, as he spoke very softly and they were a little further down the foyer.

Suddenly there was the sound of loud footsteps and the murmur of voices. I looked over my shoulder, there was a corridor to the right of me, a door had opened on it and three men came out. One was William, one was a middle aged, unknown man with a mustache, and the third man was retired Chief Inspector Crawley.

I saw The Fish and Constable Wotley stiffen up and execute a silent salute each. The Chief Inspector nodded at our little group and walked up to Marianne. She moved forward as soon as she saw him "Uncle Crawley," she said softly, putting out her hand to him. "Thank God you are safe, my dear," he said, taking her hand in his.

William was standing near the round table talking to the third man. He glanced at the staircase, then looked back at the corridor down which he had just come. "Come close everybody," he said, at last taking notice of our group. We all moved up to where he stood. "Over here, William, Briggs will find it difficult to stand, come and stand beside him," said

Marianne. We moved closer, our feet making a terrible racket on the tiled floor, shattering the silence of, to put it a little dramatically, the 'sleeping house'! And so it was, the sleeping house. It had been asleep for almost forty years, rejected by its people, packed away, buried, punished, so to speak, because its Mistress thought she had been cursed.

My eyes were on the old man, seated on the chair, his majestic faded uniform, hanging loose on him, his lined face contorted in a strange way and his eyes looking ahead, a glazed look in them. I saw William glance at him; he then turned and looked inquiringly at the third man (with the mustache) This man went up to the old man and gently patted his shoulder.

"Pa, Her Ladyship needs your help," he said softly. The old man slowly turned his eyes towards Marianne who was standing close by his chair. All of a sudden he almost jumped up from his chair and went close to Marianne.

"Oh, excuse me Your Ladyship, I cannot think of what came over me. Is the Master back? He will be wanting his drink. Ah! 'Briggs' he says to me yesterday, 'Briggs' it's only you who can mix a proper cocktail just the way I like it," he beamed round at all of us.

Marianne looked in confusion at Mr Briggs' son, who smiled reassuringly at her. "It's his mind, Your Ladyship, gone back to the old days, he does that often," he whispered to her. "He must be under the impression that you are Lady Victoria," he said giving her a meaningful look.

Marianne turned to old Mr Briggs, who was looking at her, clearly waiting for an answer. She smiled sweetly. "Yes, yes," she mumbled, a little uncertainly.

"Ah, I'd better hurry along then, mustn't keep him waiting, he must be in his study," said old Mr Briggs.

To our amazement, we saw him shuffle along down a corridor and turn a corner, his son quickly picked up a candle stand and hurried after him, we all did the same, glancing at the paintings that lined both sides of the corridor. Old Mr Briggs stopped outside a door, he knocked twice, then turned the knob, leaving the door ajar.

"Your Lordship, please excuse me, I was not aware that you had come in, Peters had been most remiss in neglecting to inform me, I shall have to have a talk with him. Did you have a good ride now?" he spoke loudly and clearly as he shuffled busily into the room.

It was a beautiful study, lined with tall wooden book shelves, dark blue velvet curtains, trimmed with gold. A grand desk stood almost in the centre, the only light was the one young Mr Briggs (as he was called) was carrying, and in it's warm glow I saw the old man act out a scene he must have executed a hundred times when he was young and all the family lived at Golden Oaks. He walked up to a corner cabinet where a tray of glasses and a large decanter were kept, he poured out a drink, holding it up most carefully, he then placed the glass on a little silver tray and slowly walked up to the desk. "Here you are, your Lordship, just as you like it." It was only now that he glanced at the chair behind the desk. "Your Lordship!" he called out loudly, "Mr Trevor, now come along, none of your tricks, where are you hiding, come, come... that's enough!" he said, his voice gradually getting fainter. There was a pause, I stared, quite shocked, at the old man, as he looked around the room, wildly. Suddenly he screamed. "Mr Trevor! PLEASE, come back!" he stood absolutely still for a second, then, slumped forward over his late Master's desk.

Young Mr Briggs rushed forward, he held him in his arms and gently lowered him into a chair that stood in front of the desk. He looked back at us, as we stood, all staring in a stunned manner, grouped together in the doorway.

Marianne was the first to react, slowly she went further into the room, glancing around. She stopped at the desk and looked at the empty chair behind it. A large portrait of an extremely handsome young man hung on the wall, just above the chair. She squinted her eyes and looked up at it. "Grandfather," she whispered in a somewhat awed manner. Her hands picked up a picture frame from the desk, she put it back, then picked it up again. She glanced at old Mr Briggs, then at his son "he was talking to my grandfather, was he not?" she asked.

"Yes, My Lady, that's so. He does that often. Loved the Master. See, look around, how clean this room is. Comes here and gets it done everyday. It's the only thing he does. It must be kept immaculately, not a speck of dust anywhere." we looked around, I moved a little further into the room.

"Look at the drinks table, Miss" said young Mr Briggs, noticing my interest. "It is ready, is it not? and the fireplace, go, look at it," he urged me. I went up to one side of the room which was quite dark. There was a great fireplace with two armchairs and a stool nearby, a cozy corner, and yes, everything here was indeed, spotless. I turned back to see young Mr Briggs looking in my direction as if waiting to see my reaction. "Yes, Miss," he said "that's so, he is here, every day, checking everything, fussing about the room..." his voice trailed off.

"It's as if he's waiting for grandfather, yes, he is waiting, is he not?" Marianne asked, turning towards William. He went closer to her and put his arm around her shoulder, all the while, looking compassionately at the old man slumped in the chair. Marianne looked up at William, I heard her say softly, "oh, William, he's waiting, waiting for grandfather..."

"These forty years, Your Ladyship, Lord Trevor was so loved by them all, Her Ladyship, Lady Cecilia, Father, none of them remained themselves once he was gone. Pardon me, Milady, but that's the way it was," said young Mr Briggs, almost apologetically.

Marianne smiled sadly, "yes, it is true," she mumbled.

"Lady Victoria shut up the house so abruptly...all life here ceased. Father was so miserable, walked about the great, empty house all day. Mother urged him to leave, but he simply wouldn't hear of it. He would say, "I must take care of the house, they will come back one day, and then all will be as it was..." said young Mr Briggs with a wistful note.

Marianne went down on her knees beside the old man's chair, she put both her hands on either side of his wrinkled face. "Wake up, Briggs, wake up, it is I, lady Marianne," she was sobbing softly, William put his arms around her trying to pull her up, but she shrugged him off. "Oh, please, dear Briggs, I'm so sorry for the past," she sobbed quietly. We all looked on, helplessly. After about five minutes the old man stirred, he opened his eyes and looked at the beautiful face, so close to him. I moved closer to them.

"Ah, Your Ladyship, shall I get the servants in order? We will need to reorganize ourselves now that you are back," he said in a clear, loud voice. Poor Marianne, she looked so confused, staring dumbly at the unfortunate old man.

"Yes Briggs, you do that. Her Ladyship needs you to organize the household," William said, kindly. The old man beamed at both of them, his face breaking into a smile for the first time.

"But Pa, we need you to help us with something else first," said young Mr Briggs, throwing William a grateful look.

The old man looked at his son, "what is it?" he asked, haltingly.

"Lady Marianne needs to find something that was lost a very long time ago, we will have to search for it," said William softly. The old man stared uncomprehendingly up at him.

"A very long time ago grandmother had lost something precious, we think it is somewhere in this house, can you help us with where we should look?" enquired Marianne, speaking slowly. Again, there was no reply.

"Lady Victoria has misplaced something, she has sent Lady Marianne to find it, ask old 'Mr Briggs' she said, to Lady

Marianne. 'He knows where we keep things at golden oaks,' " said young Mr Briggs in a high, unnatural tone.

The old man's face broke into a smile, "yes, it is always the way here, 'ask Briggs', they say," he beamed around at us all.

William bent towards him, exchanging a glance with young Mr Briggs. "If Lady Victoria or Lady Cecilia wanted to hide something valuable, which would be the best place for it?" he asked.

"Come with me," said old Mr Briggs, struggling to get up from his chair, "but mind, only Her Ladyship," he said sounding perfectly comprehensible.

"This is Her Ladyship's betrothed, Pa" said young Mr Briggs, nodding at William.

"Oh, is that so? Why did no one tell me! I must welcome him to Golden Oaks," he looked at his son, fretfully.

"It is alright, Pa, just take them both with you and tell them what they want to know about the house." The old man nodded and shuffled towards the door, everybody moved back as he came forward, but he took no notice of anyone, he just walked out, followed by William and Marianne, and young Mr Briggs holding the candle. The rest of us quickly followed them.

We all walked back, somberly, towards the grand foyer. The quaint old man stopped at the foot of the stairs, he turned to his son and raised his arms towards him, like a child. Young Mr Briggs put down the candle stand on a nearby table, then picked up his father carefully in his arms, then slowly began to climb the stairs, nodding at William as he passed him. William took up the candle stand and gestured to Marianne to follow. The rest of us just stood there, at the foot of the staircase, staring at the strange party.

"Emma," called Marianne, "do you mind coming along?" Without a word, I ran up to join her, looking excitedly at everything around us. The walls were covered with grand portraits of Marianne's ancestors. We went up two flights of wooden stairs, even in the dim light I recognized the unquestionable splendor around me.

"All this given up for fear of a curse!" I thought to myself, sadly. I gave a start as we paused at a landing. There was a marble bust of an incredibly lifelike, fierce-looking soldier, placed on a stand. No one took any notice, young Mr Briggs moved to his right, a broad passage became visible to us, lined throughout on one side, with long windows. The windows were framed with dark curtains which were held back by ornate ribbons, so a little weak light filtered in from the outside. I stared, fascinated, down the passage. Suddenly, I pictured it. A little boy holding the hand of a beautiful woman, dressed in a pale blue gown, sapphires on her throat. I felt I could see them walking down the passage. The little boy, perhaps skipping excitedly, "let's show our ghost to Mr Crawley," he must have said, pulling at his lovely mother's hand. Neither of them must have realized how their life would be altered, after that one, casual, incident!

"Emma," I heard Marianne, from what seemed like far away. My eyes went towards her as she stood in her grey skirt, a little to my right. "Emma, come on," her voice sounded so strange, as if it had an echo, I walked up to her slowly, as if I was in a trance. She looked at me curiously but did not say a word. We walked on, the silence broken only by the sound of our footsteps on the wooden floor. I saw Young Mr Briggs come to a halt outside a large door. He looked over his shoulder in William's direction. William moved forward, a door was opened, I hurried up to join everyone as they all went in, William, shutting the door behind us.

This was an elegant, but extremely decorative room. A lady's boudoir. "The Dowager Lady Cecilia's sitting room," announced young Mr Briggs, formally. "Spectacular," I gasped. Both the Mr Briggs' looked towards me, pleased. Brocade sofas, velvet chairs, a large chaise lounge, a formal fireplace, a mahogany writing table and chair. The walls were decorated with several mirrors and paintings, "oh yes, very grand indeed!"

Young Mr Briggs had put his precious burden down on a chair. The old man sat happily, he seemed to be enjoying himself. "There, Your Ladyship, that is where lady Cecilia would write her letters, then she'd ring for me. 'Briggs,' she would say, 'see to that for me, will you'."

Marianne was walking around the room, she picked up one or two things, looked at them, and put them back. William had placed the candle stand on the dresser. He was opening and closing the drawers of cupboards and desks. I moved around the room, looking around, completely fascinated. "No one stayed in here ever, not since the Dowager Lady left." said young Mr Briggs, softly. He must have noticed my interest.

"Gosh!" I said, "so many years ago, yet it looks..."

"Yes, it does, does it not? Father here insists the private apartments of the family are regularly aired and kept in order," said young Mr Briggs, pride in his voice. Marianne looked at the old man, tears in her eyes, but she said nothing. "In here, Your Ladyship, Lady Cecilia's bed chamber." Young Mr Briggs opened a door, I hurriedly went towards it, almost colliding with Marianne. We both went in, and William followed with the light.

"Goodness gracious!" I thought. The light revealed a glorious room, done in gold brocade, a lot of heavy carvings on the furniture, a formal dressing table, and, at the centre of the room, a spectacular bed. "Truly fit for a queen," I said.

Again I was given a look of approval from young Mr Briggs. "But of course, Miss, the Winwood's have always been one of the foremost families in these parts." I glanced at Marianne, "she's so simple and unaffected, yet born to all this," I thought to myself. William walked around, again opening various drawers and then going towards the wardrobe. Marianne was going through the drawers on the bedside table. "Look here, Emma!" she called, I hurried up to her and looked into the drawer she was pointing at. It contained some handkerchiefs, an empty snuff box, and a few very delicate looking scarves. We both looked at each other and smiled.

"You will not find anything precious in there," said a strange voice. My heart in my mouth, I looked up in the direction of the voice. A shadowy figure stood in the doorway, it was old Mr Briggs. He walked slowly towards a wardrobe, his son following him closely, his hand on his father's elbow. Old Mr Briggs pushed his son's hand away, clearly irritated. He seemed very excited about something. "Here, Your Ladyship," he said. He was standing in front of a tall, wooden wardrobe, that was twice the height of an extremely tall man. He pulled at the door and then, to our surprise, stepped inside it. We all rushed up to him and joined him inside the wardrobe. It was quite dark; old Mr Briggs was fumbling at something, and lo and behold, to my utter amazement, a sort of hidden safe opened up somewhere in the wall of the wardrobe. I noticed even his son seemed surprised.

"No one knows of this, but for me, it is in here that Her Ladyship kept important things, not in the huge family safe, 'that is only for precious crockery, Briggs,', she would say. 'Thieves, always remember, are bound to go there first' " said old Mr Briggs, chuckling delightedly at the memory. "Now, everyone, step back, we must leave Her Ladyship to look into the safe," he looked sternly at all of us. Obediently we all moved back and Marianne went forward towards the safe.

"Some light, please," she asked. William went to fetch it. I stared around me, into the dark cupboard. "Must have held beautiful, formal dresses at one time, the safe, hidden by the long dresses, I suppose no one would expect there to be a safe in the wall, quite clever," I thought to myself. Marianne seemed to have something in her hand. We all moved forward excitedly, she held it up for us to see, it was a large box. She peered into the cavity in front of her and said, "that's it! There's nothing else in here, come, let us go out and look at it."

The candle stand was put on the bedside table, and the box on the bed. Marianne sat down next to the box and we all stood around, unsure for a moment of what was the proper thing to do. It was a rather beautiful, medium-sized box. It had colorful flowers painted on it with heavy, gold outlines. Marianne pulled at the heavy handle that was on its lid, it did not open. She tried again, and it still wouldn't budge. William went forward and peered at the box, he turned it upside down. Still no luck. Young Mr Briggs and I moved forward, just then I heard a chuckle behind my back, and old Mr Briggs' claw-like hand pulled at my shoulder, trying to push me aside.

"It is a trick lock, sir," he said to William "you will never get it open like this." we all stared at him, for he looked absolutely thrilled, like a child having a special treat. Young Mr Briggs signaled to William (almost apologetically), William slowly placed the box back on the bed. Marianne was staring at the quaint old man.

"Please Briggs, you are the only person who can open it, it is as Her Ladyship often said...," it was William who spoke thus, in an uncharacteristic voice, and sure enough it had its effect.

Old Mr Briggs beamed round at us all and moved forward. "Yes, what would they have done without me. Let me, Your Ladyship," he said in a formal voice, looking at Marianne as if for permission. She nodded, dumbly. We all looked on, fascinated, as he fiddled with the box for about five seconds and then stepped back. "Now try, Your Ladyship," he said softly, his eyes gleaming in the candlelight. Marianne's delicate hands tried to open the lid, it fell open and we all bent forward, over the bed, staring at the strongbox. Her hand shaking a little, Marianne took something out of the box, it was a little miniature in a decorative frame. The picture depicted the face and upper body of a rather fierce looking gentleman, sporting a magnificent mustache. Marianne looked at it and then read out aloud, "Lord Augustus Macmillian C. Winwood. My Great grandfather!"

"May I?" I asked.

"Of course," she handed it to me, then turned back to the box. She took out a large, silver frame, immediately I recognized the handsome face of Lord Trevor Macmillian Christopher Winwood. There were several likenesses of his all over the house, you could not miss them. There was one more portrait in the box. This one was more recent, it showed a young man dressed in a dark, formal suit, standing on the deck of a ship. The man in the picture bore an astonishing resemblance to the man in the first miniature, except for the mustache and the clothes. I placed them both side-by-side on the bed. "Look!" I pointed to Lord Augustus, then to the third picture, "Isn't it most extraordinary?" Marianne picked up the third picture and placed it against her heart, "Father," was all she said. "You're proper knocked out, poor darling," William looked tenderly at her.

There were three letters in the box, carefully wrapped in a white, linen handkerchief. Marianne went through them and said that they were letters written to Lady Cecilia by the three men, whose likenesses we were there before us, nothing to do with the necklace.

"With your permission, I should go through them just to make sure. Its my job," said William quietly. She smiled and handed them to him.

Next, she took out a little jewel box, I leaned forward as she opened it, a huge emerald with a thin border of diamonds gleamed at us, carved into the inside of the lid was an inscription. "To my dearest Bobby, with all my love," Marianne read out loud.

"Who is Bobby?" I asked, unable to stop myself.

"No idea," she said, taking the ring out and trying it on. "It's beautiful, isn't it?" "What else do we have here?" asked William, a little impatiently. He pulled out a long narrow box, it had a pipe in it. William held up the pipe against the candlelight. "exquisite craftsmanship, eh Briggs?" he said.

"Beautiful," agreed young Mr Briggs.

The box did not contain much more, just a pen, in a silver box, and a pair of brown, suede man's gloves, wrapped up in a muslin cloth. These were the things most precious to Lady Cecilia Winwood. Things that she had kept in her special hiding place. I looked at them as they lay before us, tears pricked my eyes as I thought of the old woman taking them out and perhaps reliving her memories and thinking about her loved ones. Marianne carefully picked up each thing and put them back just the way they had been when we found them. She then got up, walked up to the wardrobe, and put the box, very gently, back in its hiding place. The safe clicked shut as she pushed its little door.

"Well!" I said. "Let us go to grandmama's room," said Marianne, moving towards the door. We all followed, going back into the corridor, our footsteps sounding very loud on the wooden floor. Young Mr Briggs stopped at the end of the passage, again William moved forward to open the door and we all went in.

I felt it immediately, the same strangeness I had felt in that bedroom in the Dowager house where I had found the photograph of Lady Victoria. The candle stand was placed on a large Elizabethan chest of drawers, next to an empty flower stand. There was a mirror hanging on the wall behind it. I looked around at the others, but they didn't seem any different. Old Mr Biggs had been seated on a large armchair, near the grand fireplace, which was of early renaissance style. The others were moving around the room. This was a small, rather cozy sitting room. The curtains were drawn and were of a floral design, and so was the fabric on several sofas that were scattered about the room. A delicate writing table stood in one corner. One glance around the room and you could get a fair idea of its owner's personality. It was almost imprinted all over the room.

"Look, Emma," said Marianne. She was standing next to a large, leather armchair, placed near the fireplace, the only piece of furniture that did not merge with the rest of the room. "Must be for grandfather," Marianne smiled as she ran her hand down the back of the armchair. I felt it again, that great sense of sorrow. That chair was so different from everything else in the delicate and feminine room, it was strong and masculine, it was just right. You could almost picture the handsome Lord Trevor sitting there, perhaps chatting with his beloved wife. I stared at it, slowly I felt a chill down my spine, I shivered and looked over my shoulder, there was nothing. Yet I felt very strongly that some force was there in that room, trying to communicate something to me.

"The bedroom! Where is it?" I asked, my voice sounding shrill, even to my own ears. Everyone looked towards me with surprise. "Please, let us go to the bedroom," I urged, looking towards young Mr Briggs. He moved to his left and I followed quickly. He opened the door and I went in hurriedly, straight into the room that was pitch dark. "Oh yes, the feeling is here, very definitely," I thought to myself. I stood still, my eyes closed, every sense straining, trying to listen. God knows for what. Then the light was brought into the room, slowly I opened my eyes and looked around. A pretty room, it's windows dressed with dark burgundy curtains, quite simple and cozy. There were a few mirrors, a tall chest-of-drawers and several comfortable chairs. The only thing formal in this room was the bed, it was very old, rather beautiful, and majestic, hanging directly over it, was a portrait of Lady Victoria, her husband, and their son standing in their garden.

"Emma, anything the matter?" asked Marianne, looking tensely at me.

"I do not know Marianne," I whispered "I think I feel...a little odd. Do you feel strange at all?" She did not answer, but looked around, fearfully. I walked further into the room, looking carefully at the little pieces on the tables, the picture frames, little pieces d'art, and several, depressingly empty, flower vases.

"Lady Victoria must have filled her room with flowers, going by the number of empty flower vases here!" I thought, to myself. I walked around the room maybe a couple of times. "What is the matter?" I asked myself, my mind was searching for something, I looked up, all around the room, all the drawers and cupboards here were quite empty. I went back towards the bed and stared at the portrait. They looked so contented, almost serene, the three of them. They must have been completely unaware of the sadness in store for them. I looked at Lady Victoria's beautiful face, her eyes gleamed in the candlelight, the artist had made them so life-like, it was frightening!

Marianne later told me that my manner at this point became a little strange and unnatural. I don't quite remember how it happened, but suddenly, in a loud and clear voice, I said, "it all started in the nursery." I felt all the others pause whatever they were doing; their startled eyes turned towards me as I continued staring up at the portrait.

"It is the child, he will not take no for an answer, he wishes to show Mr Crawley the ghost." Marianne put a hand on my arm, I shook it off, I went on, my voice getting louder, and a little fierce I think, as I stared at Lady Victoria's face. "Thomas will have his way, the guests are about to arrive, there is no time to divert him, he will be unhappy if he does not get his way.... Alright.... Just this once.... Only for five minutes.... Let us go to the Queen's chamber! But, who has put this idea into his head, it worries me..." my voice abruptly stopped, no one moved, they stood where they were, staring at me, I looked searchingly at the portrait for a minute, then turned at last towards the others, "come, we must go there, it is there that this business started, and it is destined to end there. We are wasting our time." I simply walked out of the room, everyone following me.

Outside, in the gallery, I turned to my left and walked into the darkness, for once, unafraid, Marianne close behind me, the others at a slower pace, bringing the light with them. It was very dark, and the light, weak. The walls loomed up around us, and then, we saw it, just Marianne and myself...

We turned a corner and stood, unsure of which direction to take, a slight movement across the landing attracted our attention, something went past, very quickly, someone in a white dress, with long, dark hair! Marianne grasped my arm, I shrugged her off and started to run in the direction of the apparition. I heard Marianne whisper, "Emma, no, don't," as she tried to pull me back.

"let me, Marianne, we have to know," I said.

"What's happened?" said William, a little breathlessly, for once, unsure of himself. "What's happened here, whatever's the matter?"

"We saw someone!... THERE!" Marianne pointed across the landing.

"Someone? how do you mean...?" asked William, frowning.

"A sort of...vision?" I said, uncertainly.

"What?" William said loudly, "what are you talking about?"

"Yes.... A woman, in a white dress, with long, dark hair, just went past there!" I pointed across the landing, my voice sounding nervous and shrill.

William looked at Marianne, then at me, frowning. He stared in the direction, at which we were pointing, then, as if shaking himself, he hurried across the landing, all of us following close behind. There was a small, wooden arch here, dwarfing the entrance to a smaller passage which led off from the wide gallery.

"Here, here I think, she walked by..." I whispered.

"Yes," agreed Marianne.

William bent low to avoid hitting the arch, then turned to try the doors that led to the rooms on the passage, they were all locked.

"The keys are kept in the cottage, sir," said young Mr Briggs, a little breathlessly, as he was still carrying his father. "Shall I go and fetch them?"

"I think we should go down to the others," stammered Marianne. "It is the ghost and she does not want us to come here!" she grasped Williams arm and looked up at his face, imploringly. William was staring ahead into the shadows, he was lost in his own thoughts and did not seem to hear her. "Come on!" she urged, "its not worth it, look what happened to grandmama!"

I went up to Marianne and put an arm around her shoulder, we stood there, both of us rather frightened, I must admit.

"Emma, what did you see in Lady Victoria's room?" William asked, abruptly.

Ignoring his question, I said, my voice a little hoarse and low, "we should go to the Queen's Chamber."

"Yes...yes, we will certainly do that...but there is something else...something about the child insisting on showing the room.... Oh yes, that's it, who put the idea into his head?!"

"Yes" I nodded, "yes that's just it, someone must have, why should the child suddenly make a scene and insist upon going to the forbidden rooms. After all no one went there, and he knew quite well that he was never to go there..." I paused, looking up at William in the semi-darkness.

"Who could it be?" he said softly, under his breath.

"There is no doubt, it's the person we are looking for" I said, Marianne clung to me, looking nervously over her shoulder.

"You are right, let's go to the Queen's Chamber..." William's voice trailed off...

"It's as if the past sorrow needs to be put at rest," I whispered, no one said anything.

"Shall I lead the way sir?" asked young Mr Briggs in a subdued voice. He then turned back the way we had come, towards the long gallery, we all slowly followed him.

"Should we call the others?" I asked William "we might be better off with numbers..."

"Yes, but then we will have to call EVERYBODY..." he answered meaningfully, "they are all together, and if my suspicions are right.... Yet, how...?"

Silently, we walked on, through the corridors of the beautiful, old house. It was almost unreal how well 'shut up' it was, at places a chair covered in a white sheet or a statue standing forlornly in a corner, a rejected house, a sad house. The girl beside me walked somberly, it was her heritage, this strange situation and at this moment, I think she felt the full impact of it.

"The nursery wing," announced young Mr Briggs. It was just as Mr Crawley had described, the long, wooden gallery, and the paintings hanging on its walls. I felt the dust, as I placed my hand on the wooden balustrade near me.

"Here, Sir," young Mr Briggs gestured to a large, dark, wooden door, "might be locked...."

William put his hand on the handle, "good, it's open. We all moved forward as the large door swung open, William walked in, holding the candle stand high up, for us all to see the nursery.... It was a traditional nursery, done up for a little boy in the fashion of around fifty or sixty years ago. Yet things were lying around as if they had just been used. Except for the dust and cobwebs all over the place one would not think it had been unused for so many years. Marianne walked into the centre of the room and stared at everything; she looked a little shocked.

"So it was here that the little boy invited Mr Crawley for tea, maybe they sat there around that table," I pointed. Then I turned towards the doorway where young Mr Briggs stood looking curiously at me. He had put his father down on a dusty, straight backed wooden chair that stood against a wall on one side of the door. The old man was looking at all of us intently. William stood next to the fireplace on the other side of the room, having placed the candle stand on top of the mantel piece.

"Then she came in, perhaps to hug her son goodnight before going to the main entrance to greet her guests...she must have looked magnificent in her pale blue dress and her great jewels. The young man must have looked up towards the door when it opened, and been completely fascinated by the vision in front of his eyes," I went on softly, in this strain, as if unable to stop myself. "Then the child must have sprung up and run towards his mother. Mr Crawley must have got up..., I want to show our ghost to Mr Crawley..." I said loudly.

"Oh no, Oh no...please stop!" screamed Marianne, sinking onto the floor. William reached her, in two or three long strides and bent down over her, lifting her up.

"I cannot bear this," she sobbed softly into his shoulder.

"Try to calm yourself, sweetheart, we have to get to the bottom of this now, or it will stay with us forever," he said in an uncharacteristically emotional voice, "Please go on Emma," he said looking up towards me.

"Then the child threw a tantrum, perhaps rolling on this very floor, the mother gave in.... 'Alright just this once, but do not tell father...he will be extremely angry.' They must have trooped out, the child now excited, knowing they were going somewhere which was forbidden to them." I moved towards the door, "Out of this door they went."

Young Mr Briggs moved aside, "There miss," he pointed down the passage, staring at me as if he thought me quite strange.

"Come everyone, we are now ready to go to the Queen's Chamber, finally I think it is time," I said. I did not turn back but could hear them all moving behind me.

✦ ✦ ✦

16

I looked at the oak archway, with its elaborate carvings set quite low (in fact William and Young Mr Briggs had to bend while crossing it) I climbed up the two steps and stood still. For there it was, a large wooden door, again very elaborate, with a huge brass door handle, the Queen's Chamber! My heart missed a beat.

It was darker here than in the other parts of the house as everything around us was made of dark heavy looking wood. At the far end of the passage, was a long high window with black iron bars. No light came in through it as it was half covered by some heavy curtains. I shivered and looked over my shoulder at the others. Young Mr Briggs was lowering his father gently on the floor. "I'll get a chair for you," he murmured.

"Certainly not," admonished the old man, "I am going in there," he pointed at the ominous looking door.

"But Father...it is not..." began Young Mr Briggs.

"You new fashioned people must think it proper to desert your masters, we were simply not brought up to do so," stated the frail old man, suddenly speaking very clearly and coherently, "It is my duty to stand by Her Ladyship."

I glanced at Marianne. She was standing staring at the door as if lost in another world. Old Mr Briggs put his hand in his pocket and drew out a large ring with several keys hanging from it. William moved the candlestick closer, so the old man could select the one he wanted. He did so and handed it to William.

"My eyes are not so good Sir, you open it." I moved forward and took the candle stand from William as he bent a little to look at the padlock staring at us. The key fitted the lock and the latch was drawn back. William pushed at the door handle, but the door seemed to be stuck. He put his shoulder to it. Eventually it took Young Mr Briggs and William to put their weight on it, before we heard a creaking sound and then it moved, first just a fraction.

William was the first to step in. He moved to one side and I hurriedly handed him the candle stand. There he stood holding the door back with one hand and carrying the candle-stand with the other, peering around in the dark and mysterious room. We all crowded closer to the entrance.

"We need more light," I said softly. I moved ahead of the others, my heart now thumping wildly. "So this was the Queen's Chamber," I thought. It was very dark and looked rather sinister in our weak light. The heavy faded curtains were fully drawn, a very tall, somehow a little frightening, four poster bed made of dark wood stood in the centre, the curtains that framed it on all four sides hanging, depressingly free from their stitches in several places. I noticed the bedspread was crumpled as though someone had just got up from it and no one had bothered to straighten it. A high footstool stood on one side of the bed. Here again there was dust and cobwebs everywhere. No one had covered the furniture with any dust sheets, even the chandelier hung free without any cover.

Looking around carefully I noticed a large Elizabethan fireplace in the far corner of the room, above the mantel piece was engraved the Winwood family coat of arms. There were two wooded straight-backed, rather uncomfortable looking chairs near the fireplace. Even the rugs were left scattered on the floor, I almost tripped over one as I moved gingerly into the room. Putting my hand out to steady myself, I caught the corner of a tall stand and looked at it in alarm. "It's only some sort of stand, relax," I told myself, my hand on my heart.

"Here Emma, looks like there's the remnants of a candle," said William, peering into the huge glass holder that stood on the tall wooden stand. He proceeded to light it and lo and behold a surprising bright light flickered in the glass holder and a warm glow came into the musty room.

I wrinkled my nose as I moved further into the room. "There is a horrid stench in here," I whispered.

"Been shut, these forty odd years, miss, actually more, as none of the servants wanted the caring of it!" said Young Mr Briggs who had followed me into the room. "First time I have been here myself."

"Gosh!" I whispered.

"No, you don't." We all turned at the loud fierce words. It was William; he had physically lifted Marianne and was carrying her out of the room.

"William!" she screamed.

"No ma'am, you stay out of here," he said a little hoarsely.

"But William, I must, please..." she entreated.

"After hearing about the 'curse', not a chance," he said, trying to speak softly.

"Don't be fanciful," she snapped. He lowered her onto the floor, still holding her tightly. "Call me fanciful or whatever, after hearing your grandma's story I do not think I would feel at peace if you go in there," he retorted, for the first time sounding really angry with her. They stood there in the shadow of the dark doorstep glaring at each other as the rest of us looked at them.

"Please, Marianne, for my sake," he whispered, his voice changing, holding both her arms and looking into her eyes, almost pleadingly. "Please," he entreated again, "even your grandfather would not approve." There was silence. He looked towards us after a few minutes. "Briggs, come here man," he said loudly, "Be so good as to stay with my lady."

"Certainly Sir," said the other, moving to do as he was bid. William strode into the room suddenly halting as the old man caught his arm. "Good Sir, very good that was. A wise thing to do, we cannot afford to antagonize the old Spirit, Sir." he looked at William meaningfully. William stared down at him frowning. Old Mr Briggs had not finished, clinging on to William's arm he went on, his eyes gleaming in the candlelight. "Yes...yes. You are not being fanciful. Some of us thought we were, but look at what happened...." His voice drifted off, "We cannot afford more sorrow in this house." I shivered and looked around searchingly. Then I saw the tall faded gold screen in one corner of the room, just as had been described to us. Instinctively I moved towards it, and sure enough, somewhere near it, was the door.

"William over here," I called. In four or five strides he was beside me. We both stared at the dark wooden door which stood ajar in front of us. "Gosh!" I whispered.

"Yes," William said, comprehending my meaning. "Now give me the light," he almost snatched the candlestick which had been in my hands, and moved forward. I followed him, quite scared, I must admit. I saw the dark, wooden paneling on three sides of the room, a gap in the paneling on one wall made place for a large painting of a young mother and her little son looking tragically ahead. I glanced towards the end of the little chamber.

"Look!" I gasped, turning to William; he was standing, erect, and staring at the tall looking-glass with a heavy decorative, dark frame, which was standing innocently in the corner. We both went closer and looked at it, it was quite an ugly piece, very old, with a sturdy stand. William touched it, a little hesitatingly, he tried to look behind it. "We will need more light to examine this..." he murmured, "too dark."

"There are cupboards here, look!" I said, noticing a subtle-looking handle attached to one of the wooden panels, I pulled at it and it opened to reveal a large walk-in closet. "Wow! Truly fit for a queen," I said, "rather dirty, of course. Imagine long gowns hanging here, or perhaps cloaks and things, satin shoes lined up there..." I spoke dreamily.

"We are here to look for the necklace," interrupted William, a little roughly, "I suggest we get on with our job."

We looked everywhere in the dark cupboard, proper sleuths, we were! William tapped the walls high up for any hidden crevices; I worked at the lower end. Tap-tap we went, on and on, until my fingers hurt. It was quite stifling in the cupboard, in fact this little dressing room was quite airtight, I found, to my discomfort. After a while I straightened myself and looked around.

"I think we should search the bedroom," I said softly.

"You go," he mumbled.

"No, not alone," I whispered, "please, come with me."

"Oh, alright then..." He said, shrugging. We both went back, rather thankfully, into the bedroom. The large candle on the stand was still burning bright, the door to this chamber was ajar, I could see the vague forms of Marianne and young Mr Briggs standing, just outside the door. I glanced towards the curtains and gave a start, "God!" One side of a threadbare velvet curtain had been drawn and someone was sitting on the window seat. I saw the long window, stretching from the ceiling down, almost to the floor level, with its criss-cross dark bars. My eyes went back to the dark figure I could still see.

"Emma, get a hold on yourself, it's only old Mr Briggs," said William, irritably.

"Oh, so it is.... Of course," I murmured, heaving a sigh of relief. "But, what is he doing?" Instinctively, I moved closer to William, who was looking at the bed.

"Heaven knows! Perhaps he's apologizing to the old spirit for intruding on her privacy. "

"God bless my soul," someone screamed from the doorway.

"What...the!" cursed William, as he ran towards the door.

"What is it?" I muttered, as I ran up, to Mr Briggs and Marianne. They were standing in the shadows, staring ahead, Marianne was looking pale and ashen, one hand on her heart, Mr Briggs was crossing himself repeatedly. I looked from one to the other, they seemed to be quite speechless. Both continued to look at the far end of the passage which ended with the long window, William hurried down the passage, looking around wildly as he went. When he reached the end, he moved to his right and disappeared from our view. We waited patiently for quite some time, absolutely silent, till at last we heard his footsteps coming back towards us.

"Nothing," he said, from a distance, as he came closer. "There's a wall here," he gestured to one side, "I could not see anyone or anything for that matter, what did frighten you?"

"The Lady, sir, it was her alright," blurted out young Mr Briggs, quite worked up. "I fear no living soul," he added, again crossing himself.

"Marianne?" enquired William. Slowly, she met his gaze, "a woman, in a pale gown and long black hair stood there..." she almost sobbed as she pointed towards the long window at the far end of the passage. I made as if to say something, she looked at me, "yes, yes, the very same, she stood there and stared at us, her face so strange, so ghastly, so inhumanly pale, oh William! We must leave this house at once. It is truly haunted!"

William looked down at her, his expression, quite troubled. He glanced towards young Mr Briggs, frowning. After a minute or two, he seemed to pull himself together. "There is no question of turning back now, you two, stay here, there is no one there."

"Exactly so, Sir," interrupted young Mr Briggs, giving us all a meaningful look.

"Come one, Briggs, ten to one, there is a logical explanation for what you saw," In fact, it looks to me like someone is taking a lot of trouble to scare us away..." his voice went on, "that someone is perhaps using the atmosphere in this deserted beautiful and rather old house, to suit their purpose." His voice got stronger as he spoke and somehow it gave the rest of us some strength in that moment as we each stood, frightened and perplexed.

"Come, Emma, let's get back in there," he almost pulled me back into the room.

Although I went with him, I was not quite so sure of myself, feeling as though I was walking in a dream and something bad could happen at any moment. I found myself in front of the large, high bed. Numbly, I bent down in front of it, I put my hand on the heavy wood half expecting something to jump up at me!

"Look for any irregularity in the structure, I will not be surprised if there is a hidden cavity somewhere," whispered William, "there must be.... Indeed, there has to be," he spoke rather harshly.

"We worked in silence for a while, me, almost crawling on the floor, my fingers feeling the woodwork on the bed, there was a majestic crest on the foot of the bed, but I was too intent on pressing the wood, so could give no attention to its beauty. I moved to one side of the bed, I tried to look under it, now, completely unmindful of the dust; in fact, I was quite plastered with the dust around me, there was a long wooden panel of the bed that reached the floor, so I could not see under it. I glanced up, raising myself on to my knees, my hands, on the velvet cover of the bed. In doing so, I got a view of the long casement at the far end of the room.

"What is he doing?" I blurted out.

"What?" said William, turning to look towards the windows. I think he had quite forgotten about old Mr Briggs.

That gentleman seemed to have completely taken leave of his senses, he was on his knees in front of the window seat, gesturing wildly, looking straight at me. He kept waving his hands about and mouthing some silent words. William raised his eyes heavenwards, shrugged his broad shoulders in a hopeless manner, and went on examining a rather large and clumsy looking chest of drawers.

I looked curiously at the old man, and as I looked at him a cold, now familiar feeling almost crept up on me. I got up to my feet very slowly and moved towards the old man as if in a dream. I knelt on the floor besides him, frightened half to death, I looked inquiringly at him. It had suddenly occurred to me that, perhaps this strange old man that everyone was treating most kindly, as completely 'senile', might be the one to be helpful to our purpose. After all, he was the only one who had known all the concerned people, as he knew this great, big house. The only link with the past, as it were. I had realized by now, that looking for the necklace was not as easy as I had thought. A gigantic house, full of innumerable cupboards, chests of drawers, desks, endless shelves, and book-cases, not to mention wardrobes, presented a little bit of a hopeless situation. There might be, indeed there must be, a great number of secret hiding places, as the place was crammed with antique pieces of furniture! I looked around in the dark, candlelit room, from the vantage point of the floor, the shadows we cast made the room appear to be mysterious, as if it guarded many secrets. This room had a definite undercurrent of sorrow. I shivered involuntarily. "Get a hold on yourself, Emma," I admonished myself, sternly. "Oh!" I screamed as I felt a strong tug on my arm.

"What now?" said William, irritably, not bothering to come up to me, as he would have, had it been Marianne calling out.

"Nothing, someone just walked over my grave," I mumbled. Then, stealing myself, I turned to look at my arm and saw the cold, claw-like, shriveled hand of old Mr Briggs on it, slowly, still scared, I lifted my gaze up to his eyes. Sometimes, in my nightmares, I see those eyes again. They were light grey, and were blazing in sort of a fanatical way, as if on fire! I felt I could hear my heart pounding in that quiet room. I stared at the old man who went on clinging to my arm, rather ferociously.

"What is it?" I managed to whisper, after what seemed, to me, to be ages. He continued to press my arm and stared into my eyes, I felt quite paralyzed with fear, at that moment I was certain that he was out of his senses. I was too frightened to push him away. At last, I tore my eyes away from his and looked towards William, I do not know if I cried out for help, but, miraculously, I saw William turn towards us. He looked curiously in our direction, then slowly walked up to us. I stared at him, still unable to move. He bent down and sat on his haunches next to us and looked intently at the old man, ignoring me completely. The old man moved his head just a little. William followed his eyes. He did not say a word, but got up and walked, very slowly, towards the fireplace. He stood in front of it. The mantelpiece was heavy-looking and stately, with sort of channeled columns, architrave and frieze. I felt a movement near me, I turned to the old man, he seemed to be struggling with himself, I wanted to pull my arm away but could not, his hold on me was surprisingly strong. I moved, trying to get on my knees, thinking I could try and scramble up, but he pulled me back onto the floor. To my horror, I found myself struggling to get up, the old man, clinging to me. I started sobbing as I found myself helpless. William was not looking at us, and somehow, I could not call out for help. The old man whispered something and I looked at him, my gaze going back to look into his eyes as if hypnotized.

"Yes, My Lady, I did not tell anyone," he murmured at last very, very softly looking straight back into my eyes. I continued staring at him in horror, his eyes had almost a crazed look in them.

"He's mad," I thought to myself, "I shouldn't have come up to him."

"No one has touched it," he said, this time very loudly and clearly. In two seconds William was beside us, I was almost thrown to one side, and old Mr Briggs was lifted to a standing position and held there by William's strong arms.

"Touched what?" William asked him, softly.

"No one has touched it..." repeated the old man monotonously, still looking towards me. William almost shook him.

"Touched what?" he asked, menacingly. To my surprise, the old man chuckled, William was so shocked he almost dropped him.

"You want to know, don't you?" giggled old Mr Briggs, now hugely enjoying himself. William was bristling with anger, he looked down at old Mr Briggs and this time shook him, but the peculiar old man continued smirking and staring at me, completely ignoring William.

Slowly, as if collecting my wits, I struggled up to my feet and moved close to him. "Where is it, Briggs?" I asked in a high pitched, authoritative voice, as if I was giving him an order.

To my amazement, the old man's face went through another transformation, the crazed look vanished in a second and the well-trained, perfect butler was back. I saw him struggling in William's hold. I gestured to William to leave him. Hesitatingly, William let him go. Old Mr Briggs shuffled his way to the great fireplace, we both followed. He looked up at the mantelpiece, then pointed at something. Over the fireplace was an in intricate carving. Looking carefully I saw engraved there, were rather fierce looking monsters holding what looked like family arms. There was a dragging sound, I turned and saw William pulling a chair forward. I hurried and pulled up a table that stood near me and climbed onto it, then studied the wall in front of me. The monsters over the fireplace were ugly and held ominous looking weapons. I put my fingers on the wall, rather gingerly at first, trying to do what Williams was doing.

"Here," suddenly whispered William hoarsely.

"What? What?" I asked excitedly.

"See...see here...the moulding, it's thicker here than elsewhere, can you see it?" he murmured pointing at something. I looked carefully, straining my eyes, but could not see anything different in the carvings near where he pointed.

"Look," he said, motioning me to get nearer.

It was the stomach of one of the terrifying looking monsters. When seen very carefully it was a little bulkier than the rest of the background. William pressed it, I looked breathlessly. We heard a soft sound, the monster's stomach opened up just a little bit, a dark hole appeared in the wall in front of us. William and I simply stared at it for a moment, each of us quite sure we had found what we were looking for, a hidden safe.

William tried to reach into the safe, "it's too small," he whispered.

"Here let me," I said moving closer to him. I placed one hand on the wall to steady myself and the other into the dark cavity, my heart thumping wildly.

"What?" said William, almost into my ear, I could hear him breathing heavily beside me. The opening of the hiding place was extremely small, but the space inside was surprisingly larger than what I expected. I had to lean forward, it was quite frightening I discovered, why, there could be any sort of insects inside, maybe even a scorpion. I almost pulled my hand out, but then bit my lip and tried to be brave. At first nothing, then I felt it, a soft, small little bundle.

"It's here," my voice sounding strange to my own ears.

"Shhh," he whispered, "gently, now." I could sense the excitement in his voice. I started to drag the bundle towards the opening with the tip of my fingers.

"Oh, it's stuck," I mumbled dejectedly.

"Listen, keep calm, try and fold it," he suggested. I tried but it was too difficult with one hand, that too without being able to see anything. I tried to lean closer to the wall, almost falling off the table.

"Easy there," cautioned William, steadying me with his arm.

"My God, I can't!" I blurted out panicking a little.

"Relax, and keep trying," he said, "after all someone did put it inside."

"Yes, yes, of course," I said. I took a deep breath "Will it be alright to snatch at it, I mean supposing it breaks," I whispered anxiously glancing at him.

"Never mind about that, just try to get it out of the safe," he said softly.

I snatched at the little parcel with my nails, now I felt something stiff inside it. Bravely I almost folded it and then tried to pull it out of the small opening. We held our breaths as the cloth appeared in the wall. Together, we dragged the bundle out.... At last, we had it! There in William's hand, was a little dark velvet pouch with something stiff inside it. For a moment, we just stood there simply staring at it. Then William took a step down from the chair. Hurriedly I too got down from the table.

"Here," he said walking toward the bed.

"Careful," I cautioned, quite unnecessarily as he placed the bundle on the bed.

"Here goes, this is it," he said, his eyes gleaming in the semi darkness..

"Come on," I said "untie the ribbon, I cannot wait."

He grinned at me, quite excited now, like a schoolboy, and turned to untie the little knot that held the velvet cloth together. "Such a neat little bow," I thought to myself, "must be Lady Cecilia's own hand," I said aloud wonderingly, looking at the bundle on the bed.

"Imagine, all those years ago, she folded it and tied it up and put it into the wall! And now, you and I are about to open it after all these years..." I stopped abruptly, as the velvet cloth unfolded. A thin, white muslin cloth appeared. William gently unwrapped it. I blinked in astonishment at the sight before me. There, lying on the old, quite thread bare, bedspread, was the most beautiful precious necklace in the world.

"William!" I gasped, grasping his arm.

"Good Lord," he said.

We exchanged shocked glances, then turned back to look at the necklace. It had a multitude of rubies and emeralds and hanging from the center was the largest tear-drop diamond I had ever seen! The stones gleamed in the candlelight. I stared and stared at it, completely amazed by its radiance. Even to my untutored eye, it was obvious that it must be worth a fortune. No wonder someone was taking so much of trouble to get their hands on it. This thought, suddenly brought me back to reality. Instinctively I glanced over my shoulder. It just occurred to me that there had been no sound from Marianne and Young Mr Briggs for some time. I could see Old Mr Briggs sitting on a chair by the fireplace absolutely still, lost in his own world. I moved a little closer to William, at the same time the silence was broken by a loud voice.

"I'll have that, if you please!" We both turned our startled eyes towards the direction of the voice.

"What the....!" I heard William curse under his breath. At the same time he grabbed the necklace and stuffed it into his pocket, taking a couple of steps towards the door.

"Not so fast," said the shrill voice "You hand it over quietly and no harm shall come to our beauty here. William stopped in his tracks. I saw his body tense, his head moved to one side trying to see the doorway better. I saw someone in a dark suit, a man or a woman I could not tell. It was too dark. The person appeared to be either a man disguised as a woman or a woman disguised as a man! The clothes were those of a man and yet the voice sounded very strange and a little feminine. I felt a chill, as the person dragged forward, what was unmistakably our friend Marianne, a gun to her head!

"You see, I mean business," said the thin voice quite pleasantly. "Hand over the necklace and take the lady."

Marianne stared ahead absolutely still. I looked at the doorway and at William, halfway to the door, a cold dread in my heart, remembering the secret meeting of the gang that we had been witness to.

"What shall we do, Emma?" said William; rather conversationally to me looking over his shoulder, he spoke lightly and somewhat casually. Confused, I hesitated to answer him, not wanting to mess up whatever he was trying to do.

"The necklace or our friend here," he said, speaking slowly.

"He is playing for time," I realized. There was a pause. I looked at the figure standing there with a gun leveled at Marianne's head. Really, it was too fantastic. William took a step forward.

"None of your tricks young man, stay where you are," said the voice menacingly, at the same moment Marianne gave a cry as she was hurled to the floor at the feet of her captor, her head held up by her hair and the gun leveled once again on her head.

"No, no, stop, leave her be," shouted William not daring to move forward. "She knows nothing about the necklace."

"That maybe, but you do," came the answer, "What did you think, you could simply walk away with it, after all the trouble we have taken," the voice got a little intense and high pitched.

I looked at the figure curiously, who was it? For a moment I thought it was a woman, and then I thought it was a man. I dared not move, but strained my eyes trying to make out the identity of the person holding Marianne. William and I had spoken together of our suspicions. It had to be someone we know, of that I was now quite sure. As, whoever it was, had clearly been aware of our intentions to search Golden Oaks.

"Right, now throw it over," barked the figure in the shadows, "Now." At the same moment Marianne screamed with pain.

"Oh no," I cried. "Give it please, William."

William pulled out the necklace hastily and threw it towards the great door of the Queen's Chamber; it landed where Marianne was crouching. The person holding her, bent down, while keeping an eye on William. I watched tensely, ready to spring forward, if required. Then just for a second, Marianne's captor's eyes left William and turned towards the necklace. That was enough for William. He let out a sort of a primitive yell and lunged forward towards the door. I ran after him, but our villain was too quick for us. Quicker than light he pushed Marianne aside, grabbed the necklace and fled down the passage.

I went to help Marianne to her feet, and looked around anxiously, "We'd better go too," I said breathlessly, "Hurry."

"No, wait," whispered Marianne, "Mr Briggs."

"Never mind, he'll be alright in there," I nodded at the door of the Queen's Chamber. I was already moving down the passage, I could hear faint footsteps of the two people running ahead of me.

"No, no, not him," said Marianne, "It's young Mr Briggs," she pointed to a dark corner a little ahead of us.

I turned to look and gave a start, "My God, is he dead?" I said. Young Mr Briggs was sort of huddled in a corner, clearly unable to move or speak. I went up to him and put an arm on his shoulder, he slumped forward, his head hanging over his chest.

"I think he's knocked out," said Marianne, peeking meekly over my shoulder.

"Anyway, there is nothing we can do right now, let's not wait any more time," I said a little callously, and ran down the passage.

Poor Marianne, her kind heart really troubled her. She hesitated. "Marianne," I called as I ran, "you'd better not stay there by yourself, or you might have a similar fate, and I doubt if your William will like that." I heard her hurried footsteps following me.

"Really Emma, you are too much!" she mumbled breathlessly as she caught up with me.

"It was just a mild warning," I said pausing. "Shhh, listen, which way did they go."

We were standing in the upstairs gallery, it was darker now and we had no candle with us, the only light came from outside, whenever there was a window. Luckily there were large high windows, several with no drapes, so we managed to see our way about.

"The moon must have come out," I whispered rather unnecessarily. There was silence; I strained my ears holding my breath, my eyes darting around. These old houses have so many corridors and dark corners that there are endless places for a person to hide. I looked down and saw a sort of hall with a grand fireplace on one side and long windows on the other. I could see no sign of life at all, no artificial light, no sound. We stood there silently, in the semi-darkness, for what seemed to be ages, hanging on the balustrade. My body was beginning to relax after a few minutes. I recovered my breath and turned to Marianne in order to consult with her about what we should do, when all hell broke loose.

Quite close to us, there was huge crash, we both screamed. I wanted to run but somehow could not move. I stared at the direction from which the sound had come, and then I saw a dark figure bound out from a passage to our right. The figure darted past us without giving us a glance. Behind it came a larger figure; they whizzed past us so quickly, we just stared at them, with our mouths open.

"Come on Marianne," I called after a moment and began to run behind the two figures.

"Oh! Should we?" exclaimed Marianne but she began to follow me. We ran round the gallery behind the two figures. I had almost caught up with one figure when, to my horror, it stopped abruptly. Unable to help it, I ran straight into Mr Goddard, who caught me by my collar, glared at me, one hand risen to hit me.

"Oh no," I screamed loudly, recognizing him at once, "Marianne, run."

"You interfering wretch!" he growled at me, "I'll teach you not to meddle in our affairs." I closed my eyes tight, bracing myself for the blow, which was most certainly about to come my way. At the same time, I tried to wriggle out of his strong hold. He hit me, the blow fell somewhere on my shoulder, as I was struggling like mad, making it difficult for him to aim. I fell down, with the shock of the blow. He cursed me loudly and freely in an extremely crude language, and came rushing at me, his hands raised to strike again. I tried to get up to run, but just then someone appeared right beside Mr Goddard and caught hold of him. Mr Goddard screamed terrible curses and hit out wildly, but was unable to free himself. I scrambled up to my feet, staring at the struggle before my eyes.

"Easy now, no use hitting out, you're caught, good and proper," said a breathless voice. It was my poetic friend Constable Wotley, his plump arms tightly round the prisoner's waist. Mr Goddard was a strong man and continued to struggle energetically, all the while screaming colourful curses. I looked around wondering how to help, for I was not at all confident that Constable Wotley would be able to hang on to the fierce man for too long. In fact, I could see that his hold was already beginning to slacken. All of a sudden, Marianne came forward. A little hesitatingly, she raised both her arms, I got a glimpse of a long brass plant stand in her hands. She looked at me, her arms still raised.

"Go to it," I cheered her, quite fascinated with her uncharacteristic initiative. She screwed shut her eyes, and brought the stand down over Mr Goddard. He fell down with a loud thud. I clapped my hands. "Bravo," I said a little weakly, as my shoulder hurt, thinking it was just a matter of chance that it hadn't landed on Constable Wotley!

"Thank you young lady, not that I couldn't have managed on my own," said Constable Wotley, a little haltingly, trying to get his breath back without showing it.

"Have I killed him," Marianne asked timidly, looking over Constable Wotley's shoulder at her victim, lying on the floor.

"Oh no, ma'am, killed him? Indeed not...I shouldn't think so," said the plump Constable, stammering a little, not impervious of Marianne's beauty.

"He is a poet after all!" I thought to myself, "luckily for him, she hit the right man."

"Come on, someone help me," I said a little irritably. It occurred to me that no one seemed to be realizing that I had been assaulted by the villain. They both rushed to my side.

"You alright, Miss Emma?" enquired the Constable, looking genuinely concerned and gently pulling me up from the floor.

"Not really," I said leaning on the Constable a little and trying to look like a martyr. "But I will not complain for it is all for a good cause." My voice sounded tragic.

"Emma, really," admonished Marianne, frowning at me. Constable Wotley on the other hand looked approvingly at me.

"You have the right attitude young lady, we should all stand tall in adversity. This reminds me of a poem I once composed... it went something like...

"When you fall,
You must stand tall,
For it is a call,
To demonstrate your all!"

I smothered a laugh as I saw Marianne's startled expression. She was staring at the Constable, quite shocked. He had really got going, his voice getting louder doing full justice to his poetic reputation.

"Very nice, very nice," I said, interrupting his recital. He paused to hear my praise. "Now Constable, what are you planning to do with him?" I asked him, nastily bringing the poet back to reality.

"With him?" he enquired politely.

"Him," I said poking Mr Goddard with my foot.

"Oh him," he repeated after me. I looked at him exasperated.

"Perhaps you are going to tie him up. He will come round any moment you know," I said slowly.

"Yes, yes, to be sure, precisely my thoughts," he mumbled.

"Well?" I said, nudging him along.

"Well," he repeated. Marianne looked at him quite surprised.

"Well, you must be having handcuffs on you, you are a policeman. Maybe you are thinking of putting them on his hands, sort of preliminary to arresting him," I suggested, my eyes on his face (one has to be very careful with Constable Wotley, he hates to be told what to do, he must think it's all his idea)

"Oh yes, precisely, quite...quite," he said, getting official and pulling out a pair of handcuffs from his pocket. "Now stand back ladies, this may turn ugly..." he said, almost falling over the unconscious man as he tried to pull his arms behind his back in order to handcuff him. Marianne and I held on to each other, trying to smother our laughter. I leaned over to the balustrade wincing a little.

"Oh dear, you are hurt," said Marianne softly, wiping tears of laughter from her cheeks.

"Shhh," I put my finger on my mouth, "I think I hear a sound."

"What sound, I did not hear anything," said Marianne.

"Wait," I whispered, "someone is coming." We both leaned back into the dark a little but kept our eyes over the hall below. There was silence, I moved forward again looking down. Then a faint sound as if someone was moving about very stealthily. I moved back into the darkness. Yes, sure enough I heard a step. The wood in old houses will creak when walked upon, no matter how softly one moves. Someone was definitely moving around downstairs. Impulsively, I turned and began to walk towards the great staircase, Marianne close behind me.

"Hey," whispered Constable Wotley "Where are you going?"

"Shhh," I reprimanded him sternly, looking back over my shoulder. "Look he is moving," I pointed to Mr Goddard who seemed to be coming round. I watched attentively as Constable Wotley picked up Marianne's plant stand and gave Mr Goddard another bang on his head. Our villain sank back on the floor. Constable Wotley looked up at me. "We cannot leave the prisoner," he mumbled.

"Correction, YOU cannot leave the prisoner, you stay here," I said, quite unkindly and hurried off. Marianne did her best to suppress her laughter at his obviously disappointed look, but kept close to me.

We went down the wide, imposing stairs, pausing on every step and looking around us. We had descended one flight and turned a corner. Before us stretched the final set of wide, wooden stairs, leading on to the marble floored hall below. Suddenly, Marianne pulled at my arm, I turned towards her, at the same time there was an unmistakable sound of hurried footsteps. We both stood still, holding our breathes, waiting. Again all went quiet, we continued standing where we were, as if frozen. After a minute or two, someone ran across the hall. We stared as another person came into view, clearly chasing the first. "Edward," I said softly, recognizing my friend immediately, "good work." I saw him stretch his arm as if to catch the dark figure ahead of him, I do not know what went wrong but just then there was a humongous crash and Edward went sprawling on the floor. "Oh no!" I exclaimed, moving forward instinctively and thinking all was lost, as I could see that the villain was almost at the great door. However, just then, by a stroke of luck for us, the person at the door made a fatal mistake, he or she paused, just for a second, as if turning back to see what had happened.

"Oh!" squealed Marianne, plucking at my arm and pointing. I looked round. From the far corner of the hall, a small, round, dark figure seemed to bound in at full speed. "What is it?" screamed Marianne, quite scared. I stared frightened, yet fascinated as the figure made for the feet of our villain, who, taken completely unawares, fell forward, rather like a tree cut down with a single blow! Never one to hold back, I charged down the stairs, Marianne following me at a more cautious speed. As we moved into the hall, several people appeared, through the various doors leading to and out of this, the formal entrance of the grand house.

Edward was slowly extricating himself from the parts of an old coat of arms which he had run into. "Typical," I thought, unforgivingly. Julia was there, somewhere, looking rather shocked. I distinctly saw Chief Inspector Crawley walk in slowly through a door at the far end. William was there, holding on to the furiously struggling, mysterious figure on the floor.

"Who is it? WHO IS IT?!" screamed a childish, very familiar voice. I turned to look down, quite stunned, at the little 'round, dark figure'. No dog, this, no, none but my little brother, David!

"My goodness!" Floppy said, pushing his spectacles up his nose, as he hurried up to William's side. "How did you get here?" he asked David, an arm on his shoulder. "Oh, who is it? who is it?" squealed David, ignoring Floppy and jumping up and down, excitedly, next to where the mysterious thief was being held with some difficulty, on the floor by William.

The Fish ran in just then, quite breathless. "Sir...you've got...him...her," he mumbled, rather unnecessarily, at the same time, bending down to assist his Inspector.

The 'mystery' thief was lying flat on his face, I moved closer, at the same time, Marianne came up to us. She had brought a candle stand from somewhere. In complete shock, we all stared in the weak light at the head of a familiar grey hair, dressed in a surprisingly neat bun. William and The Fish tipped the prisoner over.

"Oh!" squealed Julia. "My goodness!" exclaimed Floppy. I stared, shocked, at Mrs Weston's strange looking face. "You!" exclaimed Chief Inspector Crawley, loudly.

I moved closer, staring at Mrs Weston's heavily painted face. "Why does she look so strange?" "There is too much make-up," I said softly, bending down besides the group on the floor. William glanced at me and turned back to look searchingly at the prisoner, at the same moment, Mrs Weston let out a screeching laugh, it was so loud, shrill, and harsh, that I fell back on my haunches, besides her, staring in alarm at her.

"I know that voice," suddenly said Juila, a little meekly from the shadows nearby. I raised myself on one elbow hurriedly and looked curiously at Mrs Weston.

"Well, it is Mrs Weston?" said Edward, slowly, walking up to us.

"Is it, indeed?" murmured William, looking thoughtfully at the prisoner.

"No, not Mrs Weston," said Julia, haltingly. Then, to my utter amazement, my meek friend walked up to Mrs Weston, bent down over her and pulled at her hair. Mrs Weston snarled at her and made as if to attack her. But she was held back on the floor by William and The Fish, the grey bun was in Julia's hands!

"Oh! it's a wig..." said Marianne.

"Not Mrs Weston, then" I whispered.

"No, not Mrs Weston after all," stated William. "Rather a crude attempt, it could only succeed when looked at from a distance..."

Julia was kneeling on the floor, her forehead knitted in a frown. Everyone was quiet, there was a loud sound of thunder, I glanced around, it was quite dark, a weak light came in, here and there, through gaps in the heavy curtains, otherwise, the only light in the hall was provided by the single candle Marianne had brought. The atmosphere had suddenly become quite tense. There was another loud rumble of thunder, followed by a crackle of lightning. For a second, the hall was lit by it. I looked at the person on the floor, she looked so queer with her badly made up face, then, in a flash, I got it.

I moved closer to her and peered at her, then boldly I reached forward with my hand, somewhere near her hairline, everyone crowded closer and looked curiously. My fingers felt something strange, and I pulled.

"Oh my God! What are you doing, Emma?" said Marianne, "don't dear, please, it's quite horrid!."

"You're pulling at her face," said Floppy, rather matter-of-factly.

"Why are you doing that? why are you doing that?" squealed David.

"Ahh, ahh, get your hands of me, you pest..." snarled the prisoner, wriggling furiously.

My fingers got a good grip, the strange substance gave and I pulled what looked, at first glance, like second skin but was really a thin, rather crudely made wax mask! "Oh!" said a few people, almost simultaneously. A loud crash of lightning illuminated the hall as I pulled off the mask. "I can't believe it!" I said, falling backwards, quite shocked. The person in front of us raised her head and spat at us. She screamed abuses that are quite unpennable, suffice it to say. I ran to David and put my hands over his ears, he let me but kept his eyes firmly on the now not-so-mysterious thief.

"Ladies and gentlemen, let me re-introduce you all to Mrs Maria Rogers, secretary to Mrs Weston at the Winwood Manor School..." said William formally.

He was interrupted by Marianne. "But that is..." she could not complete her sentence.

"Yes, you have recognized her, she is an old associate of your family, owing her very job to lady Victoria's recommendation." He looked grimly at the woman on the floor, then turned to look at the Chief Inspector. "I think you too have met her Sir, under quite a different name...does Miss Mamble mean something to you? That very same Miss Mamble, who is the daughter of Mrs Mamble.... The nanny of Thomas Winwood..."

The rain came pouring down then, rather heavily, making quite a loud noise as it hit the window panes. "Of course, Maria, it does make things clearer," I thought to myself. I looked intently at the retired Chief Inspector, just for a moment I saw a strange look on his face, as if he was furious about something, then in a second, it was gone, and he was his usual mild self.

William and I exchanged glances, then I moved towards my right, the atmosphere extremely strange, as if we were all in a dream, everyone around me, as if sensing something, stood absolutely still and there was complete silence. Everyone, just watching. The only sound was my own footsteps as I went down a corridor and into the dark, as it were.

Before long, I made my way back to the grand foyer of the house but this time, I was not alone, behind me walked, an extremely tall, erect, grey-haired, handsome old gentlemen, neither of us saying a word. They were all standing in exactly the same places as before. I stood in the shadows for a moment, as if bracing myself, then a firm hand took mine, the man behind me said, reassuringly, "come, little angel, let us bring this business to it's end."

We moved further into the foyer, all eyes on us. I was looking at Inspector Crawley, and saw the start he gave as my tall companion became visible to the group. Calmly, William came up to us and shook the gentleman's hand, he then turned to the rest. "Let me introduce you all to Sir Arkwright, Lady Victoria's lawyer, and the missing piece of the puzzle," he said quietly.

Then, slowly, very purposefully, William walked up to Chief Inspector Crawley, "you, of course, are not surprised to see your cousin here?"

"No.. of course no.." murmured Inspector Crawley, rather unintelligibly.

"I thought it best to rescue him from the dungeons where he had been prisoner for the past two months!" stated William in a loud, but flat voice.

There were many gasps in the room, several eyes turned to look in shock at the stranger. I kept my eyes firmly on Inspector

Crawley, and I must say, he was very calm. He must have known where we were heading, but he gave nothing away until the very end.

"Do you want to know who kept him prisoner over there?" said William, slowly, moving still closer to the Chief Inspector, his voice sounding a little harsh now. Everyone looked on, as if hypnotised, at William, then at Inspector Crawley. No one made a sound, not even David. Just then, another loud crackle of lightning lit up our strange group standing around in that foyer of Golden Oaks, it was quite a dramatic moment, almost like a theartical production, and then, as if on cue, William finally said it. "You, Sir, it was you all the while..." he said it slowly, looking straight into Inspector Crawley's eyes.... "Why? Why, Sir? All this...for a necklace...?" William asked, a little emotionally.

"A NECKLACE?!" exclaimed retired Chief Inspector Crawley, breaking his silence at last, as if he could not help himself any longer. "You call it a necklace, say THE necklace, if you will! You fool, you don't have any idea of its value, do you?!" he looked around at all of us, a strange fire in his eyes, it was as if he had become another person, I was completely fascinated, he stared intently at Marianne, she almost cringed, poor girl, at the venomous look he gave her. "Her and her grandmother! Would THEY miss it...? TELL ME!" he turned to William, who stood stoically, his arms folded, his legs slightly apart, looking a little shocked at this change in the hither-to-mild-mannered old, retired Chief Inspector. "I tried to make John understand, but he would not budge.... He would not give me Lady Cecilia's map, that's all I wanted, all you had to do was keep your mouth SHUT," he snarled at the man standing so erect and stiff, next to me.

"Did you kill Lady Victoria?" suddenly blurted William, his voice cutting, like a knife. Another shocked silence, then I moved towards Marianne, who was sort of shrinking back into the shadows around us. Everybody waited, expectantly, for an answer. Retired Chief Inspector Crawley never answered that question. We all stood around, not knowing what to do with ourselves as The Fish went to the great door and opened it. We heard his familiar, shrill whistle, and then, after about five minutes, trooped in noisily, several uniformed policemen, they stood by, as if waiting for orders.

William put his hand out to Inspector Crawley, "I'll have THE necklace now, I think," he said softly. Inspector Crawley expressionlessly put his hand in a pocket and took out the priceless Winwood necklace, he gave a sort of laugh, and turned as if to walk away, William made as if to hold him back. The Chief Inspector looked over his shoulder, gave him a contemptuous sneer, and threw the necklace behind him, and simply walked out. The policemen quickly moved to escort him and his accomplice out, and into the waiting police cars.

We all remained motionless, simply staring as these events unfolded, I looked around to see where the necklace had landed, as I moved forward, I saw everybody moving aside, all eyes on the floor, clearly tracing the path of the necklace. I saw it first, there it was, miraculously, at Marianne's feet. She stood, frozen, just looking, almost with horror, at her family hierloom, restored to her in this unexpected fashion. I bent at her feet and picked it up. I held it up for her to see, she didn't say anything. Then I moved round showing everybody this Winwood treasure.

It was a few minutes later, when the necklace had been taken into safe custody by Sir Arkwright, that I remembered Constable Wotley and his prisoner. William almost grinned as I whispered to him. A couple of policemen followed me to rescue Constable Wotley. I must say, he was standing there, exactly in the same spot we had left him in, gallantly guarding his prisoner. I have a feeling he kept knocking Mr Goddard down with Marianne's plant stand as he came round, so as to avoid any unpleasantness that might arise if Mr Goddard tried to make a run for it. As I have already said, several times, Constable Wotley is an artist, not an athlete, and he fully understands his own limitations.

✦ ✦ ✦

17

It took a while for our party to find our voices after Mr Crawley and his 'gang' had been sent off. William requested young Mr Briggs, who had come down at some point and joined our group in the foyer, to guide everyone to a comfortable sitting room.

It was a smallish, pretty room, with a large floral sofa over which hung a portrait of a mother and her baby. Several comfortable arm-chairs and little tables were scattered around. There was a large fireplace with a mirror hung over it along one wall. As soon as I entered this room I got a feeling that I may have been there before, then I remembered Inspector Crawley describing this room to us.... At least there he had been speaking the truth!

"Come on, gang, snap out of your trance!" I blurted out, looking around at Edward, Floppy, Julia, and Marianne, as they stood by me, as if waiting for instructions. I glanced round at them and shook my head.

David tugged at my hand, "I'm hungry!"

"Come to think of it...I'm starving," added Edward, finding his voice at last. Several voices joined the call for food, and soon we were back to our old selves, everyone talking at once.

Marianne smiled and moved towards the door, "Briggs," she called. It was old Mr Briggs who came shuffling in, almost immediately, as if he had been waiting outside, his face bearing a broad smile. "My lady, you called?" he said.

"Yes," she said, smiling at him, "we're all rather hungry, is there...?"

"Yes of course...it is all arranged. We have a grand supper waiting for you, we shall serve it in the great dining room..." he paused, then gave an almost shy smile and said, "the Master had ordered it," he beamed at Marianne, I smiled at how readily he had accepted William as 'The Master'!

"But, Briggs," I interrupted, "can we not have some tea and biscuits right away?..."

"We're ever so hungry!" entreated David, looking up angelically at the old butler. Old Briggs smiled happily, and patted David's head "certainly, young man, and for you I shall look out for some cakes," he turned and left the room.

Just then, William, Sir Arkwright, and The Fish came in, followed by Constable Wotley. As they entered a sort of hush came over the room.

"Come on everyone! Cat got your tongues?...you lot never been this quiet!" suddenly said The Fish, grinning in what can only be described as, strange as it may seem, fondly, at our little group.

"Come on, sit down," said William, himself moving towards the large sofa that was opposite the door, and almost falling down on it. He put a hand out to Marianne, who went up to him and put her hand in his, a little shyly, she sat down beside him. I sat down on a chair next to them, opposite me sat Sir Arkwright. David came and squeezed in beside me, I put my arm around him. Everyone sat around somewhere or the other, except Floppy, who stood in front of the fireplace, that was just behind me.

"What just happened?" Floppy asked, of no one in particular.

"Yes, please tell us!" said Julia softly, looking towards William. There was a knock on the door.

"Come in!" said William, loudly, "hope to God it's tea...." Old Mr Briggs came in and stood by the door, he gestured to someone, then, young Mr Briggs came in, followed by an unknown lady, both bearing large trays. One with a grand tea kettle and several cups, and the other with biscuits, scones, muffins, and cakes. Needless to say, all explanations were put off for a while, as everyone attended to their respective stomachs.

"Put supper off for a bit please Briggs," said Marianne, as he supervised the clearing away of the tea things. "We'll call when we're ready."

"Yes m'lady," said old Mr Briggs, beaming happily at the young couple and silently shutting the door behind him.

"Well, that feels good," said Julia.

"For once, I whole-heartedly agree with you," I murmured.

"Me too!" agreed David, snuggling up to me.

"Well? Come on, tell us!" said Floppy impatiently.

"It was all Emma's doing," said Marianne, in her characteristic, soft voice, "she's so clever." I blushed a little at this direct praise.

"Oh no," I mumbled.

"True," said William, grinning at me, "the efficient Miss Emma just would not let it be.... She had to get to the bottom of the mystery! Why don't you tell them?..."

"No, you go ahead, you made all the arrangements, quite flawlessly, I have to admit," I said to William. He bowed his head.

"Tell them when you first began to suspect the Chief Inspector," he urged.

I sighed, "well, it was like this. It was after we had rescued Marianne, I was thinking over the whole affair in my head. It just would not make sense, something was irritating me." Everyone laughed.

"Typical Emma!" said Edward.

"I was talking it over with David, and we went over the whole affair bit-by-bit, from the very beginning," I paused, looking around, and then went on. "You see, it occurred to me that all we knew of past events in Marianne's family was from Inspector Crawley, no one else was there to either confirm, or contradict anything he had told us."

"That got us thinking," added David.

"i repeated Inspector Crawley's narration of his interaction with the family at Golden Oaks to David...I asked him to think of all possibilities, I myself began to imagine any different set of events that could possibly have occurred, just in case Inspector Crawley's story was not completely true."

"Most interesting..." murmured Floppy.

"You know, I was only trying to look for clues back then, I was not suspecting the Inspector, I was looking to see, if perhaps, there was something else we were missing," I continued.

"Then Emma said it!" said David, a little loudly, sitting up straight.

"Said what?" enquired Julia, looking quite round-eyed, from David to me.

"She said, THE LAWYER! what about THE LAWYER?!" stated David in a slow, rather dramatic way.

There was a hush around the room, everyone was looking at me, quite awed. I tried to look modest. "Fantastic," said Floppy, "well done, old chum, how come no one had thought of the lawyer up till now?," suddenly his eyes fell on sir Arkwright, sitting in front of him, and he reddened, "sorry Sir," he mumbled, apologetically.

"Not at all," grinned the lawyer, "I'm just glad someone thought of me eventually."

"Yes, Emma said, 'we must find the lawyer' and pulled me up and we ran to look for William,'" said David, annoyed at the interruption "and, we would have found him sooner had not Constable Wotley stopped us to recite some poetry to Emma," he continued, directing a nasty look at the poor, embarrassed, poet.

Constable Wotley blushed, "now, master David, the artist's mind is very sensitive, it cannot be rushed for."

"Never mind that, let Emma finish..." interrupted David, ruthlessly. Constable Wotley gave him a contemptuous look and lapsed into a sulky silence.

"Well," I said, smothering a laugh, "then William said that he would start some inquiries."

"Now, looking back," began William "I wonder how we didn't think seriously of THE LAWYER earlier, sorry Sir," he smiled at Sir Arkwright, who raised his hand, while shaking his head, ruefully. "In fact, we had made some regular enquiries at the very start of our investigation.... My men were told that Sir Arkwright was on a sea voyage and had left no contact behind.... It was Sir Arkwright's valet, who had told us about a necklace in the first place that started our investigation...." There was a notable gasp in the room, he put up a hand and said, "one moment, I'll come back to this.... On the whole, I think Inspector Crawley's whole demeanour, his credentials, were all so credible, so beyond suspicion, that no one looked at the problem from any other angle, except the one presented by him," explained William, almost apologetically.

"Everyone except for Emma," added Sir Arkwright, smiling at me.

"Well, go on!" prompted Floppy, a little impatiently. after a minute or two of silence.

"Oh yes," said William, as if rousing himself, "the necklace...Sir Arkwright's valet said that his master had suddenly gone off on a voyage without any members of his staff and very little luggage, but had left behind a letter about some, unexpected, urgent, case.... The letter was typewritten. Although at that point the valet accepted this, he was not quite easy in his mind about certain goings-on, he said he overheard his master talking on the telephone to someone in a loud, and agitated manner, the only word he caught was 'leave the necklace where it is!' Now, as Sir Arkwright was a bachelor, the valet said this was very uncharacteristic and seemed a strange thing for his master to say. He also told us about two strange men calling in the house at that time, and his master actually seeing them. Again he heard sounds of arguments from the study.... When we restarted our enquiries, we found that Sir Arkwright was still abroad. By now, the valet was quite frantic and seemed relieved to see us, his secretary too, expressed a deep concern about his employer's whereabouts, saying that he had been to the local police station as he had not been able to trace the lawyer in spite of his efforts.... In fact, the secretary seemed extremely concerned. Soon it became clear that no one really knew when he had gone or when he'd return, we found out that a ticket in his name had been booked on the QUEEN MARY to sail to New York, but no one seemed to recognize him from the photograph we showed in the course of our enquiries, there seemed to be no record of him either boarding the ship or leaving it. In short, he seemed to have disappeared into thin air. From then on, the whole picture began to gradually make sense."

"In fact, it looked as if he had been 'spirited away'," I said.

"We traced him upto Lady Victoria's house, about two months back, that is where he was finally discovered, imprisoned in the cellars!" William stopped.

Everyone looked quite horrified, and so they may well be, this whole adventure had been most dramatic from the start, with all sorts of unexpected twists and turns.

"Once we found Sir Arkwright the whole situation changed," continued William, "as he had rather a different story to tell."

Everyone turned towards the Lawyer, he looked around the room, and took the stage, as it were. "Yes indeed," he said "well, not VERY different, that is to say, the story you have been told is not absolutely untrue, it is the angle that must be slightly shifted..." the Lawyer smiled around at us. Several puzzled faces stared at him.

"Tell us, Sir," urged David suddenly, his voice loud. I gave a start, as he had almost dozed off next to me.

"You see, certain aspects of Crawley's narrative were quite true," Sir Arkwright paused, and again looked round at us all.

Then, he sort of cleared his throat and began to speak, in rather an official manner. "Many years ago, when I was a child, I lived here, in this village. 'Greenwood', our ancient, large, tumbling house, is called. You know the kind of thing, lush green woods around it (hence it's name), lot's of unused, rather musty rooms, long, dark passages, heavy furniture, basically steeped in history. There were not too many such houses around here, so the ones that were there, kept up a social interaction with each other. So it was that Vikki (Lady Victoria), Trevor (Lord Winwood), and I grew up playing together, so to speak. Neither of us had any brothers or sisters. Trevor lived here with only his mother for company. He was the nicest chap I've ever met with the patience of a saint." Sir Arkwright paused, smiling a little at some memory or the other. "You see, lady Cecilia, Briggs, Mrs Hubert, the formidable housekeeper, in fact the entire household at Golden Oaks, quite doted on him. They constantly fawned upon him. Before he reached the door, it would be opened, the minute he came into the house someone would come running with his house shoes, someone would run up with a glass of sherry, someone would take off his coat and each person would be extremely hurt if he even tried to shrug them off. Poor Trevor, that's how I always thought of him in our growing years. Lady Cecilia adored him, he was a loving and dutiful son, still it was a lonely life for a young boy with only the company of an old-fashioned and autocratic mother! So, we ended up spending most of our free time together, I lived with my father, a lawyer by profession, and my grandfather, who too had been a lawyer. Ours was a man's household, with an unmistakable smell of tobacco everywhere, rather untidy and noisy," he laughed.

"And Lady Victoria's?" asked Julia softly, blushing a little.

"Old Vikki lived at 'Hunter's Lodge' at the other end of the village, with her white-haired, rather grouchy, grandfather who had the most glorious moustache, General Blunt, he was called. Vikki's mother, Mrs Dunford, was a sweet, soft-spoken lady who served the most delicious teas. Trevor and I went there countless times and sat on the table with the General presiding rather vocally. He would almost always lecture us and would end up admonishing us about our 'new-fangled' ways!... So there you have it! Our background." There was a pause, we waited patiently for the Lawyer to continue. After about a minute or two he resumed.

"Of course as we grew up, Trevor and I both fell in love with Vikki. Nothing dramatic, we just lived under her spell, so to speak. She got to be prettier and prettier and I must say, ended up bullying us must of the time! We both knew of each other's feelings. Indeed everyone (our families, that is to say) knew. But our friendship did not change, we spent rather idyllic years growing up around here, picnicking in summer, walking in the woods in autumn, or huddled around the fireplace in winter, we were together most of the time. Then, the time came when Trevor and I both went off to study at Oxford and Vikki to Switzerland. We would come back for our holidays and do our usual things. Again, nothing changed. Then, the time came when we both offered Vikki our hearts and our hands, she accepted Trevor's. I was heart-broken, but again, so far as our friendship was concerned, nothing changed, except that now Vikki was Lady Winwood and lived here with Trevor and Lady Cecilia. During those years I started spending a lot of my time in London as I had to start work at a law firm there, so it was that my father was left to carry on work here on his own. At times it got a little heavy, and he would take on the occasional assistant, one such person, a distant relative, was a young man by the name of Humphrey Crawley..."

There was a sudden tension in the room, we looked at the story-teller, almost frightened to hear the next part of the story, at least I did not want this lovely picture spoiled by the entrance of one who, I now knew to be, in simple terms – the villain of the piece!

"At first, Crawley seemed alright, he was thorough and hard-working and handled basic secretarial work. I asked him round for a drink now and then, at my father's urging. One day, he came up to Golden Oaks with me to meet Lady Cecilia. I remember walking through the front door and handing my hat and coat to the footman, there was a slight sound, I turned and looked towards the steps. There she was. She came running down, smiling delightedly at me, as I had come after rather a long absence. I moved towards her, "careful, Vikki, don't take a fall," we greeted each other affectionately, then I turned to Crawley. I saw him staring at her, just for a moment, Vikki and I exchanged a glance, something here was not quite comfortable. It was just the way he looked at her, it is hard to describe. All I can say is that at that moment we both felt uneasy, but shrugged it off. You see, people often stared at Vikki, so we didn't make too much of it. I put it to Vikki's beauty, and ignored it. Wish I hadn't..." his voice broke off a little here.

He collected himself and resumed. "Briggs had appeared somewhere behind me, so I asked him to take Mr Crawley to meet Lady Cecilia as my father had sent him with some papers which needed her attention. Crawley went off with Briggs, and Vikki and I forgot all about him...for that day at least. How often he visited Golden Oaks and what excuses he contrived to do so, I have no idea, but on my next visit to Cheltern Common, as I was walking up to see Vikki and Trevor, I was quite surprised to see him playing with young Thomas, the nanny, a Mrs Mamble, standing by. I remember Thomas running up to shake hands with me and Crawley looking a little victoriously at me (I could not fathom why), and the Nanny was blushing furiously. 'Very curious, what's he up to? why is the man so strange?' I thought as I continued my walk up to the lodge.

" 'Why are you frowning, old man?' " said Trevor, giving me a painful thump on my back as I handed my coat to Briggs.

" 'What's Crawley doing with Thomas, Trevor?' " I asked bluntly.

" 'Who's Crawley?'" asked Trevor, innocently, walking with me towards his study, his strong arm around my shoulder.

" 'God! Trevor! There is a man playing outside with your son in your grounds, don't you know why he's here?' "

" 'I will find out directly', " he said in mock-obedience, his voice boomed, " 'Briggs!'" he called out.

" 'My Lord', " came the prompt reply, Briggs was always near Trevor, if he was at home.

" 'Who is outside with master Thomas?' " he asked.

" 'Ah, that would be the gentleman from Sir Arkwright's office'," replied Briggs, referring to my grandfather. 'He does come rather often, my lord'.

" 'Why?'" asked Trevor, 'what's his business with Thomas?,. I saw he was frowning now, I think we both were standing there in that passage, looking uncomfortable.

" 'Well Sir, he comes to meet Lady Cecilia and then always seeks out master Thomas and Mrs Mamble and spends an hour or two with them,'. Briggs looked at us, turning from one to the other.

" 'Strange' I mumbled.

" 'Well, maybe he likes children, Arthur?' Trevor looked at me.

" 'I don't like it,' I said bluntly as we went into his study.

" 'Not a nice chap?, he asked me, sounding concerned.

" 'Something about him is not quite right. It has been my feeling from the moment I set eyes on him. You see he comes from a poor family, so my father will not hear of sending him packing,' I sort of murmured.

" 'You've tried? you really are worried...' said Trevor, his handsome face looking intently at me.

" 'Yes, quite frankly, I'll feel better if you make sure he doesn't spend too much time here. Why should he anyway? He should just do his job and leave...', I said softly, fiddling with something on Trevor's large study table. We both looked at each other, Trevor seemed a little puzzled at my concern. The door burst open just then, Vikki tripped in and the subject was dropped.

"I know he kept an eye on Crawley after that, or at least, he put his 'lads on the job', because on another visit of mine, he told me that I was right, and that Crawley was a 'creep', in fact he nicknamed him Creepy-Crawley! He mentioned that he had told him off. As far as Trevor was concerned, this was the end of the Crawley chapter. I was somehow not so sure..."

"Sir Arkwright, what about the affair in the Queen's Chamber? When did that happen? If it did happen..." asked Julia softly.

"Indeed it did happen. Despite Trevor's telling off, Crawely had continued his visits. Vikki, who had no idea of Trevor's talk with Crawley, allowed his visits. Crawley had ingratiated himself with Thomas and the Nanny, and had learnt of the ghost and the family curse through them. After the incident in the Queen's Chamber he knew that Vikki regarded him as her confidante. It was somewhere around this time, that Trevor discovered that Crawley still visited the house and admonished him once again, this time, most vehemently. I was relieved and thought that things would settle down. But of course, the worst was yet to occur. A week after that.... Just a week.... Trevor was killed in that dreadful accident on the London road." Sir Arkwright exchanged glances with William, I noticed the look.

"Do you think Mr Crawley had anything to do with that accident?" asked Edward, suddenly, sitting bolt-upright and looking from one to the other of them.

"We will never know," sighed the distinguished lawyer, quite wearily. "But there were those of us who did wonder.... But there was nothing to connect him with the incident."

"Nobody must have investigated along these lines..." said William.

"You're right.... You can't accuse a man without proof, which would have had to be collected at the scene of the accident, and since no one thought along those lines...I did try to suggest the possibility of foul play to the local authorities, but without any proof, simply on a hunch, who would believe me!," said the Lawyer.

"But Inspector Crawley said he had become friends with lady Victoria, was that true?" asked Julia.

"Yes, yes...oh, he managed, the swine! Sorry children.... He used the fear of the curse to gain access to Victoria. He, sort of, made it his bond with her. I tried to get him away, but she wouldn't listen to me. It was as if she could not do without him. I realized then, what a mistake Trevor and I had made in shielding her from our suspicions regarding the strange behaviour and personality of Mr Crawley."

We all looked at him, the full horror of the sad story beginning to sink in. "And so, Lady Cecilia did, indeed, tell him about the necklace..." I said aloud.

"Oh yes, very innocently, never did she suspect him of anything. She had begun to look at him as one of Vikki's many friends. It was only I, who thought and thought of the coincidence of Trevor dismissing him and shortly having the fatal accident!" a hush fell over the room.

"Our mistake, Trevor and I, we tried to keep our concerns from Vikki so as not to worry her, and later, she would not listen to me, when I begged her not to trust him. She said, 'what harm can he do? he only visits me and talks...' I knew she had become addicted to discussing her fears of the 'family curse' with Crawley. It really was as if he had put a spell on her, I told her it was nonsense, even scolded her for it, I said she mustn't be fanciful.... So she stopped talking of it with me...another mistake that I made. You see I should have let her speak of her fears with me, rather than with that man. So everything went his way, and he made a firm place for himself in the Winwood household."

"Horrible!" I said.

"Yes, yes..." nodded Sir Arkwright.

"Poor Sir Trevor...and no one suspected..." I murmured.

"No, according to the police report then made, it was a straight-forward accident," added William. "But of course, not one person had looked at it from any other angle."

"And his family became close to the very man who..." whispered Julia.

"Yes...yes...that's it," said Sir Arkwright. "Vikki and I drifted apart. You see, when we were together, we felt the unmistakable absence of Trevor.... His absence that was always with us..." His voice trailed off.

"So sad," whispered Julia, a tear in her eye.

"But why, after all these years, did he want the necklace?" said Floppy, who had been quiet for a long time.

"Money," said William loudly, "you will be surprised as to how many times we come across this very basic motive, just... money."

"Mr Crawley was in dire need of a huge amount of money, our recent enquiries found that he was facing a financial crisis. Apparently he had gambled away the wealth he had accumulated over the years, and he had taken huge amounts of loans to cover his gambling debts," The Fish explained. "Last year, he managed to embezzle some police funds. It was very cleverly done and we think he had full plans to put the money back, to safeguard his reputation, which was a very respectable one, but his luck didn't change. Some months back, he became aware that an audit had been ordered into that very department he had borrowed/stolen from. He panicked. A discovery would not only mean a complete loss of his reputation, but even imprisonment, and he could not bear to expose that part of himself to the society in which he was so highly respected. He was indeed in a fix."

"It must've been at this point that he remembered the 'Windwood necklace'," added William.

"He asked me quite casually for the envelope Lady Cecilia had given me, claiming that Lady Victoria needed it. Of course I refused to give it to him, telling him in no uncertain terms that she would have to speak to me personally," said Sir Arkwright.

"I think, slowly he became desperate, you see, his deliverance was so easy. He must have realized that all he had to do was to locate the necklace, which was in one of the Winwood properties. He knew the Winwood household quite well including several members of the staff. By now he had full access to the family," explained William, "and Lady Victoria herself was completely unaware of the existence of the necklace!"

"It was easy for him to hire Mr and Mrs Goddard, some small time crooks he knew of, from his days in the police service," continued The Fish, "perhaps he had worked with them earlier, who can say?."

"And Miss Mamble or should I say, Maria?" asked Floppy.

"Well, he knew of her as Mrs Mamble's daughter, Mrs Mamble, who had been the nanny of Thomas Winwood, and she, of course, had always been in love with him...and so did whatever he asked of her," explained William.

We all must have looked quite shocked and perhaps a little comical, for William and Sir Arkwright looked 'round at us all and then at each other and suddenly started laughing. Sir Arkwright got up and stretched, then, as if wanting to sum up the whole affair, hurriedly said, "and the rest of the 'gang' were hired to play their parts, child's play for him with his police background."

"My God!" said Edward, "unbelievable."

"But what about Grandmama? why did he harm her?" said Marianne softly, looking at Sir Arkwright, her eyes filled with tears.

"I'm not so sure, my dear. Oh, He had been obsessed with her from the moment he saw her, of that I'm sure. He was somehow responsible for Trevor's accident, of that too, I am sure...even though I will never be able to prove it. But why he poisoned Vikki, how he brought himself to do it, I will never understand!"

Sir Arkwright continued..."I can only guess that she must have fallen out with him at that point, perhaps she finally began to suspect his intentions. She made no secret of the fact that she sent for me and maybe it was then that he felt cornered and desperate, perhaps thinking I would tell about The Necklace and of his interest in it. So he decided to sacrifice her, or maybe it was sheer greed," Sir Arkwright spoke harshly.

"What a sick man!" I said.

"Oh yes, he was sick and cruel. The deadliest kind of villain...the kind that looks pleasant and benign, as you have all seen with your own eyes. The kind that hides his intentions so cleverly, the kind, that operates under the cover of unquestioned respectability. The kind that will stop at nothing to get what he wants...whether it is a woman he has set his heart on, or even that very woman's wealth," finished Sir Arkwright.

"An utterly ruthless criminal," agreed William, his arm around Marianne who was looking ahead pensively, lost in her own thoughts. A strange poignant silence fell upon the room. After a while, Floppy said, "and you, Sir, how did you land up in the cellar?" Everyone laughed at the way he put it.

"Simple, young man. Oh, it quite maddens me to see how it was all so easy for Crawley, whenever he did something, no one suspected him, he caught us unawares. He kept me alive only because I had the all-important white envelope in my possession. Vikki sent me a message that she was suddenly taken ill and wanted me to come and see her. She said she had a premonition that she was dying, I scolded her, like old times. We spoke of our old life, of the people we loved, especially Trevor. She said, 'sorry Arthur, you know it was always, and still is, only Trevor for me. I can see him you know, before me, always, large as life.' We had laughed, I admitted to her that I too thought him the better man, handsome and dashing, we felt quite like our old selves! We spoke of legal matters, mostly regarding Marianne's inheritance, and then, much later, she came to what it was that worried her...in short, Mr Crawley. I can hear her voice – 'What is he going on about? some hidden jewellery in my house...he says he must find it for my sake, he says there is a gang of robbers after it. He sounds so strange, I have sent him packing...but I am a little fearful, I admit it to you. I'm sorry Arthur, I know I should have listened to you sooner. You were right, there is something very very wrong with him, he has a strange light in his eye, he gets obsessive,' she had whispered to me. I had told her that she had taken rather a long time to figure out the truth about Mr Crawley and then of Lady Cecilia's deed. That set her off! She laughed and laughed till tears ran down her cheeks. She said to me 'Oh Arthur, what a crazy old dear she was'; 'crazy is what all you Winwoods are!' I said, smiling ruefully at her 'is it really Trevor's necklace, and she kept it all this while, hidden somewhere.... My goodness, and you had to bear the secret...poor Arthur, we never let you alone did we? Why didn't you marry, settle down, and forget all about us...?'

I looked into her eyes, 'well you see...just as it was always Trevor with you, it was always you with me...', she smiled then, and held her hand out to me. I took it, then bent down and kissed her forehead, I said to her, 'you know Vikki, I wouldn't be myself without you and Trevor' my voice broke with emotion. We looked at each other and I told her to rest and not be a sentimental old fool, and make me one too. We laughed as I left the room, 'come back tomorrow!' she ordered, I looked over my shoulder and nodded at her before shutting the door behind me...I never saw her alive again."

There was a long pause, we were all rather amazed with this oh-so-romantic tale. Then Floppy asked, somewhat relentlessly, "and?"

Sir Arkwright smiled and said, "well, it was simple, really, as I left Vikki's room, a maid came up to me, saying some gentleman wanted a word with me. I followed her, a trifle lost in my own thoughts, to a quiet part of the house and stood near a staircase...and that's all I can remember. Someone must have knocked me out!"

"Gosh!" said Julia.

"When I came round, I was in the cellar, and there I remained till Inspector William miraculously found me."

"There now, you have it children, the whole story..." said The Fish, looking round at us all in a fatherly way.

"If not for you all, Marianne and myself would have been in deep waters indeed," said Sir Arkwright.

"Gosh, little did we think all this would happen when we first ran into Marianne in the grounds of the Dowager house..." said Julia haltingly, "you know, Edward went back for Marianne." Edward blushed a deep red, William laughed, and Marriane said "stop it William."

"And then of course, our young leader got into the act, our busybody, Emma would not rest till she solved the case," said William.

"What case?" asked Julia, looking confused.

"What case, indeed, a good question...what shall we call it? perhaps the Winwood Ghost!!!" enquired William of us all.

"Oh no!" said Marianne.

"No...not that," agreed William softly, looking lovingly down at Marianne.

"The curse of the Winwoods..." I said quietly.

✦ ✦ ✦

18

Much later, after a simple, but delicious meal, comprising of hot chicken soup followed by lamb chops, mashed potatoes and home-made bread and butter, we all slowly moved towards the front door, some quiet and pensive, others talking softly. I looked around me as I stood just under the grand chandelier in the entrance of the house, I could not help shivering a little as I thought of the deep sadness it had witnessed...yet, from all accounts, it had been a happy house once...I pictured Lord Trevor coming in through the main door, someone running up to him for his hat and coat, he must have walked through here and towards his study with Briggs close behind him. At times his wife and his mother must have come down and sat with him there, the child, young Thomas, playing nearby, perhaps on the carpet. And then, one day, someone came to the house, saw the beautiful mistress and formed a lasting obsession for her...that's when it all went wrong. I sighed as I looked back at the now-so-familiar staircase, someone put a hand on my arm, it was Marianne, we looked at each other, in the semi-darkness, our eyes wet with tears, an understanding passed between us then, and from that moment on we formed a bond of friendship which lasted us our entire lives.

A cold blast of air hit us as the great door was opened, we all moved out into the cold, down the steps, towards the waiting motorcars. I walked a little ahead, the grass felt cold and wet, I turned back to look at the outline of the house against the early morning sky. It must have been about three or four o'clock. My eyes moved towards the west wing, where the Winwood necklace had been hidden for so many years and where it is said that the ghost of an unhappy lady wanders. Love, then, causes so much suffering, I thought to myself. If you look at it, it was love that bound Sir Trevor and Lady Victoria, love that bound Sir Arkwright to Lady Victoria, and an obsessive sort of love that Mr Crawley developed for lady Victoria that ruined her entire life, and eventually destroyed her...

"What is it, child?" Sir Arkwright said, walking up to me.

I sighed, "I was thinking.... Love can destroy and give so much pain, a pain that, it seems, cannot be forgotten.... Do you believe in The Ghost?"

"I am a rational man, Emma, and always have been. I had never thought that there was anything to this story, knowing of it forever...nor did Vikki or Trevor for that matter.... Yet, Victoria got so obsessed by the 'curse...' Sometimes I think what was it? Could there be something in the story...?" his voice broke and his head bent down as he tried to hide his emotion from me.

"Forgive me Sir," I said simply.

"No, no" he said, "this has been a strange time.... But you know, she ended up believing in it...Vikki...it was as if it took over her life, once Trevor was gone...no, even before. It was as if she was waiting for something to happen after she thought she had seen 'Mary' in the Queen's Chamber.... And the fact is, that we will never know what really happened in the chamber that day..." his voice drifted off, we stood together silently, the others had got into the motorcars and were waiting for us, we kept looking towards the long windows of the Queen's Chamber. "Perhaps, somewhere in her subconscious she had always had a fear of the 'Curse of the Winwoods', Crawley sensed it and used it to gain control of her thoughts, and he succeeded to a great extent.... As I said earlier, at one point she got so addicted to discussing it with him she became dependant on him, I know she regarded him as the only one who understood the fear..."

He put a hand on my head and turned and walked, tall and straight towards his motorcar. He didn't look back once at the house; suddenly, I held my breath, for I had a strong feeling that there was someone there, oh yes, I felt it very strongly, the presence of someone close to Sir Arkwright as he walked across the grass towards the porch for the very last time. I stood there, a sense of shock and wonder as I tried to fathom what exactly it was that I was sensing. Strangely, I felt no fear, only a satisfaction that the man who had caused the tragic events in Lady Victoria's life, was finally exposed...and would never be able to harm the Winwoods again. But then, my heart almost twisted with sorrow, I felt breathless, a gust of wind went through me, I felt as if my heart sank...she had lost Trevor, she had lost Thomas, she had lost all happiness, she had lost all peace...and that could never be returned. I stood where I was, standing straight, staring at the house, unable to move. Till this day, I cannot understand what emotion it was that took control of me in those five minutes, why I felt at one with Lady

Victoria's plight, but the fact remains that I did. Although all of us were associated with this adventure, from the start, it had always been me who had the eye-opening experiences that guided us along, as if there was a hand on my shoulder, prompting me to go on, it was not just me.... Call me fanciful, whatever...but it is the truth, as I felt it then.

For anyone who is interested, Marianne and William were married in a beautiful and simple ceremony, we were all invited and Mrs Weston took us (by the by, she never knew how much we suspected her at one point during our investigation!) Also present were Sir Arkwright, The Fish, and even Constable Wotley, who incidentally cried throughout the ceremony. Marrianne and William did not live at Golden Oaks. Old Mr Briggs and young Mr Briggs went and lived with them in a large brick-red mansion that belonged to William's family. It was a beautiful, cheerful house, that, some years later, I had occasion to visit. It was Marianne who called me urgently. "A perplexing problem worrying me Emma, please come!" was the telegram she sent.... But that is another story for another time....

✦ ✦ ✦